The Lone Dragon Knight

By D.C. Clemens

Table of Contents

Prologue

Staring out a tall, thin window was a young woman with a golden waterfall for hair. She donned a flowing white gown, which reflected the silky moonlight that cut through the glass, giving her a divine glow. It was a warm night, so the cool gray stone felt nice under her bare feet. She turned when she heard the nursery door open.

"What did you see?" she asked the old woman ambling into the spacious bedroom. Her deep green eyes gained a sheen of concern when she caught the old woman's drained expression. She instinctively drew closer to the stalwart, bearded man that had been standing nearby. "Gods, what is it, Clair?"

The wrinkled woman sat on a small divan by the window. She had not wanted to exhibit her feeling of dismay in front of the queen, a young woman she had known as a babe, but her mind was much too weary to hold back the truth. She needed to recover a moment.

"My Queen," said the seer after taking that moment. "Forgive me, my visions are rarely so… vivid."

"And what does that entail?" asked the lofty king. "Is Odet still asleep?"

"Aye, my lord. Soundly. Your newest daughter remains undisturbed by my endeavor. What you must know, my lords, is that no vision, even the most pristine, is faultless. The gods themselves admit as much."

"Yes, Clair, we are aware of the impreciseness of even the best seers, but your visions have admirably aided Alslana for decades. There might not even be a kingdom today if your gift did not help guide Leandra's family. So, what did you see in Odet?"

1

The old woman sighed hoarsely before raising her coal colored eyes to meet the queen's. "I saw her as a young woman, my lords. As striking as her mother. She was walking down a mountain path with Beatrice and a younger child."

"Another child?" asked the king.

"Yes. Another girl, in fact. This one has your darker hair, my king."

The royal parents smiled at one another, but the old woman kept her stern reserve.

"They were in the middle of a pleasant walk, laughing and relishing each other's company, but then a great shadow swooped over them all. I tried to look up at the reason for the darkening sun, but its dense power did not allow me a glimpse. They ran hard, but whatever was chasing them always stayed above their heads. They reached the border of the western capital. This was where Odet stopped. She made a choice. She would fight to defend her sisters and her people. I was proud as you would be... but then it roared. Gods, how it roared. It rattled my bones and forced her to shed tears from her stoic face. A torrent of flame showered down upon her. She held her ground, lifted her arms, and cast her family's ancient shield. The spirit shield held against the flames, but the inferno only burned more ferociously around her. It reached the capital and began turning everything to ash. Blocking her completely from my sight were two vast wings of shadow. My trance was broken by another roar."

Chapter One

I couldn't remember who I was. I couldn't even remember when the serrated chain-whip had been embedded around my left arm, or what it once belonged to. I only knew that the curved teeth were as dark a red as dried blood. There came a point when my past no longer mattered. Nothing did. The boiling pain coursing my veins at every second of the day removed any real semblance of thought. However, I did recognize one thing—some hard bread and muddy water came into my lightless, dank cell if I killed whatever I was presented.

Time was impossible to keep track of, so I didn't know how often it happened, but my cell gate would occasionally slide open, signaling me to step out into the arena. Lit by unknown means, and burning my tender eyes, three paltry torchlights would then light up the curving wall of stone that rose fifteen feet to a domed ceiling. Ten yards away, just beyond another cell gate, a section of the stone wall would open. A brutish creature would come through it every time.

The first one I remembered with any clarity was a scrawny wolf. Its wall closed behind the fuming beast and its gate skidded open to release it into the arena. The desperately hungry jaws bit down on my leg before I gouged out one of its eyes with my fumbling fingers. Killing it required a few blows to its head with a fist sized rock I found on the dirt ground.

Other times I faced snarling, rabid dogs, along with other beasts whose names often escaped me. There were these thick things with coarse hair and tusks in their mouth, and there was once a three-eyed, two-legged, hairy thing a little less than my size. I quickly learned to use my jagged arm on them, especially on those that had a tendency to use their jaws as a

3

weapon. I would get them to bite down on the barbed arm and then lash out with a punch, kick, or rock. It took a lot of energy to kill something with nothing but sheer brutality. I perhaps should have felt some amount of remorse as they yelped or choked on their blood, but I wasn't permitted to experience such things, or anything at all. If I tried to think on my own, my back would burn as though it was being branded by a searing piece of iron.

I lost consciousness after any victory I had. I would revive in my locked cell with a bowl of water, a plate of bread, and an empty bucket. There would even be fresher rags for me to wear every now and then. There ultimately came a time when I faced off against other people. They were feral, malnourished beings, and the closest thing I had to a mirror. Physically, they were actually easier to kill than the beasts. Consciously, they were about the same.

When the torches lit up for my next challenger, a long sliver of dull steel glinted on the ground. Soon after I picked up the rusty short sword, the other gate opened to reveal a man wielding the same weapon. He slashed away at me, but I treated his sword no differently than teeth and claws. His blade caught on one of my chain-teeth long enough for me to run my blade through his stomach. He crumpled to the floor with a gurgled shout. The scream was cut short when my sword pierced his neck.

This was my life for anywhere between a month to a thousand centuries.

Chapter Two

I awoke from my dreamless sleep on my back, the only way I could sleep without my jagged chain cutting into my skin. My cell opened, but something already felt different. I stepped out into the total darkness. It stayed dark for a long time. Then the wall beyond the second cell gate opened to reveal the brightest light my eyes had ever seen. My instinct told me a falling sun was responsible, but after I recovered from the initial blindness, I saw that the luminance came from a simple torch, only much brighter than the ones that hung from the wall.

Carrying the flame was a sane looking young man wearing a crimson cloak. Though lean, the brown topped boy still looked fat to me. Walking alongside him was an older, but still unwrinkled, red haired woman. She wore a cherry colored cloak as well.

Despite my reaction to all others who had entered this domain, my feet were nailed to the ground. Somewhere in the unknowable depths of my mind, a bubble burst. Its echo told me that I should be attacking them, but an unseen force compelled me to do nothing more than stare at the ground as they drew nearer.

As the woman looked me over, the holder of flame said, "I still don't understand. What makes him a failure? None of the other subjects have come close to doing what he's done."

The woman's clean, pale hand lifted my chin so that she could stare into my limp eyes. I simply looked past her. She let my head drop and said, "Our master requires perfection, not 'good enough.' The subject's combat skill is indeed at a high level, but his body is still not completely assimilating with the corruption."

"How can you tell?"

She took my right arm and turned it so that its underside became visible. "See the laceration by his elbow? Similar wounds have healed within five days. This one has been in this state for eight. No, the corruption is doing more harm than good at this point. It won't be long until it begins to eat away at more than his memory. I give him another five years before the insanity creeps into his psyche."

"Five? Most have gone crazy in less than one. He's already been exposed for two."

As she pulled out a thin metal chain from underneath her cloak, she said, "I've seen this level of assimilation before." The end of the chain had a collar, which she opened to put around my neck before locking it again. "I might be off by a few months, but it's inevitable." The veteran handed the apprentice the end of the chain. "Still, he has been rather valuable. Now we know who to look for in our next expedition. Take him to be cleaned and give him some of our more decent clothes. His buyer doesn't like to feel like he's gotten anything cheap."

I was led down the tunnel and into a side room, where I entered a metal tub filled with ice cold water, though it wasn't all that bothersome. If anything, the numbing sensation it brought over my scorching body was as pleasant as any sensation beforehand. After my handler spent a few minutes scrubbing my face and torso, I was pulled out of the tub and given some dry, plain clothes to wear. Before I put on my tunic, my handler wrapped a strip of cloth around my left arm, likely hoping that prevented my arm's teeth from tearing up the attire.

After a long walk through some dimly lit tunnels, where I sensed the air become crisper at every step, we entered a particularly narrow passageway. At its end was the woman from before. She placed her hand on the flat rock wall and a small flowery rune simmered with a yellowish glow

6

before fading away. The wall responded by quietly sliding open, allowing a brisk breeze to enter the space. A strange, almost blue light invaded my vision.

I wanted to acclimate to this odd gleam, but I was forced to walk into the light, my thin sandals stepping on to a white, powdery material. As I was made to continue my walk through a silent woodland, I saw that the light came from a huge icy orb hanging in the sky. I knew its name, but it was back in my cell. Why was I missing that cell?

My short stroll took me to a brown horse with a dark mane. It was strapped to a small cart that I was pulled into when the man took a seat in it. The woman hopped on the beast and grabbed the reins, snapping them to begin a leisurely trot. As they did not speak much, only the stamping hooves and the churning wheels crunching the snow produced any kind of noise in this new, wide open world.

The youth seemed wary of me, his light brown eyes twitching over my figure every so often. I didn't know why he was nervous. I only moved with the cart's eccentricity, and my own eyes, when they weren't idly staring at the cart's cracked floor, were busy examining my new environment.

For some time we traversed the empty woods, but as the sky brightened, we reached a smoother trail. This we followed toward the rising ball of flame. I hated the strengthening light. Even the minimal heat it offered was unpleasant. I was forced to shut my struggling eyes for the next few hours, only sporadically opening them so that I could try to get accustomed to the penetrating beams. When the rays were at their most intense, I started to hear a few other travelers on foot or horseback, though none paid any attention to us. I didn't want them to.

A little after passing a solitary man walking in a tattered coat, one of my blurred glimpses distinguished several buildings of rough stone or splintered wood, most emitting lazy wisps of gray smoke from their chimney stacks. Before entering this little village, the cart made a right to an overgrown side road that went toward a little stone hut. Closing in on it saw three men step out from the shelter's draped opening, two of them being particularly brawny and all had some facial hair. We stopped in front of them.

The brawniest man in the middle of the trio asked, "Is that him?"

Not bothering to step off her mount, the woman answered, "We said he was young."

"Sure, but the boss wasn't expecting a damn kid to look after."

"He might have just exited childhood, but I can assure you he'll last longer than the others. I give him five years before he breaks. Your boss won't even have to reinforce the mind rune on his back for another few weeks. Oh, and his left arm has a fiend's tail wrapped around it, so I would be careful if you touch him there." She took out a small scroll from the animal's pack and tossed it to the man she was speaking with. "That's the incantation to link the boy to your boss's wishes."

The catcher of the scroll nodded to a heavily bearded man, who lobbed a clinking pouch at the woman. On catching it, she turned to face my handler. The cue had him step out the cart so that he could hand the end of my chain to the middle man. With that done, the first two rational people I remembered began to retread their route.

The three men and I entered their hut, which was a cozy fit, where they then began re-eating their half-eaten meals—a veritable feast of unknown dishes. After inconspicuously sitting in a corner for a while, one of the men put his bony leftovers in front of me, which I gingerly picked at. They all spoke of topics that didn't involve me and that I didn't quite understand. Their only goal seemed to make the others holler with laughter, as that's what happened more often than not. When they finished eating, the one in charge told a man named Sams to get the horses ready. When Sams returned with the familiar animals, I was put on top of one by my new handler. We moved much faster than in my first ride, quickly passing through the village to get to a new road.

Chapter Three

The light was finally dying down when I saw the outskirts of a much larger town than the one we had left. The forest cleared up to make way for larger structures and wider streets, many of which were paved with cobblestone. We stayed at the fringes, going only a bit deeper when the men spotted the building they sought, which was a large timber home that looked more extravagant than any I had seen yet. Surrounding it was a rundown wall seven feet high at its tallest.

The horses trotted up to a break in the wall, where a group of men, their guard dogs, and an open metal gate were standing. They all heartily greeted one another with what I was pretty sure were expletives. I was taken inside, where half a dozen women milled around a flourishing fire pit.

"Where's Garf?" my handler asked a gaunt woman, who adjusted her almost nonexistent top when she saw him.

Looking grimier and cheerier than I, she said, "Not even a hello, Heaton?" Heaton stepped up to her and planted an open mouth kiss on her scrawny lips. After a moment of this, she pushed him away and stroked his chest. "Brooks will be back soon, but he'll be gone later tonight. I'll be on that big bed all alone."

"I'll keep you alone if you don't tell me where Garf is anytime soon."

"Patience is a good thing to learn, honey, especially when we get in that big bed later. Garf's out back. Is that his new pet?"

"Yeah. At least he's a quiet one. Almost forgot he was here."

Heaton led me down the main hallway until we walked back outside. There were ten people in the back, all in the process of training with either

10

fist or sword. We headed for a clean shaven, well-dressed, spry looking man with silvery hair. This gentleman overlooked another man and a young woman clashing with wooden practice swords.

"Garf!" called Heaton. The older man responded by waving a hand in front of the fighting pair, ending their match. "I've brought the boy. Smaller than expected, eh?"

Garf looked up and down my frame. "Nonsense. Some food and a bit more puberty and he'll be as fine as your youngest. The scroll?" The item was handed to him. "Anything more?"

"The woman said he should last about five years before he becomes more trouble than he's worth. He's certainly quieter than the others. I don't think I've heard him talk yet."

"Another bonus. No name I take it?"

"Nah. You'll have to come up with one yourself."

"As usual. You may take the next day off."

"It might end up being longer than that. The mountains look ready to toss another fit our way." As Heaton began to turn around, he remembered something and said, "There's a fiend's tail wrapped around his left arm. I guess that's how they corrupted this one."

"His mind survived direct infusion? And he's slated to live another five years? This could turn out to be the best subject they've discarded to us."

"So you think the price was worth it?"

"I'm not concerned about the price. It seems they're getting closer to what they're looking for."

"What exactly are they looking for?"

"If the one in charge is who I think he is, then the answer is 'everything.'"

This was the man I spent most of my time with over the next few weeks. He gave me a little storage room to sleep in, with a wolf pelt acting as either my bed or blanket, depending on what I favored that night. The crime boss gradually fed me more and more, and introduced me to different foods and drinks. He never really talked to me. No one did. I preferred it that way.

The days got colder, and it was on the days when we were essentially snowed in did he open up more. He asked what I knew and what I didn't know, with every question related to my fighting potential. Through him I learned, or perhaps relearned, about the paths I could take to enhance my combat abilities. There were two ways I could concentrate on using the corruption running through my spirit energy, or prana, as it was known. On one hand, I could augment my body's strength and speed by pouring prana into my body and muscles. The second option was to use it as fuel for casting spells.

After everyone else had left the large dining room, Garf asked me, "How did you normally kill your opponents?"

"A rock... My hands too. They gave me a sword later. I liked the sword."

"A sword, eh? Hmm, then I think the name 'Saber' suits you. It also sounds like focusing on your speed and strength would be the easier course for you. I'll give you about a year to train, so I'll be able to show you some spells as well. Once you're ready, I'll send you to do some work for me. The better you do, the better your rewards. You should take advantage of them, too. You won't have long to enjoy what life has to offer, as your destiny will have you living fast and dying young."

Thus started my formal training with my new name. He would often send me to the backyard to spar or fence against his people. Sometimes he would watch over himself and hand out some pointers. He would at first pit me against a couple of other boys closer to my size, but it was soon clear that the speed and strength my corruption offered me was more than enough to handle them. I moved to training against men twice my size. They could

12

knock me down or jolt me with some spell, but the pain they inflicted was minimal compared to what I had already endured, so I was never down long.

Garf most often watched and guided my training when I held the practice sword in my hands. My handler appeared to be a busy man, so the fact he spent much of his off time training an amateur told me he must have found the pursuit an enjoyable pastime. My overseer called my overall fighting style brutish, but salvageable. He gave me several books and scrolls he had on different offensive and defensive stances. It took me a few weeks to remember how to read the symbols, which a few of the women helped me out with, but there were plenty of illustrations to match my movements to in the meantime. I looked over these fighting manuals in the hours I wasn't training, including several on incantations.

According to Garf and the manuals, it normally required months of exhaustive training to begin sensing the prana latent in all living things. As I had already gone through this effort some time before losing my memory, combined with the corruption viciously invigorating my soul, all I had to do was acknowledge the spiritual fuel seeping from my body. So when I wasn't training or reading, I meditated over some spells to purposely use this energy instead of only instinctually implementing it in my physical strikes.

A handful of Garf's people could use some low level spells to create a sword of flame or summon a weapon they had sealed away previously, but since my handler did not desire for me to accidentally destroy a part of his home, I focused on a spell that wouldn't be destructive if I succeeded in casting it. The spell I chose was an illusionary type that I found in a tome. This particular incantation would generate a visual replica of myself that could be used to trick enemies. Mastery over this incantation meant being able to cast more than one copy and controlling them over longer distances.

At first, there was little other reason for learning this spell besides the fact it was nondestructive, but the more I mulled over the concept, the more I felt a tinge of desire at fooling my enemies before I sent my blade into them. As I had few feelings that seemed like my own, I embraced this aspiration a great deal. Excluding the tome itself, the only physical item I needed to practice the spell was a mirror, as I needed to recognize how I looked like to achieve a good doppelganger.

During this time I also learned that if I had to spend time with anyone, I preferred the company of the women. They could be as verbally brash and filthy as the men, but they were not physically abusive to me and a few even had the capacity to act with kindness. This preference toward the opposite gender grew when I later noted how most women outside the criminal underworld appeared more genial still. Meanwhile, even men unassociated with Garf's life didn't seem all that different from the criminals I associated with, if not as freely violent.

Even as the spring came to make all walks of life more colorful, my handler's aspiration kept me training. There were moments when more of my own meager ambitions leaked through, but this was quickly followed by Garf reinforcing the mind rune etched on my back by reading his scroll with a hand on my back. Most others in the house saw me nothing more as an extension of Garf's will. I knew enough to know that this was somehow wrong, but the few sparks of self-thought I had were not spent on them.

Chapter Four

By the time the trees changed their leaves to brittle pigments, Garf's will wanted me to join his people in their often savage trade. Wintervale belonged to him. That's what I heard, but there were some people who needed reminding, or who outright rebelled. Most times, however, the people we encountered did not need a fistful of reminders to give Garf his due. I became more involved as the months continued to pass, though nothing that really tested my developing skills.

My swordsmanship was almost as good as Garf's best fighters. Only their experience prevented me from closing the gap entirely. The illusion spell was progressing, though I could not get my unsolid replica to keep its shape for longer than three seconds. It wasn't until I read well did I realize that the spell was probably too advanced to start with, but I had invested too much time to give up and start on something else.

Not long after my second winter in the outside world, Garf and some of his lackeys hauled me eastward to a large town called Rise. This was not his town, but he wanted it, which meant more prolific work for me. From what I gathered, the town belonged to several groups, and our job was to secure territory away from the weaker ones. Not all of this taking was done through fighting. Oftentimes, all Garf had to do was pay off some people to either get them to convert to his cause or to stay away from a future clash.

When we did take the fight to our enemy, I was regularly sent to start it, as my age allowed me to get in closer than most. I would stroll up to the unsuspecting enemy assembly and smash a few small smoke bombs in their direction, catching them by surprise. It sometimes didn't even become necessary for the others to interfere. By the time the blackish smoke cleared, a heap of two or three men would be dead or dying at my feet, my short sword dripping their blood. Someone would sometimes make a fight of it, but this was when my group would come and overwhelm them. A strong sense of disappointment overcame me when this happened. I wanted nothing more than to test myself against a worthy opponent. Whether this was Garf's will, mine, or a combination of both didn't matter. It's what I felt.

More months. More blood. I ate well, slept on soft beds with well-made blankets, and wore durable clothes, boots, and coats. My handler had gained a foothold on Rise near summer's end. It was entrenched enough so that our work was not always so constant. He and his people's revelry now went deeper into the night. Since my handler did not need my presence during these times, or during their recovery periods, I had more time to myself, as it were.

Of course, his will drove me to seek ways to better my lethal skills. This mentality sent me seeking more training manuals. Garf funded my search by giving me a few coins to purchase what I needed. I could have simply stolen them, but when I wasn't with Garf or the others, then it was inadvisable for me to attract guards when I was alone.

Rise had plenty of shops to look for useful guidebooks. One of these I found early one morning. It was an out of the way shop that had a sundry of items, including books and scrolls. An elderly fellow manned the counter, who was the only one in the small store with me. He asked if he could help me look for something.

"Training manuals."

"Want to be a warrior, eh?"

"A better one."

He chuckled. "I see. Some basic stuff is on that shelf to your right, but the more advanced booklets I have stashed in that little cabinet next to it. Go ahead and open it and see if you like anything."

I rummaged through the dozen manuals he had in the cabinet. Most were actually not that advanced, but a few of them looked worth a lengthier gander, so I took these up to the counter.

"Just these three?"

"Unless you have more."

"I do have more books on broader topics."

"I'm only interested in enhancing my fighting skills."

"Ah, but reading about history and other academics can be just as useful in becoming a better warrior. They can open your eyes to tactics that other generals have used or help you figure out how people think. Do you think the best warriors only learned from some simple guidebooks?"

It sounded like a pitch to sell more books, but there was wisdom in what he said. Enough so that Garf's desire was not averse to the idea either.

"What books would help me gain an advantage in a fight?"

He stepped out behind the counter and showed me another shelf with some history books. I bought one that focused on famous generals and another that described human anatomy. He told me to check back a few days from now when he received a new shipment of goods.

I consumed both the training manuals and the educational words over the subsequent days. For the first time in a long time I sensed there was indeed something more out there. Reading about ancient generals had me wondering about the details of their lives and the reasons for the battles themselves. Even the anatomy book showed me something beyond the immediate wishes of my handler. I went to more shops and bought more books. Purchasing them felt as though I had made the most personal decision I had ever made yet. I had more or less forgotten the old man's shop, but almost a month after my first visit, I returned.

I wasn't alone.

Chapter Five

I was walking with Hector and Miles late in the afternoon. We had been collecting this month's cut from our new sources and were walking back to our headquarters. Hector caught sight of a woman ahead of us. Only the back of her slender body could be seen, including her long chocolate hair, but this was all Hector needed to try and get her attention with some hissing whistles. The woman ignored the attention seeking calls. He whistled again. She walked a bit faster. So did we. She entered that familiar shop.

Hector laughed and said, "She's playing hard to get! My favorite game!"

He followed her inside the shop, so we did too. By the time we entered, the woman had ran behind the counter to join the old man. With her front side now visible, I saw that she was on the verge of leaving her youth. Her long face and small nose looked somewhat similar to the old man's, making it easy to assume their relationship.

"Can I help you gentlemen?" asked the guarded old man.

"Everything in here is for sale, right?" asked Miles. "How much for a night, babe?"

Trying to sound firm, but failing, the old man replied, "Now, I'll have to ask you to leave if you continue making such vile jokes."

"Who the fuck is joking?" asked Hector rhetorically. "Do you know who we're with, old-timer? This can be simple or *really* simple. I'm a fair man, so I'll give you an entire silver standard for a wholesome night of fun with the girl. How 'bout it?"

Hector took a big step forward and the old man reached for something under the counter.

The girl squeezed the old man's arm and whispered, "Dad, be careful, please."

"I would listen to her if I were you," said Miles, taking a smaller step forward while also unsheathing his sword. "Last chance to just take the coin."

The old man responded by pulling out his own sword and yelling out, "Lock yourself upstairs, Millie!"

Hector and Miles hollered with savage glee as they ran and hurdled over the counter, leaving me standing there as Hector used his broadsword to knock away the old man's desperate attempt to defend everything he held dear. His daughter shrieked horribly as she ran up the stairway located behind the counter. Hector shoved the old man to the ground and chased after her. Miles brought down the end of his steel blade with a thud, ending the old man's groans.

"Should have just taken the coin, old bastard."

Without ever looking at me, he trailed his partner's upward path, his sword's tip wet with blood. The woman shrieked again, but it was muffled before it could get to its highest pitch. Limbs and bodies hit the floor and walls. I walked up behind the counter. The old man's neck was gushing the red sap of life. His dim eyes were wide open. Despite their lifelessness, I felt them imploring me. I wondered if he had recognized me. My rune began seething.

"Miles!" said Hector. "Did you make sure the fucking door is locked? Go make sure, dumbass!"

Miles' stamping footfalls speedily came down the stairs. On seeing me, he said, "Oh, right. Saber, lock the door and keep guard."

My rune burned hot, but I was still able to lift my hand and point to some vials hoarded within the dark hollow of the counter. I asked, "What are those?"

Miles turned to see what I was referring to. "Just some fucking health poti-"

His voice stopped when my sword severed his spine and throat. I almost collapsed with Miles' body. The rune was blistering my skin and sending the pain into every nerve, pinching them at their ends. But I still had control. I straightened and began climbing the tallest stairway in my life, every step up feeling as though it required the sacrifice of more of my humanity. Only her stifled whimpers pushed my legs higher.

When half a lifetime ended and I had wholly ascended, I saw that they were on the hallway's floor, his pants-less body facing away from me as he gyrated in a roughly rhythmic fashion. The floor squeaked in my approach, but he must have assumed it was Miles, for he never stopped his revulsion. He did eventually turn his head a bit, but it was at the same moment I lunged my bladed hand forward.

There was no time for him to dodge. The sword went through his back almost as easily as it had cut through his friend's neck. He didn't die as quickly, however. He thrashed and uttered a gurgled groan, but I held my sword firmly inside of him, even giving it a twist. The woman stayed frozen on her spot, her clothes ripped. It wasn't until Hector's twitching body slumped back onto her did she return to her senses, yelping and crawling backwards. Hector tried to say something, but the blood spouting out of his mouth made the words unintelligible.

I fell to my knees and vomited. I puked the entire day's food and all of my bile until I was just dry heaving my raw lungs. The burning of the rune finally subsided just enough for me to stop throwing up and look about myself. The man was dead and the woman was holding her clothes together with one hand as she sluggishly stood back up. She eyed me nervously. My trembling hand picked up my sword, wiped it off Hector's pants, and pulled open the flap of my coat to sheathe it.

20

Below us, I heard a stranger say, "Is someone in here? Are you still open?"

"You should get the guards," I told the woman. "Tell them everything."

I walked past her to get to a bedroom behind her. I next heard her clambering toward the stairs as I saw my goal—a window. It was small and encrusted with dust, but it opened with a gripe and had sufficient space to squeeze my body through. It was a two story drop to the alley, but it didn't take much prana to fortify my legs at this height.

After dropping to ground level, I walked briskly toward the side of town Garf did not have as many eyes watching his interests, though I knew even this separation wouldn't be enough for a lasting solution. The only option I had was to get as far away as possible as fast as possible. My description would be spread to every town guard and, what concerned me the most, to every criminal associated with the underworld by morning. Besides the obvious need to escape retribution, my rune was the overriding reason I decided to run instead of hide. I wasn't certain how the rune's power worked, but I figured the farther I was from Garf's will, the less bearing it had over mine. Maybe I had to get four thousand miles away for that to hold true, but I was going to try.

I wanted to steal a horse to get a bigger head start, but there were three problems with that idea. For one, the expensive beasts were always watched. Second, in Rise's mountainous terrain, there weren't many paths to take that would allow me to easily lose my pursuers. And lastly, my only experience riding a horse came from either watching others or being behind someone as they steered. No, there were too many unknowns. I had to go by foot.

With that in mind, my only real chance at escape came in the form of the Onyx Mountains. The great peaks towered over the town a few miles to

21

the north. It was late summer, but Rise still underwent some near freezing nights. It would be worse at higher elevations.

In preparation for my first goal in life, I used much of the remaining coin I had to buy a large waterskin, a little pouch to store dried strips of meat, and a few hardy biscuits. I wanted to buy another coat as well, but I didn't have enough for one that would do me any good. Moreover, most shops were closing at this point, and I didn't want to waste any more time looking for an open shop with a good deal. I slinked out of Rise as discreetly as I could once I had what I needed. When I was sure no one could see me, I started running.

Chapter Six

The rune burned deeper and fiercer. It had been bearable after my vomiting incident, but it now seemed to be reacting to an invisible leash that stretched tighter and tighter the farther I moved from town. The blurred vision I suffered from obligated me to sprint slower than I liked, and even then I stumbled and tripped often. The debilitation soon traveled to my ears, upsetting my balance and forcing a pace that didn't look that much different from a wobbling drunk.

I was fucked if this speed held throughout my defiance, but some two hours after I stepped out of Rise, my senses started to clear up. It wasn't so much that my rune became less active, but was instead concentrating on something else—my conscious, my very will to escape. I knew it was Garf's influence coming through, trying to get me to stop. I suppose it was ironic that this adjustment helped me resume a faster run. Still, it was like running with heavy weights on my legs, arms, and eyes, but I'd take weights over vertigo at this point.

It had been a week since Garf last reinforced the rune, though I knew it should have still kept me under his influence for another week without too much trouble. I could only guess that my corruption had an effect on the rune's power over me, giving me a fighting chance. I didn't know too much about the corrupted spirit flowing through me, but neither did most others. The creature's tail I permanently sported belonged to a fiend, a general term given to any of the corrupted beasts that came from one of the summoned realms.

Only a few of these realms were understood to any degree, and it was in these that prana wielders could summon a weapon they had sealed, or, for higher level wielders, call upon a creature to aid them in battle. Fiends belonged to a forbidden realm. They carried a corrupted form of prana that, while typically more powerful than the regular kind, drove most beings mad. Due to the insane-driven destruction they caused, it was prohibited to summon a fiend for any purpose. This was now the realm abetting me.

No different from the rest of my remembered life, time remained an insensible thing to me. Only the sunrise informed me of its progress. I tried heading for areas that gave me the best view behind me, which also gave me the higher ground I sought. When it didn't take too long, I climbed some steep hills to make sure no horse could follow me. I stopped to catch my breath more often than I liked, but the throbbing rune at least stopped me from lingering too long in one spot, as it eased up somewhat when my legs moved. I was sweating quite a lot by midday, making me glad I didn't end up buying that extra coat, though the element in my waterskin was still being consumed faster than ideal.

The woodland I was traversing was thinning out, and fewer birds were singing their songs by the time the sun made the shadows long again. It became so quiet that, during one of my respites, I heard the far off sound of barking. Half an hour later and the howling had closed the distance considerably. The mind rune was not acting up more than it already was, so I theorized that Garf himself was not part of the group. Wanting to see what I was up against, I climbed a lonely tree and fixated on the land below.

I picked up nothing for a few moments, not until my peripheral vision caught a pair of little figures moving to my right. Looking at my left side had me seeing a couple of other specks exiting a line of trees. Then the dogs barked maybe half a mile out in front of me. It was a pincer movement. My clean escape was over. Hiding was impossible with dogs sniffing me out, and it was clear my slothful sprinting would only bring them closer. One plan of action remained. I would have to get rid of the central hunting party if

24

there was any chance of losing the others, however laughable that chance was. At least I found something funny in this. I climbed down the tree and ambled toward the barking mutts.

When I made my way onto a rocky plateau, I heard what must have been three separate dogs yapping excitedly. I froze beside a fledgling tree, removed my unwieldy waterskin and food sack, and drew my secondary weapon, a curved knife. Sounding much like the dogs, I heard Heaton's voice give the canines a command. Their paws unquietly navigated the gravelly slope, the steps of their masters following close behind. The three frothing animals dashed into view.

The swiftest one, a shaggy shepherd dog, charged ahead of the others. It was instinctive at this point. I raised my left arm in front of me and allowed the dog to bite down. A few of its teeth breached the skin, but not enough to bother me. I actually paid more attention to the second dog, a large hound. This second dog jumped for my throat, but its own neck met the end of my jutting knife. Its limp body collided into both me and the first dog, who had let go of my arm with a cry.

When I scrambled back up, two men made themselves known. The longsword-brandishing Heaton I readily recognized, but the other man I knew only vaguely. His name was Christoph and he evidently favored the bow, as that's what he had drawn. The last uninjured hound disrupted my evaluation of the humans. I spun behind the tree to avoid an arrow, but couldn't avoid the second hound grabbing my pant leg, almost making me fall again, but I had enough cognizance to stick the knife in its skull. Unfortunately, I couldn't easily withdraw the dagger. I quickly gave up on it and unsheathed my main blade to slash at the dog bleeding at the mouth.

The moment the final dog was out of the way, an arrow lodged into my right shoulder. It was enchanted with a flame spell, but it wasn't anymore bothersome than the rune's own oppressive heat. I reset myself behind the tree to take the time to rip out the burning arrow.

"You'll fucking die for killing my dogs!" frothed Christoph.

I heard Heaton stamping closer. I couldn't fight both at the same time. I took out the only two smoke bombs from their pocket and waited until the last second to smash them onto the ground. With Heaton caught in the blinding smoke, I rushed out of the expanding cloud and headed for the bowman. He appeared surprised by my head on sprint. He fired off an arrow as he backed away, but it was easily evaded. My enemy dropped the bow to reach for a sword sheathed on his back. I sent a surge of prana to my legs and leapt the several feet needed to reach him with my sword. He withdrew his weapon, but he couldn't swing it fast enough to prevent my sword from piercing his upper abdomen. As I extracted my weapon, I made sure to lift the blade upward to make his wound as large as possible. Christoph wilted like a ghostly flower.

I turned around in time to see Heaton about to throw one of his hefty daggers. He hurled it and I was just able to deflect it with a swipe of my sword. We then simply stood there.

"I always knew one of you experimental rejects would bite us in the ass someday, though I can't say I don't pity you…" He passed his free hand over his longsword, which responded by igniting in flame. He next pointed this fire-coated steel to the sky. A streak of fire shot up into the air before it died with a flash of embers. "Look, call this a mercy killing, kid. What were you going to do if you did escape? No one will help a corrupted. You'll be hunted for the rest of your short life. Or maybe you want to live out here like an animal? Just stop causing trouble and make this easy for the both of us."

The words that came to my mind were those of a General Mercer I had read about. Stealing them for myself, I said, "We all die, Heaton. The best we can do is to die on our own terms."

26

He rose his burning sword in a defensive stance. "Then let's fulfill these terms of yours."

I ran at a man a head taller than I was and wielding a sword almost twice as long as mine. Heaton slashed the air in front of him to send a wave of fire at me. I ducked and used my arm and sword to block the residual flame from hitting my face. The most intense of the fire missed me, but the sleeve of my coat still turned to soot. I next evaded a downward slash. I swung at his leg, but his speed allowed him to ward off my swing with one of his own. As I recovered my bearing, I was forced to duck another swing. His slash missed, but not his kicking boot, which impacted my chin, sending me staggering backward. The longsword's point aimed for me. I was just able to spin out of the way from the line of fire it emitted. I rushed at him again, knowing I had little chance at his preferred midrange fighting style.

His blazing blade kept disorienting my vision, making me wish I had more smoke bombs. My amateurish illusion spell was useless without another distraction. But what else could I use? Getting knocked to the ground the third time provided a possible answer. I clambered toward the thin tree I had first used as a hindrance. I stopped over the dead shepherd dog, grabbed the waterskin it was half hiding, and flung it at Heaton. As anyone without a shield would do, Heaton swung his weapon to defend himself against the incoming airborne object. The roasting steel promptly burned through the skin and instantly boiled the water it touched, creating a cloud of steam in front of his face.

Heaton did the only smart thing, which was to swiftly step backward as he tried wiping his eyes. He also ineffectually fired a wave of flame at my general direction. After skirting it, I opened my clenched fist and cast my illusion spell. When Heaton next opened his eyes, he saw me rushing at him. He hacked at my form, but his steel hit only air. By the time he registered the second me behind the destroyed illusion, he could nothing to prevent my weapon from slicing at his arm. I severed his hand at the wrist, taking the weapon it held with it. I would have then went for a vital spot, but Heaton charged at me with a primal shout. I was forced to backtrack to the edge of the plateau. He wanted to stop there and have me be the only one who slipped, but I was able to grab his coat and we both tumbled down the slope.

I heard my loose weapon bounce against the rock-strewn wall, and some fleeting, rolling glimpses had me seeing a grouping of shrubs at the end of the slope. I thought this would be the termination of our spill, and I was already trying to think of what my next step would be, but we didn't stop. Our hurtling bodies crushed the desiccated line of shrubs to reveal a ten foot long crevice in the ground. With no time to avoid it, both of us fell in.

It was deep, that was immediately clear. The light from the sun could not breach through most of the darkness, but there was still enough to reflect off a lake three hundred feet below. I would have simply closed my eyes and hope for the best if I had been alone, but falling with Heaton had me doing something else. I rolled my body to get closer to him. I think he realized what I was trying to do, as he attempted to get his own body over mine, but his lack of a hand made it easy for me to repel his frantic attempt to save himself. Half an instant before we met the water, I was able to get him beneath me. I heard a loud smack as the front of Heaton's body crashed into the lake. The cold water sheathed my body next.

I never swam before. Never needed to. I simply copied what I had seen others doing. Combined with the sheer force of my churning limbs, my brutish technique allowed me to keep my head above water. Swallowing a good amount of lake water, I gradually churned to the smooth rock wall of the underground lake. I followed it for a few dozen yards before seeing the shadowy edge of a pebbly shore. On finally pulling myself onto dry land, I took a few moments to collect some cool, inert air to replace the water I was coughing up. I laid as torpid as the air I sucked in until my numbing skin

28

started soaking in the frigidness of my wet clothing. After making sure the lake was truly still, I removed all of my clothes and squeezed as much water as I could from them.

As I sat cross-legged on the shore of a gloomy, subterranean lake, I did something I was unsure I was even capable of—I laughed. It was really more like a chuckle to any ghost watching, but for me, it was akin to hysterical hilarity. For the first time in my memory, I was in charge of my life. Maybe I was eternally stuck down here, but they couldn't get to my rune, they couldn't get me to listen to them anymore. Fuck them.

Taking off my thin undershirt had ripped most of it to be nothing more than an unwearable piece of cloth, so I instead used the strip to delicately wrap it around my shoulder's arrow wound. When the rest of my clothes were adequately dry, I put them on as well. In rummaging through my pockets, I discovered all I had was a little dagger I had completely forgotten was inside my inner coat pocket. Otherwise, I only had a half-eaten piece of venison jerky for food and a stagnant lake for my water.

When my eyes adjusted to the rocky netherworld, I could see that the lake was larger than I had first assumed. The slim cavern opening above actually lined up fairly close to the shore. The rest of the lake stretched for two hundred yards more before it met the other end of the broadening cavern wall. This warped wall only broke up on my little coastline. The shore extended down a tunnel of pitch black darkness. I walked a few yards down this burrow, but a probing holler told me it went down a long way. At least it gave me some hope that I wouldn't die of stagnation.

Before the meager light would pass away completely, I skimmed the area for any kind of food, but the best I saw were a few fluttering moths near the fissure. The lake might have had some fish or plant life to nibble on, but the cold waters would make it too risky to dive in and search randomly, particularly with no way of catching the fish or knowing if the plant life was

29

poisonous to eat. For all I knew, the water itself was bad to drink. I began wishing I had learned a greater variety of spells.

I heard stifled voices high above me, though I didn't pay attention to their rabble. I was exhausted, and wanted nothing more than to shut my eyes for a couple of hours, but my fatigue was still not severe enough to overcome my rune's persistent burning, which the cold water had not diminished. To kill two birds with one stone, I strove to drain all of my energy while also finding out if the tunnel led anywhere. I placed a hand on the left side of the wall and started walking, counting my steps as I went.

Even with eyes accustomed to the dark, a hundred steps into the channel eliminated the sense entirely. Only with touch did I perceive my surroundings with any exactness. I moved slowly, knowing there could be a steep drop anywhere, or a large crack that was waiting to twist my ankle and force me to hop everywhere for the rest of my existence. My sense of hearing could make itself useful later on, but it only presently allowed me to pick up the echoing booms of my palpitating heart.

I took several trips down the tunnel, switching which wall I traced on every attempt. I kept returning to the lake after I added another hundred steps or so to my memory. It was mainly to give me an idea of what I was heading into before I went all in, but I also didn't enjoy being in total darkness for too long. It was as though I were in a kind of limbo, waiting for the gods to judge my life and do whatever it was they did to our souls.

When night made my shore dark, I forced myself to sit down and shut my eyes until sleep overtook them.

Chapter Seven

There was a hint of sapphire moonlight shimmering the lake's surface. Whether it was the same moon I went to sleep with or another night entirely, I didn't know. It had always been difficult for me to tell how long I slept. The arrow wound stung and my muscles felt tender, slowing down my movements for a while. Once I drank some water and ate the last piece of jerky, I restarted my mapping of the tunnel.

Employing some advice that Garf imparted to Heaton's son a few weeks ago, I took it slow at first, knowing that the buildup would pay off later. So the next several hours were spent mentally mapping as much of the tunnel system as far as my brain could take it. I soon learned that the lake tunnel branched off to two other right leaning channels half a mile from the lake.

I didn't know how underground caves normally worked, but I started to get the sense that these three tunnels had not been naturally designed. Their floors and walls felt unusually flat, and they rarely deviated in width or height. My problem now was choosing which one to take. They each seemed to go a long way. Since the one farthest to the right appeared to incline upward ever so slightly, I decided to try it first.

Not minding if it would spur my descent into insanity, I often talked or hummed a bard's song in order to hear any changes in the channel's size. This method also made me think that another tunnel opened up to the left at some point, but I kept my hand to the right wall. A thousand steps later forced my attention back to the previous passageway, as a total collapse blocked my progression.

More darkness, more tunnels, and more collapses ended up wiping most of my map clean. I couldn't even be sure I wasn't just heading back toward the lake. I rested at times, but knowing if I was actually napping or not was difficult to figure out in the realm of nocturnal. Yet even her potent power did not stop a trace of light from sneaking in.

The first light I had seen since the lake came from a little patch of glowing fungi, which I already knew were toxic. My appreciation for this small gift was demonstrated by sitting alongside this beacon. I soaked up its greenish light for a few minutes before I tried to see how long they glowed after plucking one up. A handful of seconds was the answer. More coalitions of these fungi appeared down my latest tunnel, which felt marginally more humid than those before. Thinking this meant some kind of progress to somewhere, I accepted an increase of pain to squeeze through a partial collapse of the tunnel a short while later.

Another minor development occurred when I entered a large space that echoed back my random words. The walls here were extra smooth, so I assumed I entered an artificial chamber of some kind, and recognizing that the other end still had the continuation of the tunnel, I also assumed it was not a room people had once actively lived in. Perhaps they were rest stops? I walked into another of a similar size some six thousand steps later, but the darkness made it impossible to determine anything more than what I already presumed.

Faceless time didn't permeate the underworld, but I could still keep track of it when I paid attention to my growling stomach and drying lips. I expected bugs to appear so that I could eat them at some point, but no worm or beetle showed itself. Were they sensitive enough to hear me coming and hide away in a crack or under a stone? Or were there none around to begin with? In any event, going by the far-flung and sporadic scuttling I heard, there might have been something alive with me. The penetrating dark might

32

have just been playing tricks on me, but I made sure to keep my dagger handy.

My lack of nourishment intensified my wooziness, which had me occasionally forgetting to keep my hand against the wall, so I couldn't even be certain I was preserving on the same track I had been going five minutes before. My last real impression of an idea was to always take the path that inclined skyward, though it wouldn't surprise me to learn that I had only gained an inch of higher ground than I started out with.

Then, as I rested my legs, the leash of the rune suddenly became less taut. Did my handler think me dead? No, his will wasn't completely gone, just subdued. Was I a lost cause to him? Was he merely asleep? Whatever Garf's exact state of mind was, the longer tether afforded me some ease of movement now that every part of my spirit wasn't having to resist the rune's influence. Of course, this improvement did nothing to put food in my desolate stomach or water on my cracking lips. No small part of me wanted to go back and get a drink from that cold lake water.

Gods, that icy liquid sounded good to me. The memory of it taunted me. I could almost feel it tickling my skin with cool droplets… Wait… I wiped my forehead to feel that I was sweating quite a bit. Why was it suddenly warmer? The tunnels had stayed within a cool temperature range, but there was an unquestionable spike during the last hundred steps.

At one point, when I turned at one of the few sharp corners I experienced, there was the softest of glows at the end of a tunnel. The orangish luminescence was quick to brighten at every stride. The heat rose as well. In fact, it was warm enough to where I needed to remove my coat. I draped it over my shoulder as I crept toward the rising radiance.

When the light finally became bearable to my feeble eyes I started to see that the smoother gray stone of the tunnel was being replaced by bare, rough rock. In addition, the passageway was widening, permitting even more light to pervade my visual organs. Then I smelled a foul odor that made me gag. Something was burning, something that smelled like rotten eggs mixed with burnt meat. My ears joined the rest of my senses when it heard something that resembled a bubbling, slow-moving river.

Stepping out of the damned tunnel and into the wide open space I now found myself in was overwhelming. Most of the ceiling was two hundred feet up and the light appeared to emerge from a long fissure on the ground that stretched for as far as I could see to my right. To my far left I saw what appeared to be an avalanche of rock obstructing anything from fashioning a path.

The space beyond the fissure stretched for fifty yards before ending in a fragmented wall decorated with dusty murals and worn carvings. The wall was speckled with a few tunnels three times wider than mine. There were also several stone doors that were either destroyed or left open. My side of the wall looked much the same, though the tunnel entrances were smaller. It was an ancient, dead place I felt I had no business being in, but here I was.

I drifted the forty feet to get to the edge of the putrid crevice. Looking down at its precipice showed me a thin river of molten rock steadily eating away at the mountain. I could fall fifty feet before touching it, so I guessed the crack had been much fuller years ago. The noxious gases it was giving off were hopefully no longer sufficient to kill me, but I backed off to be safe.

I walked alongside my wall, examining what once were brilliant murals and intricate carvings of various scenes. The most intact representations appeared to depict larger-than-life battles by a grand mountain range, which I supposed were the Onyx Mountains.

I searched my paltry memory for "lost nether city." A few scraps of related information surfaced to my awareness. Yes, there was something about this mountain range I had either read in a book or heard spoken as a

34

fable. Indeed, one of the generals I read about fought in a "War of Dragon Fire" not far from Rise, though this great war of many names had really involved much of the world.

The details I did not learn, but I did know that this globe spanning war had ravished the lands a half millennium before. A group of nations had allied themselves with one of the dragon elders, who led an army of his kin and a group of rebel dragon knights. They then proceeded to conquer kingdom after kingdom. At great cost they were driven back to their strongholds until they were ultimately defeated. Fearing that each race was only debasing the other, the surviving elder dragons were convinced to sever their realm from ours. The only dragons left in Orda today were untamable beasts no wiser than wild bears. With no intelligent dragons to ally with, the dragon knights ceased to exist as well.

Was that the answer, then? Local legend stated that one of the subjugator's strongholds had been nestled in these mountains. What was its name…? Nam-, No… Nim. Yes, that was better. Nimbra? Nimbri? Nimbria! That was it. Was this where I was? The ruins of Nimbria?

For the first time since seeing Heaton flop into the lake, some movement caught my eye.

Chapter Eight

I gazed beyond the blazing pit to see a two-legged, lizard-like creature darting into a tunnel entrance. Seeing as it couldn't have been much bigger than the average dog, I actually felt better about not being alone in this place. That changed a minute later when a larger tanned lizard dashed from one tunnel and into a doorless room. With a longer view, I noted that this particular creature was about as tall as I was. It had two long legs that ended with four claws and its two scrawny arms held a single curved talon. What stood out the most was its wide front-facing frill that it used as its entire head. Two beady eyes were kept at the lower outer edges of this fan-like face, along with a snapping jaw at the bottom.

I had seen illustrations and mentions of this creature before. They were known as scamps, one of the most common types of fiends there were. In addition to not being difficult to summon, they were one of the few summoned beasts that adapted well to Orda's diverse environments. Like the rats people compared them to, they ate any and everything and hastily populated a region when left unchecked. Many didn't grow all that big, and a single scamp was never as much trouble as any other feral creature, but when one was famished and in an unobserved ruin with only a finger-long blade in hand, it wouldn't take much to overpower this vulnerable person.

In any event, their presence did give me the hope that something edible wasn't far off, supposing they just didn't consume themselves. Of course, it likely meant I would have to fight them to get to it.

As I continued to explore the ruins, I discovered some bones scattered about rooms or just inside the tunnels. Many looked half eaten. I only now realized that it was possible that some rocks I kicked around in the

36

tunnels were actually shards of skeletons. Most looked too small to be part of a human, but a dusty skull missing its lower jaw bone confirmed that at least a few once belonged to my kind. Were the scamps only brave enough to gnaw on bones, or were they willing to go after those still owned by the living? I think they normally hunted alone, but if a big enough meal was nearby, they were known to gang up on their prey. I saw a few more scurry about and take jerky glimpses at the new curiosity in their midst, but if they were truly interested in me as a meal, the vast gap in Orda kept them at least thirty feet away.

After passing the initial cluster of tunnels and doors, my side of the wall primarily became the rock of the mountain itself, while the scamp-filled side continued to display tunnel entrances, door openings, and most intriguing of all, a few staircases. Since the other side looked to be the true starting point of the nether city, I had the sneaking suspicion that I would have to cross the gap to get any closer to liberation. I thus had my eyes open for some way to cross to the other side.

Except for a couple of heavily rusted blades, cracked clay pots, and several pieces of flimsy metal sheets that probably once belonged to complete sets of armor, my watchfulness did not offer any answers to the unpassable barrier. Its narrowest points were still too wide for me to attempt a leap, and the ruins held nothing I could use to construct a makeshift bridge. There wasn't even a sturdy pole to vault me over.

After about a mile of tracing the lava river, I noted two things. First, the air was slightly cooler. Looking into the crevice showed me that it was less filled and less active than I had perceived half a mile behind me. This also had the effect of making the mountain hollow darker. Second, the river began to curve toward my wall. It was subtle at first, but a hundred yards later had the sizzling river veer sharply in front of me. It cut into the mountain itself, blocking off my advancement on this side.

37

A brick of discouragement hit my stomach, but a closer scrutiny of the gap revealed its sharp turn was also a weak point. A large section of the upper pit opposite me had collapsed into the blackening lava, which was relatively shallow here. The fallen pile of rocks was enough to cut the lava flow's width by half. That was my only answer. I would have to climb down the gap and then climb back up to escape my side of the city.

Just putting my head over the breach was enough to make me uncomfortable, so I knew I would have to suffer a few burns to scramble in and out. The only protection I had available against the water-sucking heat and the sickening gases was to begin tearing off strips of my coat and to wrap the cloth around my hands, forearms, neck, and lower face. I couldn't, however, make the strips all that thick on my hands, as that would hinder my climbing ability. I took some time to study the inner fissure, trying to plan out the trek as best I could. The fissure's uneven walls looked to have plenty of cracks and projections to grip, but their stability was harder to judge. After popping every bone there was to pop, I began the descent.

The first dozen feet went well enough, but it didn't take long for my breathing to become raspier and my vision to blur. I used my unwrapped fingertips to feel out my handholds before going all in. As for my feet, I was content in just digging in my boots as deep as they could go. After closing in on twenty feet, I experienced more lapses in focus, more slips of a finger or foot. The gases were a bigger problem than I thought they'd be, which, given my worn out state, I should have predicted. My searing sweat also made its way into my eyes. I cursed the gods. I didn't know all that much about them, but I cursed them anyway.

The effervescent heat was rippling the air when I reached the halfway point. I had to speed things up. My energy wouldn't last much longer at the pace I was going. I looked behind me to see I was still lined up with the fallen rock pile. What I was thinking of doing was risky, but that

38

was redundant at this point. I focused on sending as much prana as I could into my legs. I then used them to push off the wall with all I had. I twisted my body in midair to face my aim ten feet away. My body crashed just a foot from the lava flow, but I felt as though I landed in the molten river itself.

I was on fire. Every breath felt like I was guzzling down a bowl of boiling water. I had to shut my eyes and just blindly start climbing the rock pile. I was lucky it sloped fairly evenly, allowing me to gain a quick fifteen feet of separation from the pit's lowest point, but I was still at the verge of bursting into flames until I had ascended another ten feet. I wanted to throw up, but the only thing left to bring up was the stomach itself. Whatever did come up actually felt cooler than the surrounding air, so I didn't bother removing the cloth over my mouth.

Something in my ravaged body started reacting to my death climb. It was helping me move upward, but at the cost of my soul. It was my corruption. I was instinctively handing it greater influence so that I could use more of its power to heal and drive my body forward. My madness would come sooner, but perhaps that was as redundant as anything.

Still feeling like I was being cooked, I pulled myself up to level ground. I collapsed face first onto the comparatively ice-cold floor, far too weak to flip to a more comfortable position. I only pulled off the cloth I had around my mouth so that I could exhale all the heat I could with every sore breath and wait for my skin to stop its roasting...

Did I lose consciousness? It didn't matter. Something had forced me to open my eyes and lift my head. It sounded like a large croaking frog. In a hazy hallucination, I saw a scamp cautiously creeping closer. A low croak came out of it. Another croak to my left responded. While I was still too out of it to process the danger properly, a deep-rooted compulsion forced me to stand up. I wobbled, my vision was incoherent, my red skin was tender enough to be agitated by the air, and my trembling hand dropped my dagger.

As I stooped to pick it back up, more scamps appeared from the tunnel in front of me. They croaked in spurts at one another. I began sidestepping to my right, where only a smaller scamp was in the way.

They maintained their guarded distance as they continued to observe me with voracious beady eyes. A few of the smaller ones were the ones to make a probing jump at me before taking a quick step back. The mock bravery of the smaller ones gave the bigger ones real courage. They began taking longer, dashing charges, many making an odd growling croak as they did so. I followed their example and took several rushes at them, which succeeded better than I imagined. The scamps scattered like a flock of pigeons.

Nonetheless, like the flock of birds, they didn't go too far. I'm sure they never even took notice of my near non-existent dagger. They just didn't know what to make of a creature as big as their largest brood. As our game of chicken took an ephemeral respite, I skimmed over my surroundings, looking for anything that could get me out of this new, but foreseen, situation. I especially wanted to find a stairway.

I walked more briskly, keeping my back toward the lava pit. When a scamp decided to get bold, I would charge at them to force them back, but I knew they would eventually learn that I was more bark than bite. I could try killing one to make an example of it, but they were far too swift to waste energy chasing around. Of course, I might not have to do any hunting. The little bastards in particular were quickly learning that they were at least faster than I was and were becoming less intimidated, waiting until I charged almost on top of them before they retreated. They also began snapping their little jaws at me and croaking more excitedly, encouraging the bigger ones to do the same. More started showing up from every side.

Then I saw it—a staircase. I used a charge to send most of them back a few feet. I was planning to sprint upstairs, but getting just a few yards closer told me that would be impossible. The stairway had suffered a collapse, obstructing any attempt at ascension. This breakdown also affected the room beside it. Most of its wall was rubble, exposing a space that had once stored away weaponry, going by the multitude of rusty sticks I saw. Having nowhere else to go, and hoping not everything was unusable, I made a beeline toward the open room.

I stepped over the debris and useless weapons to enter the center of the large, meagerly lit room. In it I spotted two things I did not expect to see—two intact skeletons. The one closest to me had its legs buried in rubble, but its upper body was still whole and had bands of disintegrating cloth over and under its bones. The second was donning a simple corroded helmet and the rest of its body wore a heavy set of greenish armor. It was in a sitting position up against the deepest corner of the wall. They looked to be fragile as dust, but they had been clearly left alone by the bone eaters. Why? The packed croaking behind me forced me to overlook the dead.

Five hundred years had done its work to these cheap, unenchanted weapons and pieces of armor. I scrambled behind a stone table for the defense it supplied. The scamps were at the fringes of the room, looking wary about entering. Did they think I was setting a trap? I spotted something interesting in the middle of another desperate visual sweep. Behind the shadow of the sitting skeleton was an undamaged, leather-encased scabbard. It was in the shape of a longsword, and a black grip, silver crossguard, and silver pommel were jutting out the sheath's opening.

I sprinted to it, knocked over the skeleton in the way, and picked up the red scabbard. My hand trembled. Not from weakness, but from the quivering of the sword itself. All the scamps croaked timidly at the same time. Then, as though my corruption had gained a voice, I heard a ferocious growl coming from deep inside my head.

Chapter Nine

The growl and quivering died away, but their reverberations still ricocheted in my body. I unsheathed the dynamic, double-edged blade to reveal its polished steel and the central groove running up all the way up its flat sides until it stopped near the tapered tip. Mocking my weak body, the sword seemed to weigh little more than my dagger, and the enchantment that was surely on it meant its lightweight did not take away any of its strength. Its length was still a tad too long for me to handle with real grace, but grace was not a luxury I cared about at the moment.

The scamps began backing away. I took an unyielding step forward and they backed away further. The inside of my head produced a low snarl.

"What are you?" I whispered at the sword, not sure what to expect as an answer.

With a voice that kept the rumbling aspect of its growl, the internal reply was, "Your only hope, boy."

"You can get me out of here?"

"It would be in both of our interests. Scare off the damnable iknni so that we can speak in peace."

I assumed he meant the scamps, so I rushed at them with conviction. They dispersed as fast as they their legs could take them. I felt as if I had grown ten feet taller.

"Why are they scared of you?" I asked the blade, keeping an eye on my flanks.

"The weak fear the strong, do they not? I can sense your own power, boy. I can sense the rune suppressing your potential. Do you wish for me to remove the troublesome incantation?"

"Are you a fiend?"

It snarled loudly. "Does my power feel attuned to your wretched corruption? My power is of an undying flame that can easily remove your mind rune and restrain that trivial corruption of yours."

"Just that simple, huh? And what do you want out of this?"

"That should be obvious. Do you know the history of this place? How long I've been stuck down here? If we reach the surface, then I'll be grateful enough to make your goals my own. Think how much you will be able to accomplish with a dragon aiding your cause."

I wanted to ask more questions about this self-proclaimed dragon's past, but I was forced to care about solving my more immediate problems. "What do I call you?"

"Humans call me Aranath. My real name would be unpronounceable in your tongue."

I was about to tell him my name, but I stopped myself when I realized I couldn't keep "Saber" if I reached the outside world again. Likewise, I had no desire to keep using a label that meant nothing to me. Choosing the only other name that came to mind, I said, "All right, Aranath, you can call me Mercer. Now, if you will, remove the rune."

"Then sit down and stay still, boy."

I did as bidden. The hand that held the hilt then started to tingle. This tingling was warm, electric, and oddly pleasant. The sensation crawled up my arm, ran over my shoulder, and connected with my rune, which reacted by lighting the room behind me with a yellow glow. I felt the leash become taut as ever, and while it felt as though Garf's will was suddenly looking over my shoulder, there was no desire for me to follow his wishes. His will was only there just so Aranath could turn it to ash.

As the light faded and the tingling sensation disappeared, an outpouring of raw prana started to fill my body. It was like a dam had burst

43

and the loose lake behind it was quenching a desert. But whose prana was it? Was it Aranath's? It certainly wasn't the corruption taking a greater hold.

"The rune is removed," said Aranath. "Even the original caster won't be able to resurrect it. Indeed, you are now immune to such mind-altering runes in my presence. It was more potent than I anticipated, but the corruption had already compromised it."

"Do you now have your prana running through me?"

"Ah, as I expected, the corruption has spoiled some of your mind already. No, boy, only master dragon knights can absorb a dragon's prana. A mind rune is a type of incantation that suppresses prana so that one's inner self can then provide little resistance to an external will. Your prana is now free to breathe, as it were. I'm also taking the liberty of restraining your corruption, which the little prana you had free was busy trying to resist. Mind you, I cannot cleanse such corruption, but even if I could, I would advise against it. With me here to stop its spread, you can use its enhancing power all you want, and in cases of dire need, I can even allow some corruption to spread a little more to augment your power for a brief time. If you're the type of human to seek silver linings, I would also say that the experience of resisting both a potent mind rune and the corruption has strengthened your prana beyond most humans your age."

"I don't know what my long-term feelings are on silver linings, but I'll take whatever I can get at the moment. So what now? Getting back full control of my prana is nice, but I still need food and water. Do you know where I can get either?"

"Sustenance is all around you."

"What are you talking about?"

"The iknni."

"The scamps?"

"You now have the means to kill them easily enough."

44

"And do you have the means to cook the meat for me? I don't exactly know a flame spell."

"I cannot cast spells for you, boy, though I can later show you how to summon a bit of dragon fire when you have the energy. Regardless, their fresh blood is as close as you can get to water until you find another source."

"Fine. What about you? Do you have a plan to get us out of here?"

"My sight into your realm is dependent on your own field of vision, so you will have to show me what paths are still open. These accessible routes will determine what course we take next."

With sword in hand and prana to spare, I commenced the hunt. Wanting to take advantage of the lava trench's light, I headed back in the direction I came, as the curving crevice robbed the city beyond of light. My inadequate experience in hunting had me merely move as quietly as possible in search for a scamp. I saw or heard a number of them, but they heard or saw me well before my senses picked them up, often fleeing down a dark tunnel.

It wasn't until I cornered a mid-sized scamp in a dark room did I get my first chance at a fresh meal. Seeing no other option, the accosted creature lunged at me, making it easy to land my new blade's edge on its neck. I didn't send all that much prana down my arms, but it was still enough to effortlessly lop off its head.

I dragged my prey into the light and began cutting off its limbs. I then used my dagger to skin its leathery legs and get to its thickest muscles. I cut off bite-sized pieces of bloody muscle before gulping them down with haste. The satisfaction in my stomach prevailed over the awful, sort of sticky taste left in my mouth. I ate what muscle I could from the other leg before stopping. The rest of the reedy creature didn't look worth the effort of taking apart, despite Aranath suggesting I dig for some organs. Alternatively, after my stomach settled down, I left the corpse and resumed my hunt for more leg muscles. So as not to incite the scamps or another bloodthirsty creature by having fresh blood on me or the sword, I took off my last shirt to wipe away the gore before it could adhere to me or the blade.

I brought death to a few more scamps, most about the size of the first. It was impressive how quickly I recovered my stamina after just a few more mouthfuls. Once I had a gratified gut, I investigated the openings of tunnels and stairways for Aranath. He seemed to be looking for something in particular, but didn't really explain beyond telling me to etch an "x" next to a tunnel or stairway he found noteworthy.

Despite the ages of isolation, the sword didn't appear to enjoy chatting all that much, and I was indebted enough for his help that I didn't try and trouble him with any frivolous questions as of yet. I had my suspicions, of course, but even if he had been allied with this stronghold's old owners, it wouldn't bother me. Holding ancient grudges was a problem for nations with long memories. On the other hand, I was all in favor for seeking reprisal for recent wrongs, and Aranath could aid me on that front nicely.

I don't know if it was due to the raw meat, lack of sleep, or some other toil, but a strong headache hit me all at once. With Aranath on hand, I did not fear the scamps getting too close, so I found a dark room to rest in. I succeeded in getting my first real relief since running away. I awoke without the headache and went hunting again. After ingesting more scamp legs, my own legs traversed the ruins for Aranath's benefit.

As I looked up an intact stairway, Aranath said, "We need to go back to the last tunnel you marked. That's our best option."

"You sure? These stairs look okay."

"No staircase on this level reaches the surface. Most lead to soldier barracks or storerooms."

"I see."

46

"Actually, you won't. I doubt there will be many more lava trenches to light our way."

"Again, a fire spell would be nice."

"Yes," he grumbled, "I was getting to that. Now that you have nourishment available to you, I can spend some time teaching you to summon some of my flame. You've never summoned anything, correct?"

"Right."

"The process is fairly straightforward. The biggest obstacle summoners have is finding or creating a realm to call upon their sealed items or making a pact with a summoned creature. You have easy access to both. Find a smooth stone so you may learn to engrave the rune key to my realm."

I found a fist sized obsidian rock a minute later that fit his criteria. Aranath then began describing what lines and shapes to carve into the rock. I apparently messed up halfway through and had to start over on the other side of the stone. The design I finished creating looked mostly like several overlapping triangles inside a circle, though there were a few other details like smaller circles and squiggle things within the triangles. According to the longsword, the positions of the smaller details were especially important.

Aranath next instructed me to find additional stones so that I could carve more of his realm's rune key. By my eighth one, I had memorized how to etch the key without his directions.

Once I finished with my tenth etching, Aranath said, "Focus on steadily sending your prana into one of the stones. When the right amount of prana is poured in, the rune will activate and will be sent into my realm. I will then chisel another rune on top of the key. Summoners will normally have a copy of the key inscribed somewhere, but as you do not have the luxury, you can use another of the keys to resummon the stone you sent to me, which will have some of my dragon fire stored into it. Pouring more prana into this stone will activate the flame. It won't last long burning a small

47

stone, but it will have to do in the meantime. Now begin practicing your summoning technique."

It wasn't difficult finding the right amount of prana to activate the dismissal of the rock. One second had it tight around my hand, and the next had it vanish into thin, stale air. A minute later and I used another stone key to call back the first, which appeared where I wanted it to—on the ground in front of my splayed hand. The returned stone was now carved with eight embedded dots and two different sized scratches from what was undoubtedly one of his claws.

Picking up the summoned stone, I said, "Um, is it safe to activate dragon fire when it's in my hand?"

"You're not expected to activate it in your hand, boy. Some of your prana was embedded in the stone when you sent it into my realm, which means you can link to it from a distance. Place the stone a few feet away from you and focus on sending your prana to it. Even disregarding the added distance, it will require more power than before to trigger the flame, so you don't have to start slowly this time. The tricky part will be initially linking with the stone."

"Any advice on how to link with it?" I asked as I sat five feet away from the rock.

"No."

My back was against a wall as I concentrated on the little rock. As always, I had no lengthening shadow or sex-seeking bird's song to tell me how fast time flowed. I do know that when I felt a spark exactly where the stone laid, I transferred as much of my prana as I could on that spot before the connecting flicker disappeared. The invisible flicker was replaced by a brilliant flash and a loud cracking bang that made me wince. Some of the bits of exploded rock struck me.

"What was that?" I asked.

48

"Hmm, I suppose I made the flame too focused."

"Sounds like I'm not the only one practicing."

With a more guttural sound than usual, he replied, "It'll simply require a minimum amount of amending. Let's try again."

It required six more stabs of "amending" to finally get the stone to burn with a steady flame. A few more attempts showed that most rocks burned for about five seconds before they just simmered with a red glow. The dragon flame was very effective at melting the toughest rock. Many had actually fused with the ground and could not be pulled out with ease.

I also spent hours learning how to incite the dragon fire when the stones were ten feet away and hidden in the dark, something I would have to do often in the gloomy city. I made more key stones, many more, including the explosive kind, and sent most of them into Aranath's realm for easy storage. I carried four stones in my lone serviceable pocket for quick access, planning to summon more whenever I used up two or three.

I went on another expedition for food, and the next muscles I ate had the benefit of being grilled on the steaming stones for a few seconds. This was enough to char them to a crunchy crisp, but I preferred this than tasting the pulpy slime. After filling my stomach to the brink, Aranath and I stepped into the darkness of the tunnel, expecting that the next reliable light we saw came from high above.

Chapter Ten

I walked with drawn steel, keeping Aranath in front of me, as it were. So if anything did decide to blindly charge, they would get to violently meet my ally before ever making my acquaintance. Moreover, my left was always gripping a summoned stone. I had to tie the scabbard to my trousers using some leftover cloth. It dangled precariously, but as long as it wasn't tugged by anything, I didn't have to worry too much about it.

The first fifty yards already had me tossing in one of the stones. Its flickering burst showed a tunnel three times as wide as any I had been in before. This tunnel also had rooms budding out every so often. The most interesting feature was at the end of the passageway just a hundred feet away, where a wide set of stairs led up to another level. What made me balk at first was seeing the silhouette of a large armor-clad warrior halfway up the stairs, but it turned out to be a statue of white marble.

"Yes, this is the right way," said Aranath.

"Who's the statue of?"

"You should stay quiet."

"If anything, the scamps will run off if they hear me."

"There are viler things down here than iknni, boy."

"Any you care to mention?"

"Two come to mind. The calvini are blind and use scent and vibrations in the ground to track their prey. Their bite then paralyzes their victims so that they can extract their inner fluids while they yet live. I don't know what humans call them, but they would look something like giant beetles to you."

"Can they fly like one?"

"No, but the second creature can. I believe you call them 'wolf-bats.'"

"Yeah, I've heard of them. A couple of hunters were killed by some not too long ago."

"That's why I'd be encouraged if we see one. They prefer hunting in open spaces, which means we would be close to the surface in their presence."

"And how far is the surface from here?"

"The battle that ruined this city began when the peaks above collapsed. I do not know how much rock is over us, but I do know that the level we are ascending to now was the level beneath the surface. However, this second level is more complex than the one before, so unless you want to make us more lost, I suggest giving me some quiet to work with... Take a right when you reach the top of the stairs."

Taking the right showed me the very dim outline of another channel, making me think that the complexity Aranath was talking about came from a dizzying tunnel system, but the passage soon came to an end. I tossed a fire stone. Even before I lit it up, its bouncing echoes informed me that I was in a huge open space. Sure enough, the dragon's light did not have the strength to expose all the area I was in. Its five second burn did reveal the most fantastic place I had ever been in.

I was on a suspended road, which was one of some two dozen more above and around me. My street led to what looked like another passageway, but other roads either ran into large stone buildings carved right from the mountain's foundation or onto extensive circular plateaus. As expected, even many of the broader streets were cracked and had at least one major fissure somewhere, but they still looked as though they could support a mammoth.

As the light died away, Aranath, with a hint of reminiscence, said, "Welcome to the heart of Nimbria."

I had to be especially careful walking the roads, as much of the fall-preventing railings had crumbled away, not to mention those holes or fissures scattered any and everywhere. Despite my first street being among the lowest, dropping a regular rock informed me it was still quite a drop to the bottom. This level wasn't as dark as the tunnels I had first used. It was a smog of darkness, to be sure, but it was a darkness with different shades of black.

Over time, my eyes were even able to make out general shapes in front of me. Conversely, without the sound of bubbling lava around, this level was as soundless as those original underpasses, though there was the occasional tumbling rock or fluttering bug's wing to break the ringing silence. Most of Aranath's directions had me follow the bigger roads that connected to large stairways.

Hours later, when we were close enough for the dragon fire to light it, Aranath pointed out two enormous columns of rock that spiraled upward and that many hovering roads seemed to lead into. "Those are our objectives," he said. "They will contain interior stairways that will take us to the uppermost roads and edifices."

On getting a few hundred yards closer to these spires, I thought I started to hear something both familiar and needed. My sultry mouth basically confirmed what I was hearing before my actual thought formed— the trickling sound of life affirming water. With our objectives already in range of the conjured light, Aranath had no qualms about me trying to search for the origin of the enticing sound.

I ending up heading toward a protruding section of the mountain wall. It sounded so close, but I ended up reaching a dead end when I entered a half collapsed building. I threw a summoned stone over the railing and activated it. Its falling light bounced off a gleaming, unreachable portion of the wall ten yards away from me. It was a little stream of water seeping out from an unseen crevice.

I hung my head in frustration and watched the fiery stone drop until it landed two streets below me. The clunk of its impact abruptly made the area alive with hissing sounds. The dying light was just able to show me a mass of insectoid bodies about the size of large dogs scuttling about.

"Those would be the calvini," said Aranath.

The next noise alarmed my ears. It sounded a lot like a buzzing wasp, but much bigger. It was arising from the mass of giant bugs.

"I thought you said they couldn't fly," I angrily whispered.

"Hmm, I know their males cannot. I suppose their females can."

"Fuck. So do I fight or run?"

"Go to the last unbroken building you were in. If they chase you, you can at least force them to join your elevation."

I threw and set off a stone in front of me to make sure I didn't stumble over something as I ran. I had to throw another to reach the building safely. The buzzing and hissing, meanwhile, spread throughout the cavern. Some of it got closer to me, but not with purpose.

A few minutes later, as some of the ruckus died down, my companion said, "You have to keep moving so that they won't eventually catch your scent and mobilize around you. You should be fine as long as you don't allow them to overwhelm you."

I tried to keep track of the pests' whereabouts as I stepped back out onto the road, which was easy to do when their wings beat, their numerous legs tapped the stone, or when they hissed to speak. As one would do, I walked as silently as I could manage to not give them another sensory avenue to pinpoint my location. I would sometimes hear one fly right over me, making me freeze and hold my breath until it passed. I wished my sweat would stop leaking out, but the best I could do on that end was to rub dust over my body and hope that concealed a part of my delicious aroma.

My pace was painstakingly slow now, and the buggers seemed to be getting shrewder. I used to throw a rock as far as I could to get them to focus somewhere else as I used a fire stone to light the next section ahead of me, but most stopped being fooled after the first hour or so. The fliers started to land closer to where I was, sniffing my trail with the four fuzzy antenna on their heads. It wasn't just the fliers getting closer. Those that had been below me were scurrying ever higher. Unlike my less versatile feet, they didn't need to use roads or stairs to climb the mountain. The column I headed for also didn't seem to be any sort of sanctuary. If anything, I was sure at least one of the columns held a hive of them.

Two hundred yards from reaching the pillar, I tossed a dragon stone. When it activated, a calvini fifteen feet away hissed at the fire and flew away. Behind her were a handful of males who hissed back at her and began dashing all along the road. More hissing came from a few nearby females above me.

"Boy, summon an explosive stone and make a run for the column. If too many get close, just fling the explosive near you to make them flee. The blast should overwhelm their senses."

I summoned an explosive stone and picked it up, but before I ran, I threw another fire stone further up to make sure I avoided ankle twisting perils. I ran past the crawling bugs easily enough, but I wasn't too worried about them. A quick jump, kick, or slash deterred them from landing a bite with their twitchy mandibles. It was the beating wings closing in on my stamping feet that gave me an inflating sense of fear.

When it sounded as though a group of fliers just needed a few more beats of their wings to reach me, I tossed the explosive stone ten feet above me and triggered it. The flash showed me that the column's large entry was just thirty feet away, and the high-pitched hissing and retreating wings told me of the fruitful scare tactic. Crossing the threshold had me toss in the second to last stone I carried. In front of me was a room of ornate pillars that extended up to the roof fifty feet up. Hugging the wall was a wide set of spiraling stairs.

"Take the stairway and don't leave until you get as high as you can."

I used what time I had to refill my pocket with more summoned stones before taking the stairs. The fliers followed me inside seconds later. Instead of wasting more stones, I put my back against the wall and hacked away when they closed in. I think my longsword hit two of them. Their skin was hard, but brittle, the sharp edge having no trouble cutting through what it struck. One hissed and backed away while the other fell with a thud. Thirty feet higher and I was forced to use another explosive stone to force back a larger group of females.

My speed was often hampered by debris or the steps themselves, but at least the stairs also seemed to delay the males somewhat. Of course, not all the males were below me. Having to kill or kick away some calvini coming down the stairs slowed me further.

I made gradual progress, going past other rooms with those supporting pillars and sensing that the darkness was not so heavy. Another hundred feet up and my eyes were actually seeing objects more than ten feet away. The air itself changed. At first it was just thicker, but a few more inhales informed me of its sourness. I don't think the calvini liked it much. The females withdrew almost all at once and the tapping of the male's legs calmed down.

"We're entering new territory," said Aranath.

"Can you smell that? It smells like crap."

"Only prana and the senses of sight and hearing can be transferred between realms with any effectiveness, but I suspect you're detecting the droppings of wolf-bats."

"I guess that's good news."

No longer being pursued, I climbed with leisure up the remaining steps. Maybe two hundred feet from where I started, I hiked into an unpassable blockade of rock. I thus went back to the last road access and threw in the proper item. The road here had several supports at the edge that propped up a curved rooftop. The end of the road led all the way to the mountain's wall, where a faint white light was emanating from the large ingress. The stench worsened, but as I had already gone through a river of fire, going through a river of sewage would be refreshing at this juncture. I simply had to jump across a six foot gap and I was finally free of the mountain's innards.

Chapter Eleven

Crossing through the threshold had me inside a massive domed structure of faded orange stone. There were many cracks both big and small on the roof, which gentle beams of moonlight were able to use to infiltrate the ruin. The cracks also allowed me to see a dam of rock encompassing the sprawling structure. It was this unpassable barrier that blocked the otherwise open door on the wall opposite mine. In the center of the room was a thick column helping to hold up the roof.

The floor was strewn with the bones of deer, goats, and other animals. A few still had rotting meat still stuck on their carcass, though this didn't appear to be the main origin of the stink. I had been without food long enough to make the flies and maggots I saw look like a tempting treat, but I refrained, knowing I was so close to getting something more substantial and less repulsive. I looked out for wolf-bats and an exit hole big and low enough for me to crawl through. Neither of things appeared, however.

I stood in the epicenter of the cavernous room, wondering whether I should head for the twenty foot tall, arched passage on my right—where I believed most of the fecal odor was flowing out from—or take the mirror route on my left. As I was coming to the easy conclusion to avoid the path of stink, the left passage began to act up. Something heavy was stomping toward me. Backing away, I also heard what sounded like something being dragged. The oncoming entity was also producing heavy grunting and snorting sounds.

I hid behind the column and took a peek around my bulbous barrier. A hulking, gray-skinned creature tread into a moonbeam. It was a seven foot tall mountain troll. The stocky legged, top heavy creature was dragging a lifeless ram behind it. Three yellow eyes skimmed the chamber after it released its kill.

"A juvenile," evaluated Aranath. "Its skin won't be too tough, and its bulk will make it slow. Aim for its throat, or at least blind it."

Despite Aranath's belief that I was willing to fight, I started receding toward the other passageway. I preferred to avoid something that could take off my head with one swipe of its ponderous hands if I made a mistake. Before I got halfway to the other channel, however, the troll started making a lot of fuss. The beast hammered its fists numerous times on the ground while bellowing like a fussy toddler. A bellowing answer came from the reeking passage behind me. I turned to see the approaching silhouette of a knuckle-walking troll. It looked a little bigger than the first.

With no place to hide, I ran back for the inner mountain road. The troll already in the room with me spotted the potential meal with one of its trio of eyes and excitedly hollered, followed by equally ecstatic grunts by its companion. I felt the ground shudder as their lumbering bodies charged. A look back showed me that they were propelling themselves with their forearms, giving them a faster speed than one would think, but I was still quick enough to keep ahead of them. I arrived at the road's gap and leapt over it. I then put a hand to the ground and summoned four explosive stones. I picked one up, but left the other three at the brink of the break. I backed away and waited to see how trolls treated obvious ploys.

The first troll continued to blatantly charge, but it did see the gap. It was evidently confident in itself and took the jump. I triggered the stones just before it landed. The beast yowled in midair when the flash-bang hit its senses. Hundreds of pounds crashed in front of me. Its legs were dangling over the brink, so it had to pull itself up with its arms. With those powerful limbs engaged in another task, I closed in with the longsword. Using one prana-enforced motion, I pushed the sword's tip into the troll's third eye, which hovered above the other two. I felt its skull split and it was dead as soon as the front end of the blade punctured its brain.

The second troll had come within ten feet by the time I was pulling out the sword from its companion's face. It stopped charging when it reached the verge of the fall and started angrily pounding the ground, as though it wanted to make the gap bigger. Luckily, the road was too thick and wide for the brute to accomplish such a feat. It gave up on its slams and began pacing, wondering whether to make the jump, but it soon quit this as well. The troll roared at me a couple of times, then released a prolonged howl toward the domed building.

When it stopped its uproar, it became immovable enough to make me think it had turned to stone. It moved and huffed again when a distant roar made a reply. The troll pounded the floor and headed back where it came, though staying within the vicinity of the dome. A half minute later and I hearing something even larger coming within earshot.

"Get out," said Aranath. "It called its mother. You have no chance if she keeps you in the dark."

"That might be better than facing the mother of the thing I just killed."

"This is no time to jest, boy."

"You think I'm fucking joking?"

"Listen, mundos can see well in the dark. She'll either block this exit until she believes you starved to death or, more likely, chase you in here until you're crushed under her fists. You can't win in here. You have to get outside."

I regrettably took the jump and peered into the dome. A pair of great lungs were snorting and the trembling mountain wall shook off loose pebbles from its steps. Then a huge mass came into view, its skin much coarser than the younger beast I couldn't see anymore. The shape was of an immense

59

troll. She was twelve feet high, but she could have elevated another couple of feet if trolls weren't always hunching over. There was more meat and bone in one of her robust arms than in my entire body. The bulging, golden eyes of the largest living being I had ever seen turned to me.

"Well, fuck."

Her response was for her to slam her prodigious fists on the ground and begin a charge. I really wanted to head back into the dark I had gotten so used to, but Aranath's growl reminded me of the only real chance I had.

As I ran toward the right passage, my sword said, "The exit can't be far. Just lose her."

"No shit," I panted out between breaths.

I purposely went around the larger boulders in the hopes of slowing her down. I didn't bother to see how well it worked. I entered the passage, which was just a channel that went thirty feet before opening up to another dome. The air in this space was dense with flies, all taking advantage of the piles of shit in various states of hardness. I ran over and through these stink heaps in my attempt to get behind this dome's column.

The end of the room was just a wall of rock, so there was no more running into other rooms. I went behind the pillar and turned to see which way the brutish mother came at me. When she picked a direction, I dashed in the other. She took a sharp turn to adjust and her shoulder slammed into the column, sending ceiling shards falling to the floor.

I headed back for the passage, not hesitating when the troll-child reappeared inside of it. When I closed the distance to it, I threw the explosive stone at its face. I set it off in midair, forcing the beast to shut its eyes for that instant I needed to pass it. The prana I sent to my legs helped give me a bit of separation, but there was the realization that losing them could not be accomplished by running alone. Looking up at a moonbeam's source gave me some inspiration to try a card up my nonexistent sleeve. I quickly studied the wall near the next passage, seeing that the right side looked the most vulnerable. I raced for a particular cavity where the wall met the floor, which was big enough to fit a fat possum. Keeping a precarious five yard lead, I slid to the chink in the wall and summoned every explosive stone I had left. A pile of thirty or so stones filled the little cleft. I stood up and revived my run just as the child-troll smashed its fists in my spot. This is when I activated them.

The strength of the blast was surprisingly strong, at least going by the initial flash and boom. Both trolls responded by roaring—the smaller one from surprise, the bigger one from incitement. Then I heard the cracks form. They were near me at first, but they swiftly moved skyward. Dust, pebbles, bits of the ceiling, and mountain rock were falling like drizzle in front of me. As the child-troll thrashed around in its blindness, I drew back until I was underneath the passage's ceiling. Aiding the development of the cracks, the continuing charge of the heavy mother troll wobbled the structure.

I needed her to stay every second possible, so I summoned every fire stone in my realm, which amounted to be as many as the explosive kind. I next swept the batch with my hand to spread out the stones. As more debris fell, I waited the extra second it took to have the mother be on top of some stones before setting them off. The dragon fire emitting from five dozen stones forced me to shut my eyes from the penetrating luminosity. My ears shuddered from the mother's deafening roar, who seemed to stop in her weighty tracks.

I opened my eyes to see larger fragments of rubble crashing onto the dome's floor. The troll, after taking a second to see that the fire was already losing its luster, took a step toward me. Using my last ploy, I cast my illusion spell. A second me appeared in front of the real thing. Just as I had done with Heaton, I sent this ghost running toward the dimwitted troll. She reacted by taking a swipe at the illusion, smothering it, but I didn't need it anymore.

A large boulder struck her left shoulder, making her stumble. In the middle of her pained howl, a rockslide obscured my view. It was as though the entire roof and the rock it held back had rained down in one whole sheet. Fearing the roof of my own passage was next, I ran for the other side. I still heard the snarls of the trolls behind me, but they were waning with every step I took. The next dome I entered had a troll-sized hole where the exit door had been. I picked up the pace, going as fast as my legs could push me. I crossed the downpour of moonlight, bolting into a world where the sky was the only roof I had to worry about.

I heard as boulders continued to tumble and crash in the rockslide I created. I was in a large plaza at first, but that ended in a blur when I reached a set of stairs fifty yards wide. Going down them I saw another dome on my left, its exact state too fuzzy for me to note. I went down two more tiers of damaged domes and worn stairs before getting to natural ground. I didn't stop when I reached the dirt ground of a dense woodland. I didn't even stop when the throbbing in my ears overtook any external sound.

It wasn't until Aranath said, "Slow down, boy. Your energy is still precious out here," did I begin thinking again.

I fell on my hands and knees, griping the hard soil between my fingers. I sucked in all the crisp mountain air I could, eventually looking up to see a full moon through an opening in the tall pine trees surrounding me.

Chapter Twelve

That night and the following day was all about regaining my strength. Sleep occurred under the low branches of a tree, where I snoozed sitting up against the trunk. When the daylight of early autumn broke through, warming up the valley to a comfortable range, Aranath helped me seek out plants he believed humans could safely eat, which included some yellow dotted mushrooms and a handful of red berries. For water, he told me to head east, where he hoped a river still existed a few miles away. I wasn't sure if it was once the river he spoke of, but I did find a small creek around noon.

As I washed my face of grime and dirt, Aranath asked, "What will you do once you recover?"

"The people who corrupted me, the people who placed the rune on me, they have to die."

"Revenge, then?"

"You could call it that if you wish. I'm not even sure I'm all that angry at them. I just feel like it's something that needs to be done."

"Whatever your exact sentiments are, the original caster of your mind rune is quite skilled. The rune would have been much more problematic if this caster was resisting me. You'll need proper training if you hope to be a match against this foe."

"You'll train me?"

"There are few other options."

"Then you'll make me a dragon knight?"

The dragon growled. "A human term propagated during the age of the Dragon Concord. Most humans started associating all human-dragon

63

partnerships with that phrase, but it's an antique job title, not the true name for an individual pact."

"Then what do you call it?"

"If you insist on calling it anything, then I'd prefer the more precise label of Veknu Milaris."

"Is that an old human term?"

"Yes. It roughly translates to mean 'fire bound,' which is as close as you'll get to what we dragons call it. It's a pact between a single human and a single dragon, and it can be agreed to for the same reasons any other pacts are created. When that contract became a civic profession it was called being a dragon knight, but we will be no such thing."

"And what does being a Veknu Milaris entail, exactly?"

"Veknu Milaris has several stages before a true sharing of power can begin. The agreement itself is the first step. The second would be for you to learn to control dragon fire. Summoning me would come afterwards."

"You sure I couldn't do that now? Flying over these damn mountains sounds pretty good to me."

"Your use of prana needs to be much more efficient for the task, and the deed must be completed with excess prana available, or you won't be able to make much use of me for long. This will make up the bulk of your initial training. I cannot teach you spells, but I can guide how well you use your spirit energy. It normally takes years for someone to reach the point of summoning a dragon, but your unique experiences have given you an advantage few will ever know."

"And I have all the time in the world now."

The rest of the day was spent hunting for a meal. The best I could do was catch a couple of rabbits by hurling my dagger at them. Cooking the first with dragon fire was not very fruitful. Dragon fire doesn't stop burning something until there is nothing left to consume, and it does so with great ferocity. Even thick branches were treated like dry leaves. Trying to beat the hasty time limit, I put the rabbit on the stick too close to the fire pit and it caught fire, turning my first meal to bony cinders. The second rabbit cooked better in the regular fire pit I made.

The next few days I spent near the creek, which ended in a small pond. I recovered my strength by catching a few rabbits, a large owl, and some little fish. Of course, I wasn't the only thing hunting. I already knew that trolls made their home in these mountains, not to mention the possibility of mountain lions and bears. Aranath told me of a way to keep back most of these carnivores was by circling my "territory" with burnt dragon stones, since few creatures would dare cross into a dragon's arena. This was how I kept safe in the nights, along with regularly maintaining a large campfire to keep away the hordes of mosquitos. The blood suckers made me miss my shirt and coat.

As for training, Aranath had me begin by working on my illusion spell. Not only did I have to work on the amount of time I held it together and how well I manipulated it, but Aranath taught me that the best way to make efficient use of my prana was to learn what was the minimum amount of prana I needed to activate the spell and then attempt to use less and less prana each time I cast it. Moreover, I needed to learn how to keep the illusion going after it went out of my sight, such as behind a tree or boulder.

I used up almost every hour of every day training and hunting, which I found comforting. A good chunk of me wondered why I even had to leave this place, but any time I looked at my serrated left arm, I was reminded of what my only goal in life was.

It was a week after leaving the mountain when I asked Aranath, "What is the best way to get to the other side of these mountains?"

"If memory serves, going westward is a trip twice as long as going east. The mountain range does curve northward some three hundred miles east, but there is a gap in the range we can use to avoid climbing over anything. Be warned, the gap lies in a tundra with little in the way of food and water. You must be at your most fit when you leave the woods."

"I don't feel too far off from being fully recovered. Another week here and I'll actually start to gain real weight."

"I would start the trek sooner than that. Autumn is short here, and the winds are already shifting. Unless you know how to make a good coat out of bear pelts, I wouldn't try being caught in an early blizzard out here."

Two nights after his assertion, I shivered from a cold breeze. It wasn't much, but it convinced me to start my journey east on the next day. The first few days of travel weren't much different from the last week. I found food and water well enough, and the woods themselves stayed an echoing image of the area I had just walked past.

It wasn't until the fifth evening of travel did I spot something new—a used fire pit. Its size suggested it had been used by a group of people, not just one or two. The only clue pointing to their identity was a small rugged knife made from bone, which Aranath guessed came from a nomadic tribe that traversed the tundra and woods during the warmer months.

"Is this tribe dangerous?"

"They were harmless enough in my time, but who knows what their disposition is now. I would stay away if you see them first."

"And if they see me first?"

"Don't try to fight or run. Assuming they didn't change languages, I can help you speak with them. I'm certain they won't be hostile toward someone who can speak their tongue."

Five minutes after moving on from the campsite, I picked up more signs of recent activity. Dried blood sprinkled the ground and on a tree, and there was some torn fur clothing in a shrub. The dirt only had scrambled impressions from footwear and bare feet, with no hint that predators were responsible for the attack on these rovers.

"Any hints as to who did this?" I asked the only being available.

"It isn't easy ambushing four or five nomads. Whoever attacked them must have either overwhelmed them with numbers or have been deadlier combatants, meaning you should keep your guard up for more than just bears."

"There's a blood trail that heads east."

"Then go north. This attack couldn't have happened more than two nights ago. There's a good chance you'll run into the people involved if you hold your direction."

So that's what I did for the next several hours. I didn't want to sleep only hours away from a bloody scene, so I kept moving beneath the moon longer than normal.

When the time came to find a place to hang my drooping head, a large shadow swept over me. A high-pitched screech of a huge bird was then heard far above me.

"Great," said the dragon with a subtle form of sarcasm. "A jengsing hawk has spotted you. They are known to ally themselves with the Boreal Tribe. Keep still and let them come. Say exactly what I say when I tell you to. At least they won't be able to sense your corruption."

"But what if they recognize the fiend's tail?"

"*I* don't even recognize what kind of fiend that tail belongs to. Still, even if they assume such a thing, your relative sanity should preclude a blind attack."

I walked toward a small clearing so that the moonlight could fully expose me. Here I stood for a few noiseless minutes, occasionally seeing the huge hawk flying equal with the wispy clouds overhead.

"I'm sure they're nearby by now. Repeat after me, and loudly—Ku ma, Orda kis-ra."

"Ku ma, Orda kis-ra! What did I say?"

"'Come on out, children of Orda.' Now stop speaking like a demented fool. They have sharp ears. Say it again."

After I did, there was a whistle behind me. I turned around to see a woman armed with a drawn bow. She wore lightweight leather armor partly outlined by some brown fur. She said something sternly in her language and I retorted with Aranath's similar sounding words. I next heard a pair of steps to my back and to my right. She spoke again and there was a response from a man behind me. Aranath told me to turn around.

I was now observing a stout man with a long blade made from bone in each hand. I called them swords, as one side did appear to have a sharpened edge, but they really looked better as pure thrusting weapons. He carefully looked up and down my frame, stopping a couple of times at my left arm and the crimson scabbard I gripped tightly on that side. The third nomad, now on my left, said something with harsh conviction. A glance showed me he was not much older than I. His weapon was a shorter sword of bone, which had a sharper edge than the longer example. The apparent leader replied to the young man with a firm tone. Aranath then told me to say something else.

The leader nodded and said, "My family often trades with southern towns, so I can speak the shared tongue if you find the words easier, but how is it you know our old tongue? Few outsiders bother to learn it. What clan do you belong to?"

"By 'clan' he means what kingdom you associate yourself with," clarified Aranath.

"No clan is mine," I answered. "The words you call your own were given to me in the same way your hawk gives you eyes in the sky."

"I see. And how does a clanless child of Orda find himself here?"

"Desperation. I assume something similar can be said of you."

"What makes you say that?"

"You're searching for members of your tribe, are you not?"

His eyes gained a gleam of urgency. "You saw them?"

"An abandoned campsite five or six miles south, then signs of a fight not far from that. No bodies, but there was blood."

The nomad spoke in his language again. The other two offered their own input.

Aranath said, "They're wondering if you're involved with the attack on their tribesmen. The male child is suggesting that your upper garment is missing because it was stained with blood. The sword is not doing you any favors either. There's no way out of this, tell them you will lead them to the attack sight and aid them in the search of the true attackers. The leader's name is Unith, by the way."

"I'll lend you my assistance, Unith," I said in the middle of their yammering.

They quieted down when Unith raised a hand at the others. "That must ultimately be our decision. If you really are not involved in the disappearance of my people, then hand over your weapons to us and they will be returned once your trust is gained."

Aranath told me to say, "You will not be able to hold my blade."

I offered the longsword's hilt to him. He clasped it with conviction, but his fingers were not there half a second before he jerked away his hand. The sword had trembled in my grasp and Aranath had said something in Unith's language.

With a look of trepidation and a shakiness to his voice that he had to clear, Unith said, "Very well, you may carry your blade, but it means any wrong move will force us to subdue you."

69

"Fair enough."

Unith proceeded to tell the other two something, to which the young man protested to, but a stanch tone from his superior quieted him. To me, he said, "Start heading for the scene of battle. We'll keep near you."

I nodded and walked past the receding woman, who never lowered her bow. Unith whistled and I began going at a faster pace. I almost reached running speed before I heard Unith tell me to not go any faster. They all stayed several yards to my flanks. They were good at residing in the shadows and making their footsteps light throughout the expedition. No talking transpired between humans, but there were intermittent bird calls coming from Unith, which were sometimes responded to by the great hawk above.

I slowed down when we neared the place of interest, and when things looked particularly familiar, I slackened to a brisk walk. My feet stopped moving when I saw the edge of the bloodstained area. The younger man and Unith scrutinized the woods for a few minutes as the woman kept her wary blue eyes on me.

"How many are you looking for?" I asked Unith when he seemed to finish his assessment.

"Four, and I count five different sets of prints here."

"My own, I take it."

"Yes. Do you still proclaim your innocence, clanless child?"

"Yes. I have no reason to fight your people."

His male comrade spoke to him with anxiously angry words. I didn't need to have Aranath tell me that Unith responded by hushing the speaker. Back to me, he said, "Do you see the blood trail?" I nodded. "Do you know where it goes?"

"No, I had wanted to avoid any confrontation with bloodletters, which is why I turned north from here."

70

"We'll follow it, then. What we find at its end will have us see what we do with you."

"So be it, but before we move on, may I ask the boy's relationship to those missing? He certainly isn't keeping a calm head over the matter."

"He is fearful over all missing, as three of the four are close companions of his, but it is his sister that makes him unlike a true warrior."

"Any relatives of yours among them?"

"His sister is my niece."

"And does the woman have any close connections to them?"

"She is my wife, so she is a niece too her as well. Why the interest in our connections?"

"Because I'm innocent, which can only mean that the violence occurred among themselves."

"We shall see how your, how do you say? Theory? We shall see how well it holds up to more information. Let's get moving."

I did my best to follow the erratic blood trail in the quasi moonlight. It stopped completely after a hundred yards or so, but there were still some footprints to follow. Aranath helped me be a better tracker than I otherwise would have been, and the trio of nomads rarely had to point out the correct path for me to take.

After a mile the tracks turned toward the mountainside, where the air started to get a little fouler. It was here Aranath told me to stop and to look carefully at a rock wall behind a collection of bushes. There was a narrow and deep vertical crack on the face of the wall, which some of the footprints steered toward. The crack went up for twenty feet, but not high enough to open up at the top, meaning their hawk could not look down on it. Getting a bit closer gave me a good whiff of death emanating from within. Unith came up behind me as I stood thinking.

"Go in," said the nomadic leader.

"Something's wrong," I said. "It feels too much like a trap."

"If it is, you will help spring it and earn my trust."

"But don't you understand? If this is a trap, who was it for? It couldn't have been for me."

"Whatever your thoughts, none of my people will enter first."

"Have it your way, but then you must do me a favor."

"If it's a reasonable request, I may grant it."

"Listen, if I'm right, then this trap was probably meant for one of your people. My request is for you to make sure that no one gets behind you."

He looked surprised. He also looked as if he might say something to rebut me, but he held that specific statement and instead nodded toward the crevice. As he withdrew into the shadows, I moved forward, really not liking that I was heading inside a godsforsaken mountain again.

The crevice was just wide enough for me to walk into without going in sideways. I quietly unsheathed Aranath when I stepped into total darkness. I next picked up a random rock and threw it in. Its impact was distant and created several echoes that signaled an open space. I waited a moment to hear if anything moved or breathed, but nothing happened. Still not convinced nothing was there with me, I swayed the sword back and forth to better judge the width of the path in front of me.

Fifteen feet in, where the crevice had gotten a few feet wider and would only continue to do so, I pulled out a dragon stone. I lazily lobbed it to make sure it remained within my twenty foot activation range. I then knelt to summon an explosive stone. Grabbing it, I activated the dragon stone and immediately prepared to cast my illusion spell. The illumination of the stone showed a small cave that had a dead boar in the corner, but I stopped paying attention when I sent in my illusion running into the cave. My trap set off the one I was expecting. Two nomads jumped out from their hiding place next to the cave entrance and attacked my illusion with excited shouts and bone swords. The instant the illusion was dissolved by their first strike, I threw in the explosive stone.

Braced for the effect, I was able to land some hard blows on their confused heads, disorienting them further. I could have killed them, but I was still unsure what the consequences of that would be. The scrawnier one I knocked out with a single blow with my elbow and his natural impact with the hard ground. The other required a strike to the head with my sword's pommel followed by taking his head and slamming it to the floor. Not a second later, a woman screamed outside. The hawk screeched at the end of that same second, making my next move clear.

Reaching the open air again, I heard someone yelling a war cry as they ran deeper into the woods. This I headed for. A few yards in and I witnessed the outline of another running figure to my right. Focusing on it told me it was that hotheaded youth. He saw me coming and yelled something at me, to which Aranath translated as a threat to keep out of their business.

"Fuck that," I said to resolve myself. "If he gets away with whatever he's doing, then I'm their next target."

I used prana to propel my legs to take longer, faster strides. Seeing this, the nomad ran toward me and cast something that glistened in his hand. He then fired this as a projectile. On evading it, I saw that it was a thick icicle. It seemed well made, but the next icicle that came at me confirmed that he wasn't launching them with dangerous speed, at least not dangerous to me.

The distance between us closed quickly. He brandished his bloody short sword. No fear emanated from him, so I knew he was an idiot. I wouldn't even need a distraction. Like an idiot, he started a swing of his short-ranged weapon far too wide, allowing me to predict its arc. I leaned backward to dodge the swing. Again, killing wasn't my goal just yet, but I cared nothing for limbs. His sword wielding wrist provided little resistance to my upward swing. His scream was cut short when I bashed the pommel to his face, knocking him down where his sword now laid. No longer a conscious menace, I moved on from him.

I didn't move far when I heard another shriek from the hawk inducing a woman's scream. I followed the auditory cue to the sight of a man-sized bird pinning a young woman to the ground with its talons. On my left was Unith standing over a dead man. He raised his weapons when he noticed someone approaching, but lowered them on identifying me.

"Did you see my wife?"

"No, but I knocked out the two in the cave and wounded the boy."

"Come with me."

To the red feathered hawk, he whistled a few bird calls. The winged creature responded by chirping and tightening its grip on the girl's back, who squealed from the pain. I took Unith to the spot I had beaten his nephew. I had evidently not hit him hard enough, as he was awake and attempting to run away, though he stumbled too much to make a good effort at it. We summarily caught up to him and Unith began yelling at him. When the answers weren't satisfactory, Unith punched him in the stomach, sending him on his knees.

"Can you watch him?" he asked me.

I nodded. He then began searching and calling for his wife. There was never an answer. The night became silent for a few moments when I couldn't see or hear Unith anymore.

It was still quiet when Unith reappeared holding his limp wife in his arms. He laid her body nearby, strolled up to his nephew, grabbed his hair, and slammed his fist into the youth's jaw. I heard it break. Unith next drew one of his swords, said a few words, and sliced the throat of his enemy.

"You say the others are still alive?" he asked me as he looked down at the dying young man.

"Yes. Are you going to kill them all?"

"The girl's fate will be decided by the Mother of Stars."

"A kind of seer," explained Aranath.

By his request, I followed Unith into the cave, where he cast a little flame spell that hovered just above his open left palm to light our way.

After slicing his third neck, he said, "I would have been the one to enter this cave if the stars had not aligned to have our paths cross."

"I'm sorry about your wife."

"Aye."

He was mute until he chirped at his feathered companion, compelling the hawk to fly back up to its domain. Unith started talking to his niece, whose back was ripped with several gashes. She had a fierce, defiant look on her face when she responded to him.

After a few back-and-forth statements, Aranath said, "Family squabbles. According to his children, it seems Unith's younger brother is better suited to lead their family tribe. Not the first or last time I'll see humans crave power over blood."

The newly broken family conversed a while longer before Unith pulled out a thin rope he used to tie her hands together. When he was finished, he said, "You've done much for me already, yet I do not know what name is yours."

"It's Mercer."

"Well, Mercer, do you mind keeping watch over my niece here as I give proper veneration to my life partner? I give you leave to end her spirit if she rebels."

A nod from me had him head back to his wife's body. The hawk perched on the top of a nearby tree, keeping its powerful vision on its

75

summoner. Whatever Unith was doing had him occasionally chant loudly in his ancient language. My charge stared at the same patch of ground for a long while. She stayed looking at it when she spoke.

In my language, she said, "You are not us. Why here?"

"The stars aligned or something."

"Kill the man and I'll be your woman."

"I don't think I'll need a deal for that to happen. Besides, I don't go for backstabbers."

Losing a battle to hold back tears, she began crying a few minutes later. I wondered if she was the one who had planned the assassination on her uncle. Or had her brother convinced her? Did it even take much convincing? Aranath said they had chosen power over blood, but had they? How much was this pushed by obligation to a sibling? Whatever the amount, if it was already this prevalent in the middle of nowhere, I shuddered to think what I would encounter in places with more than a dozen people.

As dawn approached, Unith returned and we started a two day journey to a large campsite where more of his hunting and foraging group was located. When he learned that I was going to cross the gap, he offered me safe passage with the main caravan, but I said I preferred being alone and would only take whatever supplies I could carry. So not long after we reached the group of portable huts at the edge of the forest, I began my journey across the tundra.

Chapter Thirteen

My stop at Unith's base camp gave me the chance to finally get out of my tattered garments. I wasn't sure if I had a style, but I knew the frill of fur that went with the short brown tunic and boots I was given wasn't part of it. At least they fit snug and were plenty warm. In fact, they were almost uncomfortably warm in the daylight. To protect the gift, I wrapped a rag around my left arm, though I did later shear the excess fur myself.

Other gifts included a pouch of throwing knives made from bone, little bags of seeds and nuts that would provide bursts of energy when other food was scarce, and a waterskin. Unith wished to give me some coin, but he said we would have to head for the main assembly for that, which I once again declined to do.

As for the journey itself, I kept near the woods for as long as possible, knowing there wouldn't be many trees to offer firewood when I headed north. There was also the relative protection the trees offered from wild animals. I did eventually have to leave the woods completely, but I didn't mind getting to sleep under the unobstructed view of the unreachable stars. I would even say that the nights were my favorite time of day. It was serene as shit to find a lone tree and make a little fire next to it as I focused on enhancing my illusion spell, or cooked a bird or mouse-like thing I caught. Once in a while I saw bigger things than rodents. Small packs of mammoth promenaded near any water source there was, and larger herds of bison and elk were never in one place for long, doing all they could to keep ahead of wolf packs and the stealthier saber-tooth cats.

Becoming involved in other people's complications concerned me more than running into aggressive animals, so I would lay low and hide anytime I believed I saw a human silhouette on the horizon. Since I didn't meet a soul on my way to the mountain range's gap, I considered the method a success. The gap itself was still a tall hill of rock compared to the flatter grasslands of the tundra, but I had no misfortune going through the mile wide route.

The other side of the gap was more tundra, but as I made my way southward, I saw a handful of permanent settlements where some desperate or misguided farmers eked out a living from the hard, harsh land. These settlements became bigger and more common the further down the compass I went. In due course, there were small towns I had to skirt and roads I avoided. Patrols were infrequent this far north, but I didn't want to take the chance and run into an Etoc soldier or city guardsmen. I imagined there would be questions asked to a solitary youth armed with a longsword and dressed like a nomad walking around on "civilized" trails. Likewise, roads were always good places to meet bandits who might see my sword as a nice prize.

As the weeks leisurely passed, neither Aranath nor I became anymore talkative than before, though no sense of awkwardness grew from a muteness that could last two days straight. It seemed there was an understanding that each of our pasts didn't need to be rehashed all at once. All the same, Aranath would occasionally let something slip during a training session—the only time we were each inclined to form consecutive sentences with more than three words in them. They were minor details, such as remembering a certain stance he saw a soldier productively implement in a fight, and they were always related to battle. I spoke a little more about my past then he did, but that was only because I was heading right for it.

In preparation for that encounter, the near constant training I did was producing some results. My illusion spell was lasting a few seconds longer and I could even momentarily lose sight of it without it evaporating. Adding

78

to my limited assortment of training regimens, Aranath started teaching me to better use my prana to increase my speed. He explained that he was getting better at sensing the way my prana was coursing my body and, as he put it, I was employing it in the crudest way possible.

Instead of merely pushing prana to a foot when it touched the ground, his advice was to send the prana to the foot when it went airborne, so that I had a concentration of it by the time it came back down. It was a tricky technique to master. I basically had to manipulate prana in two different places at the same time—the gathering of prana in the midair foot and the release of prana in the foot that hit the ground. I trained in this aspect hundreds of times a day, but early evaluations had me only get the timing down on a handful of occasions, and none were done on purpose.

Despite what Aranath called my "amateur station," I felt ready to see Garf. However, a significant part of my plan involved me staying incognito as I tracked him down. I couldn't do that in a guise that drew attention. So as soon as I left Unith's camp, I was on the lookout for an opportunity to acquire more clothing. I hoped to come across a recently dead bandit with my exact size of clothing just waiting to be plundered, but no such luck. It wasn't until I left the tundra behind and entered a region with actual blotches of forest did I get a chance at adding to my attire. It happened not long after I passed the largest town I had seen yet.

I thought I had gotten back to uninhabited territory, but a worn dirt path heading for a grouping of trees told me otherwise. I was going to ignore it, but a woman's shriek brought my attention back to the tree line. It wasn't a scream of fear or agony, but one of those I heard a woman squeal out when someone was being rowdy with her. Again, I was about to disregard it, but the sound of splashing intrigued me.

As I wandered closer, I began to hear one other girl and at least one guy. Passing the first line of trees had me see the shore of a small lake shimmering under the noon sun. Sneaking a bit closer had me catching sight of two girls and two young men bathing with frisky excitement about twenty yards away. It would have been a little chilly to be out swimming alone, but I suppose the youths were attaining bodily warmth by some mysterious means.

I watched them for a minute, particularly the white haired girl with two bulbous assets, before I saw a pile of clothes on and around a nearby tree. There were boots, shirts, and pants, but catching most of my interest was a dark blue cloak flapping on a low branch. With the owners of the garments focusing on places those garments had once covered, it was easy tiptoeing to my objectives without being noticed. I snuck behind the tree and grabbed the cloak and a nice linen shirt. I concluded that at least one of these juveniles belonged to a higher class than most. I slinked back behind cover and was gone before I overheard any reactions to the missing clothes.

Not wanting to carry it around or leave it behind, I wore the linen shirt over the fur-laced one, which was particularly useful during the cold nights. The cloak and its hood fit me well, and had the added benefit of concealing my sword.

A couple of days later and I made the turn westward. There were more roads branching out in different directions, but sign posts guided me in my journey to Rise.

Chapter Fourteen

I was forced to take a flat road to make my up the steep highlands Rise rested on. This meant seeing a greater concentration of travelers, but everyone minded their own business. With less area to forage and every farmer watching their crops closely, I basically ran out of food by the time I reached Rise one early morning. Thus, my first stop was at a shop where I sold the stolen shirt for a few coins, which I then used to buy a light breakfast of bread and butter at a tavern.

Not helping myself, I afterwards went over to the shop that old man was murdered in. I wasn't sure why I wanted to do it. Was it to find out what happened to the woman? That was really all I could learn, but that didn't satisfy what I was feeling. I couldn't enter the closed shop when I arrived on the desolate street it rested on, so I merely stayed observing the building from within an alleyway on the opposite side of the street. It looked abandoned, but so did the entire street.

It wasn't until the sun rose an hour higher did I see more people begin their daily routine. A few minutes after that and I saw five kids playing tag, which changed to hide-and-seek several minutes later, and which changed to a footrace after that.

When one came close enough, I said, "Hey kid, do you know what happened to the owners of that place?"

The grubby boy looked up at me for a moment before turning to look at the building my finger pointed at. He shrugged and said, "Maybe. How much can you give me?"

I reached in the pouch and showed him one of my white throwing knives, widening his eyes. "Would this be all right?" He reached for it, but I pulled it away.

"Oh, the old man was killed by some robbers. I think the lady moved somewhere else."

"Do you know the lady's name?"

"Ms. something Grayson. She was my mom's friend."

I handed him the knife. He grabbed it and ran to show his friends. That done, I left to begin the search for Garf. The growing daylight was a bad time to go sleuthing for crime lords, and while I believed a town guard could give me some answers, I couldn't be sure whether they were on Garf's payroll and thus alert him to a possible problem. Even if they were on the straight and narrow, there was always a chance they would get curious about my sword and intentions.

So with my ideas of acquiring information hours away, I decided to see if there existed a way to earn a few coins. Assuming the last several weeks hadn't seen a dramatic shift in power, I went to the side of town Garf had not secured as his own, which contained a little business district of its own. I knew the outskirts of this district had a few businesses that were always in need of woodcutters. The first work field I went to hired me on the spot after I showed the burly fellow I could split a log with a single downswing.

It was sweaty work that didn't pay all that well, but in addition to killing time, it was a good way to practice manipulating the prana in my arms. I was soon at a steady, hypnotic rhythm, a rhythm that barely went unbroken when the burly man's heavyset wife came out to offer water to the workers at the sun's highest point. On stopping a few hours later, my employer asked if I would return the next day. After taking the coin he owed me, I answered that it would depend on the night I had. To refresh my drowsy muscles, I walked a few hundred yards out of town to grab a nap under a tree.

I awoke with the sunlight nearly extinguished. I roamed the streets for an hour to make certain the night's masking shadow was at its most opaque before I headed for Garf's territory. If Garf still resided in Rise, then I figured he would be in Pirate's Cove. The name of the inn never made sense to me. The second floor of this nest of debauchery was a place I knew Garf used as his primary dwelling after he had been out and about during the day. The inn was large, made of stone, and the nights always had his people guzzling down anything with alcohol in it. Of course, Garf kept around sober bodyguards, but I knew a few tried and true methods to remove such complications.

The lodging was situated in the middle of town between shops and a large outcropping of homes, making it a popular destination for more than just the criminal sect after a long workday. The wide structure had two entrances in the front and one in the back that led into the kitchen. I used the front door to let myself in.

The inside was filled with five or six dozen uproarious people. In the center of the room was a wide wooden counter where the barkeeps worked, one of whom was a man I knew as Kent Smith, the owner of the inn and a friend of Garf. We had not really interacted before, but I knew his keen eyes would recognize me if given a good look at my face, so I made sure to keep my hood up and head down as I walked away from the huge fireplace on the left side of the room.

Next to the roaring fireplace were the flights of stairs that led to the second floor and basement levels, and next to the stairways were a couple of armed men in scale armor. They looked a bit like the city guard, but I knew they were actually employed by Garf to defend the more exclusive levels of the lodging. Whether that meant the man himself was here was not as clear.

As I strolled to the corner, I knelt down beside one of the few empty tables and rolled a dragon stone under it. I did the same thing when I reached my own lonely table. For a time I merely watched as everyone laughed and spoke with wilder abandon at every passing minute. No one took notice of the cloaked youth in the shadowy corner. The room had a couple of people I recognized from my past life, but nobody of significance. I thought a familiar woman was giving me a curious stare at one point, but she forgot about me when one of the men she was surrounded by put his fat face in her wobbly chest.

The drinking, joking, and smoking reached a fever pitch—the state of excitement I was waiting for. I moved myself to a corner stool by the counter, where I dropped another dragon stone.

When Kent got within hearing range, I said, "Kent Smith, right?" I was careful to not lift my hooded head too high.

"That's me. What you want?"

"Is Garf here?"

"Who's asking?"

"I found a valuable sword he wants."

"That so?"

"Aye." I untied Aranath from my belt and partly unsheathed the blade for Kent to see. "I would prefer to sell it to him now if he's around."

"I know Garf. He won't be bothered at this time of night, but I could take the blade off your hands now."

"I would prefer dealing with him personally."

"He never deals with small fry directly."

Getting off my seat, I said, "I have a feeling he'll see me face to face. I'll come back later."

As I made my way toward a door, I set off the dragon stones. Someone noticed the rapidly swelling flames a few seconds later. There was screaming and a mad rush for the exits. I turned back around to see one of the bodyguards go upstairs. I pushed through the scrambling crowd on my way to the stairway. The second guard saw me coming at him and rose his hands to keep me back, but before he knew what I was up to, I ducked, pulled out my dagger, and thrust it upward. Hot blood poured out from the hole I made just above his throat. I was already climbing the stairs by the time he hit the floor.

I heard the guard above yelling for everyone to get out of the building. Moments later and a group of six or seven people, mainly yelping women, went running past me. Many of them were lucky to be wearing a nightgown.

When I reached the second floor, a woman in chainmail was banging on a door down the hall. She yelled, "Let's go, Garf!" A door opened farther down the hall to show another woman attempting to put on a gown. The guard I had seen go up the stairs was running toward this woman.

When the female guard noticed me, I yelled, "Is Garf still up here!? We have to go! The whole place will burn up!"

She began saying something, but that's when I squinted and lobbed an explosive stone. It flashed its striking light in front of her eyes. I then drew Aranath from his scabbard and charged forward with all speed. My first target had no chance to react as the point of the sword punctured between the scales to get to her gut.

Then three things happened at the same time—the stabbed woman fell with a cry, the other woman screamed, and the door beside me opened to reveal Garf. Dressed only in his loose fitting breeches, Garf quickly summarized the scene in front of him and reacted by receding back into a room lit by a single candle on a nightstand. I withdrew the sword from its victim and dashed inside a room that also held one of his barely dressed mistresses.

85

I gazed at my last handler straight in the eyes. He must have realized who I was, but no sign of surprise appeared as he focused on casting a spell. A bluish light glowed around his right forearm for an instant before it was released in a lightning spell. I had Aranath in front of me, but he could not completely diffuse the electrifying effects. Every one of my nerves were firing all at once, but the spell was not debilitating enough to force my muscles to quit. Having forced myself through greater pain over longer periods, it was little matter of grabbing Garf's right arm and thrusting the edge of Aranath to his throat. He ceased his spell when the lightning began coursing his own body. His woman screamed as I put myself behind him so that he was between me and the door.

Garf's other bodyguard came in, mace at the ready, but he stopped when he saw the situation and heard me say, "Get any closer and I'll kill him. Go ahead, Garf, tell him to get more help while you and I talk. That's all I fucking want. Talk and you'll live."

"Boss?" asked the underling.

"Take Elena with you," said Garf calmly.

The subordinate nodded and reached for the woman, who hysterically babbled at me to let him go.

As they left, I asked, "Who did you buy me from?"

"You think they would tell me who they are?"

"I think you know anyway," I said, pressing the edge a little harder.

"I have a theory as to who it might be. That's not the same as knowing."

"It's all I need."

He sighed. "Riskel Rathmore. He was declared dead about twenty years ago by Voreen's Warriors Guild, but rumors have always persisted about his continued existence."

"And you believe in mere rumor?"

86

"I know the rune you've somehow removed was placed by a powerful caster, and anyone my age knows of the stories concerning the experiments that man did on corrupted prana. If it's not him, then it's someone taking inspiration from his work."

"Where can I find him?"

"I received a note eight months ago from your seller. It described how I would no longer be able to avail myself of their services. It strongly hinted of their relocation, so even if Rathmore was personally involved in these mountains, I suspect he and his team are now long gone. This is all I know about your origin."

The smell of smoke was getting thicker. I wondered whether the stone building would burn down after all. "Will you sacrifice more people on me?"

"It wouldn't reflect well on me if I simply let you go, even if that does seem like the smarter move at the moment."

"Maybe something happens that delays the pursuit."

"It's often difficult to tell which way someone went in the dark. I might accidentally send my men in the wrong direction."

"Sure. There's no way I'll head west or north, for example, so east and south are your best bet."

"Good to know."

"Lay on the floor and count to twenty."

As soon as his stomach met the warming timber, I went to the window, opened it, checked to see if the coast was clear, and dropped down to the alleyway. The slick cobblestones hampered a clean landing. My right foot slipped and twisted somewhat, but I didn't take notice of my swelled ankle until my body had calmed down later. I perceived some commotion coming from inside the inn, in what was probably a few casters trying to douse the vibrant flames with water spells. The commotion extended to the outside as well, where dozens of folk were gathering to watch the sizzling structure.

I glided through the shadows unnoticed, however, and was out of anyone's line of sight seconds later. Minutes after that and I was on my way out of Rise entirely.

Chapter Fifteen

It was probably destroyed, or at least cleared out of anything that could be useful to me, but I had to try and find the first place I remembered. I was originally going to avoid searching for this place until I trained enough to be confident in my ability to handle anything, but with Garf believing my sellers to be long gone, I figured there was no harm trying to uncover the subterranean system I had been transformed in. The problem was finding it. All I knew to start with was to head for the village where Heaton had picked me up.

Rise was miles behind me by the time the sun made its appearance. I was glad to once again find myself in wilder territory. I still had to keep closer to the road than I would have liked, but there were very few travelers going anywhere. The nights were now getting dangerously cold for most to make needless trips to other settlements if they were longer than a daylight's journey.

I did stop by Wintervale for a couple of hours to buy some food, though my main goal was to buy a map of the region. The best I could afford was one presenting the basic features of the hourglass shaped Iazali continent. I asked the shop owner about the area, learning that the next town to the west was a little place called Bronzefrost. It was also the last town in the west before the highlands became too high for human habitation. I didn't tempt fate too long in Garf's city and left within the hour.

A half day later had me arriving in the very quiet village of Bronzefrost. It had a single inn and most of the people here seemed to belong to one of about two dozen families, all of whom seemed to make their living as miners. Some snowflakes had fallen overnight and the morning sun was not strong enough to remove it. My first aim was to see if the hovel I was bought to was still there.

Sure enough, I found the lonely stone hut in the last spot I saw it. I walked up to it and pulled the tattered curtain flapping gently in the breeze to reveal its vacant space. There was only a small table with four chairs, one of which was knocked over on its side.

Snow crunched behind me. I turned to see a middle-aged man with a full head of gray hair coming over to me. He held a walking stick, but he didn't look like he needed it.

"Now, there's a perfectly cheap inn to use," he said. "I won't have squatters on my property."

"You live here?"

"Of course not. Terrible place to raise a family. It's just a venture of mine I never got around to completing. It's still a good place for summer gatherings, though. Besides, even if I was in a sharing mood, I wouldn't recommend sleeping outdoors."

"I know how to make a good fire."

"Oh, I'm not talking about the cold. This must be your first day here if you haven't heard all the stories yet."

"What stories?"

"About the screams people have been hearing the past few weeks. Most of the time they're far off sounding, but sometimes they're much closer than that. Everyone's heard at least one by now. I heard one just a few days ago."

"Where do they come from?"

"No one knows. Most think it's a fiend, but they sound a lot like a screaming woman to me. Very unsettling. A few hunters say they've even seen signs that it could be a human."

"Like what?"

90

"Oh, bare footprints, pieces of torn clothing, things like that. My nephew was one of the hunters who swear they saw somebody madly running around their campsite the whole night. They tried tracking it down in the morning, but they couldn't find it again. Some are even thinking of hiring a mercenary, but no one has actually been harmed by anything. Might be some very vocal birds for all I know." He looked up and down my frame. Then, looking around, he asked, "Are you here alone?"

"No."

"Good. You shouldn't travel alone if you can help it. I don't mean to scare you away from our little village, it really is quite pleasant, but I don't want to feel guilt-ridden for not cautioning you if something does befall."

"Thanks for the warning."

He nodded. "May I ask what you're doing way out here? Most travelers visit during the summer."

"I'm looking for something."

"Oh? What for?"

"Something hidden."

"Ah, the cryptic type. Very well, don't mind me." He turned toward the village. "Just stay clear of my property and any mad screaming and you'll get along fine."

I followed him back to the village and sought out the inn, where I bought two more hardy biscuits.

When I headed back for the western woods, Aranath said, "I take the screams are coming from some loose corrupted."

"It seems strange that they would set them free before they left. People might start investigating."

"Corrupted are difficult to keep wrangled. Perhaps a few simply got loose on their own after being abandoned. In any case, they might make searching for the secret hollow a little easier if they haven't scattered too much from their origin."

No strange screams came during the first few hours of roaming, but there was a growing sense I wasn't alone. Everything was too still, as though I was in a painting. The breeze had died down and few animals made themselves known. Then, just as the sun hovered over the horizon, an animalistic shriek echoed across the highlands. It might have been miles away, but the reticence of everything else made it seem like it could pop out from behind the nearest tree. Disregarding this audibly unnerving hint, I knew I couldn't have been too far from the hidden hollow. I recognized that the journey from the hollow to Bronzefrost had taken about half a day going at the footspeed of a horse, so my own footspeed would be comparable. It was simply a matter of uncovering the entrance.

The wind began carrying the air again, which I found annoying, as its howling gusts sometimes mimicked the scream from earlier. I stopped to make camp and built a fire big enough to roast a whole boar. Some would see this caution as coming from fear, and maybe there was something akin to dread deep within the primeval part of my being, but most of the reason came from making sure I could actually see beyond ten feet. The clouds were getting heavier, blocking out any moonlight that might have aided my eyes. Snowflakes started to fall, giving the ground a new luster of purity.

Another shriek, closer this time. It was different from before, as though it came from something smaller… Another scream, more womanly and distinct. The smaller one replied with high-pitched wails, each pained cry closing in. I drew my blade. My sight caught a dark blur at the edge of the fire's light. Then I saw its eyes, which reflected the red glow of the fire. It was half as low to the ground as I was—a cursed child.

I heard stamping feet behind me. I spun around to see a skeletal woman dashing at me with outstretched arms. With only on eye shimmering back the light, I could tell that an eyeball was missing, along with half her hair and flesh. She screamed as she pounced. I pierced Aranath through her torso, but she took no notice and moved deeper into the sword's steel. She was stronger than she looked and her bony hands reached my face, her nail-less fingers grazing my neck. She was the coldest thing that had ever touched me.

The smaller shade screamed wildly as it exited the darkness. Keeping the blade in her, I swung it to move the corrupted entity between me and the smaller form. At the same time, I slid out the weapon. That accomplished, I plunged my free sword into the corrupted's skull. The second she crumpled to the ground, the smaller one leapt over her corpse. The boy, or so I believed it to be, would have landed on my face if my reflexes were ordinary, but as they weren't, I evaded him. He instead landed on the campfire and his raggedy clothes burst into flames. He scrambled back up, only to meet my swinging blade, which had no trouble removing his head. The body fell back into the fire.

Seeing as this was better than leaving them out in the open or digging a hole, I kicked the woman's body into the fire as well. I wanted to help along the burning process, so I tossed in a dragon stone on the remains. I would have thrown in a couple more if Aranath didn't grumble something.

"What?"

"Dragon flame is a sacred power meant for the honored dead, not corrupted corpses you never knew."

"I know I could have been one of them."

He grumbled again before saying, "Just make certain this doesn't become a frequent occurrence."

A tainted soul howled in the distant darkness.

Wiping the sword with a piece of cloth, I said, "Define 'frequent.'"

Sleep was impossible to catch. Two, possibly three, distinctive screams erupted every few minutes. There were times when a bony profile would be outlined against the night before disappearing in the next blink. I overheard their hard breathing as they tramped on leaves, snow, and kicked pebbles as they ran indiscriminately. I just wanted them to attack me already, so that I could do the only merciful thing I knew to do, but most of their presence came only from the horrible noises they produced. This presence diminished altogether as dawn approached. With plenty of light to feel reasonably safe, I headed for the last shriek I heard.

Half a mile later and several uproars began to infiltrate the woods. The first unique sound I picked up was a shrill squealing. It wasn't a corrupted, but I heard one of those wailing as well. Getting nearer brought me in range of some loud grunting, which Aranath believed was coming from a bear. His prediction turned out to be correct.

As a yearling bear cub squealed from a tree's higher branches, I saw its brown mother attacking a corrupted fifteen yards away. She kept having to knock it down with her huge paws, not understanding that a corrupted soul was difficult to kill, though I did see a lifeless one nearby. As I backed away from the scene, the mother was finally able to put an end to the corrupted being by pouncing on its head, crushing its skull. She quickly spotted me when she sought out her child. She charged.

My sword was at the ready, but I didn't plan on using it. I instead summoned a few explosive stones and backed away. I set them off when she came within five feet of them. She roared and stood on her hind legs, showing me her eight foot tall frame. I chucked a couple of dragon stones and activated those too. The smell of dragon fire made her hesitate further. She roared again, but with less vivacity. I continued retreating. She started a mock charge and I threw another stone. The farther away I got, the less

94

inclined she was to pursue me. We stayed watching each other until the trees and distance obscured us entirely.

"She would have provided plenty of good meat," said Aranath.

Knowing he would figure out why I didn't kill the mother bear, I didn't say anything. The woods became much less noisy after the bear event. I even dared take a nap on top of a steep rocky hill for a few minutes around noon. The rest of the day and night passed without any result. It was on the middle of the next day that a comet of déjà vu hit my brain. I couldn't say how trees that all looked the same could suddenly feel so familiar, but they did. The awareness I was indeed close to what I wanted was amplified by a short cliff wall I discovered. To try and hear any hollow space behind the rock, I tapped Aranath against it as I slowly traced it from one end to the other.

After striking a spot that didn't sound special, Aranath said, "Wait. Tap the rock again." I did. "There's prana here. It's nearly dissipated, but it's undeniable."

A tougher scrutiny did reveal that this section of the cliff wall was perhaps too smooth to be natural.

"Is it possible to activate the rune?"

"There's not enough prana to suggest a hidden rune is here. They likely removed it when they left. You'll have to us force."

Having no other option, I dug a hole in the rigid soil next to the cliff and placed a few explosive stones in it. The result of their burst was a slightly larger hole and a few hairline fractures in the rock. With sufficient evidence to push the technique further, I began a strategy of progressively depositing a larger amount of explosives after every eruption. There eventually came a point when I summoned almost every explosive stone I had left. If anyone had been within three miles of me, they would have easily heard the explosion that shook the cliff face. I had applied much of my prana in the exertion, but it produced a conclusion.

The four inch thick bluff had cracked open a fissure wide enough for me to fling in a dragon stone. It didn't go very deep and its active light showed me a collapsed tunnel.

"What now?" Aranath asked.

"We go to Voreen's Warriors Guild and find out all we can about Riskel Rathmore. If he is alive, then someone might know something about his current whereabouts."

"Then may the hunt commence."

Chapter Sixteen

Voreen was not in my Iazali map, so I went back to Bronzefrost and asked the innkeeper about the best way to get to it. He told me that it would take a ship to cross the Lucent Sea, a five to seven hundred mile wide strip of water to the west of Iazali that separated it from the landmass of Niatrios. More specifically, Voreen was a small but influential nation positioned in the central eastern portion of this neighboring continent. With this information on hand, I started my southward trek.

Since I didn't trust that a sea captain would give me a free ride on their ship without joining their crew, one of my goals had to be earning the coin needed for a safe, question free voyage by doing some odd jobs. I also wasn't adverse to the idea of stealing some coin or a sellable item if it seemed like no affluent noble was using it. I would then head for a western port once I had saved enough. It might take months for me to gather the necessary fare this way, but I was in no great rush. Furthermore, I was confident that heading into a more populous region would grant me greater opportunities beyond log splitting.

It was slow going getting out of the highlands, and my walk was not faster than winter's coming. There came a point when the white powder became a permanent fixture in my travels. It was either already resting on the ground or in the process of adding another layer. I didn't mind the cold itself, it was the screeching winds that often accompanied it that forced me to seek shelter, which was not always easy to come by.

Thanks to Aranath, I learned of a trick to at least keep my blood warm. I would trigger a dragon stone and wait for the flame to perish. With the rock having been cooked to its core, I could then take hold of the still smoldering stone and grip it tightly in my hand. While a regular flame barely blackened a pebble, dragon fire was able to keep the half-melted stone steaming for several minutes in the numbingly cold air. Holding a burnt stone in each hand helped get me through the rougher stretchers in the weather.

The first month and a half into the cold season was brutal enough, but the next month could kill me in an unlucky day, so I resigned myself to stopping at an area where shelter was easier to come by. My map told me of a large city just east of some extensive marshlands called Mil'sith.

When I told Aranath of my intention to head for the city, he said, "'First Star' is the meaning of the name, but don't be fooled by the boastful designation. It's a place that reeks in summer and filled with gloom in winter."

"Then why the fancy name?"

"It's an ancient city, likely the first of its kind in this continent. Ancient humans must have thought that a noteworthy accomplishment."

"Anything else I should know?"

"Nothing that would be of use in this era, though being as it's a large trading hub, expect to find all types trying to sell you something."

When the city became visible a few days later, I saw that its congested center was situated on an extensive hill and defended by a sturdy, if old, stone wall. The outskirts, however, were largely left exposed on the lower ground around it. Dotting the region east of the city was farmland, though only a handful currently grew anything but the hardiest of midwinter crops. The tallest structures in the area were six slender towers at the very center of the hill. Three were constructed of black stone with narrow bands of white appearing every twenty feet. The second trio were white with bands of black stone.

"What are those towers about?"

"They surround the temples of day and night. Three gods for each side."

"What do the gods do, exactly?"

He grunted. "The smallest child knows that keeping balance is their maxim. If the day ever overtook night, the sun would scorch the world. Too much night and it's a frozen wasteland. This, of course, spills over with other aspects of life. Allow anyone to do as they please, for instance, and chaos spreads. Too much law and there is no free will. True peace comes from perfect balance."

"They don't seem to be doing a good job at attaining it."

"That's due to the impossibility at achieving such a thing, even for the gods. Too many independent influences exist for even a short lasting peace on a universal scale, but that does not make the goal any less noble."

"Is that what your war was about? To make the world more balanced?"

There wasn't an answer for several moments. The silence lasted long enough for me to think he was never going to answer it, but he finally did say, "War is always at the extreme end of chaos, the dominion of the gods of strife, not balance. Not to say war doesn't have its uses. I'm of the belief that it prevents stagnation and can bring about momentous change through sacrifice, but it is a tool few master. No, the reason for my war was as simple as any other—the attainment of power."

I entered the city limits in the afternoon and entered a large tavern called the Laughing Goose to buy a bowl of hot vegetable soup. As I waited for my order to be heated, I saw the wall to my right had numerous paper notices stuck to it. After I ate my food by the counter, I went over to see what the notices said. Many were old news bulletins from the city and from parts beyond. I only gave a cursory glance at these. What caught my interest the most was anything involving monetary rewards. Several were bounties for criminals—some of which had a sketch of the fugitive—and others advertised a job opportunity, usually some type of manual labor. Then I saw a piece of paper with a list of names, dates, and addresses.

Below the list of eighteen names was a statement that read: *'By decree of the Mil'sith City Guard, fifty silver standards will be given to anyone who can give information leading to the discovery of the above missing persons or their abductor(s). Please report any suspicious activity immediately.'*

Intrigued by the hefty reward and circumstances, I went up to the counter and asked the woman behind it about the missing people.

She shook her pretty head and said, "Talk to my husband if you like grim news. He never shuts up about it." Doing my work for me, she turned to face the man with her and said, "Robert, someone wants to know more about the missing people."

A man who must have had a great personality to land his wife, said, "That so?"

"Aye, but don't smile as you talk about it this time."

They switched places. The barkeep studied my unwavering eyes a brief moment before saying, "You must have just come into town, right?" I nodded. "Bad bit of business, that. Started last winter. It was just a couple of people at first, but it picked up quickly when spring came. It was ten by the time summer came along. Almost all of them were last seen in the Honey District, which is in the southeastern section of town. I personally believe the beekeepers in the Mammoth District make better honey, but I suppose they don't make as much."

"Anything that connects the missing people besides location?"

"Did you look at the names? All but three are women. Mostly young ones from what I hear, and all taken overnight. Most people think it's some lonely bloke doin' all the taking, but I'll stake my tavern that this involves more than one person. Maybe it's a troupe of lonely fellows, but a troupe nonetheless."

"There aren't any clues?"

"Sometimes somebody hears a scream or sees a bloodstain, but nothing that's led anywhere. That's what spooks everyone. It's like they vanish into the night herself. The guards have looked everywhere, including the sewers, but no luck."

"Do you have a copy of the notice you can give me?"

"Nah, I go over to the newsstands every week to get what I have. I always expect a new name to show up."

I thanked him for the information, bought a biscuit, and headed out.

As the barkeep said, there was another list kept by a stand nearby, which I bought and studied a bit. The addresses were of the last sightings of the victims, so I decided to start my quest on those spots.

"What makes you think you can unravel this mystery?" asked Aranath, obviously annoyed I was going about this task.

"When I was sure no one could overhear me, I answered, "I'll just spend a couple of days on it. If nothing becomes clear, I'll move on. So, any ideas?"

"Good predators seek higher ground when they hunt. That might also explain why a few males were taken. Most humans look the same from on high."

A wide street paved with stone circled all the outer districts, making it easy not to get lost as I made my way southwest. The Honey District's main street, like the north and western divisions, was mostly lined with businesses, which were currently busy with patrons. The streets that branched off from the main one led to homes and were largely left unpaved, though a few of the higher class divisions did have brick paths leading up to them. The first address I reached was a spot just off the main street, not far

101

from a line of food stalls. Taking the dragon's advice, I scrutinized any higher ground one could use to stake out a crowd of people. I tried to memorize every notable detail of the area and moved on to the other addresses.

Late afternoon made itself known by the time I finished visiting fifteen addresses. Many of them were of homes, where I imagined the family or friends of the targets lived, the last ones to see them before they were snatched up later. But why this district? There must have been something it held that aided the abductors somehow. Whether swayed by the disappearances or not, the crowds began to disperse as evening's shroud closed in, and with the clouds not taking their leave, it came quicker than normal. Meanwhile, I continued my scrutiny of the other locations still on the list.

As I headed for the last two addresses, two warrior-types spotted me. Half of the pair was a woman with black hair tied in a bun and donning a white mantle, which a few gusts of wind allowed me to see was covering a dark piece of leather armor. The other was a stocky young man with a white mantle over his bulkier metal plates. I could go weeks feeling like I hadn't gone noticed by the people I passed on the roads, but this woman took a particular interest in me. That interest was acted upon when she coxed her partner toward me.

"You there," she said, "Hold a moment by the name of the Warriors Guild." I reluctantly did as she requested. "I recognize your footwear as Borealean, and I suspect at least your trousers are as well. Where did you get the clothing?"

"They were gifts."

"Gifts? Those nomads aren't particularly friendly with outsiders. What did you do to earn their gratitude?"

"I helped settle a family dispute."

102

She eyed me warily, with her companion keenly eyeing both me and his partner. "Why are you here?" she asked next.

"Collecting coin for a voyage west."

"Quite the traveler, I see. What's your line of work?"

"Anything that pays."

She eased her stern look, seemingly satisfied with my answers. "When did you get into town?"

"This afternoon."

"Have you heard of the disappearances?"

"Yes. Is that why you're interrogating me?"

"Aye. New faces are always suspect to me, so I hope you don't take offense, traveler."

"None at all. Any suspects?"

"None right now," said her partner.

She cleared her throat and flashed him a cross look. "We don't comment on active cases."

"Anything you can tell me about the victims?"

"What's your interest in that?"

"Fifty silver standards."

"Ah, an intrepid fellow. This is beyond you. It's been a year and the entire resources of the city guard haven't been able to find a single victim."

"Then it could only be a benefit to give them resources beyond their scope."

"That's why my guild sent me here."

"Us," corrected the other.

"Sure," shrugged the woman.

I shrugged as well and said, "Fine, then I guess I'll have to find every family and friend of the victims I can and have them recount the information all over again."

103

I actually wasn't going to do all that work, but she evidently believed I was serious and said, "Wait, there's no need to disturb those poor people again. I can't imagine how many pretend inquisitors have bothered them already since the reward was advertised. What do you care to know?"

I showed her the notice. "There's a tavern a few yards back. Why don't we have a drink and you can go through everything you know?"

"A break sounds nice," said her partner.

She rolled her eyes. "Very well, but let's make this quick."

A few minutes later and the three of us were drinking ale at a table while the warrior woman told me what she memorized about the victims. She evidently took her job very seriously. She had quite a few details memorized, talking through them without saying one "um" the entire way. I let her speak without butting in with my own questions, even when my ears perked up when she mentioned that the third missing person, Trevon Apor, was a young man who had last been seen by his coworkers fixing a roof by the main street.

I otherwise learned that eleven of the missing were young women described by most as being able to marry above their station if they so desired. One had in fact already married a well-off honey farmer's son, and yet another was engaged to a banker's son. Four were older women, three of which were wed, and the three men were barely past boyhood.

When she finished with her accounts, I asked, "Has anyone tried acting as bait?"

"A young member of the city guard attempted the ruse for a week. No results were attained."

I sat back and watched her trace the rim of her empty cup with a finger. "If I remember correctly, Trevon wasn't all that far from the first two victims, while the others seem more scattered and random."

"I noticed this initial anomaly as well. So you believe Trevon grabbed a couple of girls and just couldn't stop?"

"No. Whoever is taking these people knows what they're doing. I doubt some young roofer became an expert kidnapper overnight, but I do think he's somehow involved. There has to be at least a couple of people participating in this crime. You said Trevon was a loner, known only by a few of his colleagues?"

"Correct. He was only reported missing after he never showed up for work. I couldn't find anyone else who knew him."

"Then there are the other two men... Tell me, if I went out right now and asked a woman to follow me, what would happen?"

"She'd probably scream and run away."

"And if you went out and asked a man to follow you?"

One of her thin eyebrows jerked upward. "I see. You suspect the women were forcibly taken while the men were lured away."

"Not only lured, but possibly recruited to doing some dirty work. I can imagine a few fellows being enticed to the idea of being able to have their pick of some kidnapped women."

"An interesting theory, but it doesn't get us any closer to where these people are or why so many are being taken in the first place."

"Not exactly, but I think it's pretty clear we're dealing with an intricate system that's probably been established for... Wait, the roof Trevon was working on, you said that belonged to a large two story home, right? Who owns that place?"

"The big stone house? Why does that come to mind?"

"If one is looking for easy opportunities to recruit young men, then hiring some destitute juveniles to repair a roof is a good way to meet and study them for a bit."

She contemplated a moment before saying, "The Sanderson couple occupies the home."

"Have you ever seen or spoken with them?"

"Not personally. I can't even say what they do for a living. The little information I received of them came from an interview with a city guard."

"Thank you for your time." I stood up and began to walk away.

Standing up as well, she said, "Hold on. What are you planning on doing?"

"I'm going to watch that house for a while."

"Is that all you're going to do?"

"Unless something happens."

"Just watch it if you can. I'll try and find out more about the family. If something does appear suspicious, then we can inform the city guard."

"I wouldn't inform them of anything. Based on the fact that the city guard haven't ended this crime yet, I can guess that the enemy is either keeping a close eye on their movements or have infiltrated their ranks. Find out what you can on your own, but don't rely on them."

"Hey," said the still sitting partner, "She's not on her own, you know."

Ignoring him, she said, "Would you like to know what I find out?"

"If you're willing to allow me all the reward."

"You think I'm in this for the coin?"

"Then we'll meet back here at this time tomorrow."

"Fine. What's your name?"

"Mercer."

"Francine"

"Not that anyone cares, but I'm Jacob."

While walking toward the house in question, I saw an aging caster light the tall lampposts lining the main street. The glow was only enough to dissolve a circle of darkness twenty feet wide, making anything beyond the main street just as dark as it would be without the presence of the kindled towers.

The windows of most homes told of blazing fires keeping their inhabitants warm for the bitter night, but on reaching my goal, I found no hint of light appeared anywhere inside the house. The southward facing structure was situated a couple of rows behind the main street, on the side closest to the city center. A tall metal fence and gate prevented easy access. I took the branching street it was on and strolled past it for a closer look. It had windows, but all were shut by wooden panels. No sound it emitted. Not taking a chance that someone was watching, I didn't try for another pass, but instead searched for a good place to watch it.

I eventually found a two story shop-house combination that had a large chimney stack that I thought could give me some good cover while still offering an unobstructed view of the stone house. I climbed the brick structure, sat on my perch, and began my vigil.

Chapter Seventeen

Excluding the occasional passing cart, neighing horse, barking dog, or my own breathing, nocturnal kept her secrets close to the chest. With nothing stirring in the house by the time night's sibling pierced the scattering clouds, I climbed back down to ground level. I stayed watch by the corner of another house, but I had to move when too many people started spilling out their homes. I considered this progress, however. A comfy looking home empty in the dead of winter set alight a suspicion that something was off about that place.

I later visited the last two addresses Francine had interrupted my study of. Nothing there drenched or reinforced the suspicions I had. When the time came, I went over to the meeting place. The guild members were already there and I took a seat by their table.

"The home is up for sale," said Francine the second I settled in. "Has been for months."

"That matches what I found. No activity to speak of."

"But that doesn't mean a dead end," said Jacob. "The house hasn't been sold yet because the owners are asking for a huge amount."

"I doubt they want it sold," continued Francine. "Putting it up for sale could give them a reason to move, but still continue using the home when they want."

"Have you found where they are now?" I asked.

"No. The couple seemed respected enough in the neighborhood, but they didn't seem to be particularly close friends with anyone. All I found was that Bruno Sanderson and his wife owned an inn not far from here, but sold it around the same time they put the house up for sale. I say we keep watching that house for a while and see if anyone uses it."

"I found a good spot to keep a lookout on its front side. If you can find another for the flanks or the back, I suppose that would be best."

After agreeing to meet every morning and evening to get updates from one another, we went our separate ways. The next few days were thus spent in patient readiness. During the day I would go to an isolated spot outside the city and catch up with sleep, training, and read a book on prana practice, which Aranath scoffed at. The nights would have me back on my roost, understanding that even if I was right about this house that weeks might pass without anything happening.

In lieu of weeks, it was early in the fifth night that a dimming of the nearest lamppost told me something was different. It wasn't by much, but my well-adjusted eyes perceived that the flame had lost some of its fervor behind its glass case, giving prominence to the shadows under the overcast night. Turning my attention beneath the lamppost revealed a cart being indolently pulled by a large horse. Two hooded figures sat in the front of the cart, with the taller one holding the reins, and a third cloaked figure was sitting on some of the rolled up rugs the cart was holding.

The cart turned to the street that led to the stone house. It didn't slow down any when it neared the building, but the passenger in the back began to take one of the larger rolls and lift it over their left shoulder. Along with the other passenger, the hooded figure hopped off the cart and headed for the metal gate. The unencumbered figure opened the surprisingly noiseless gate and the two soon entered the house itself, all without carrying a lantern or casting a light spell. The cart, meanwhile, continued on its way.

I wasn't sure whether the other watchers saw what I saw, but I at least knew the house wasn't going anywhere, so I decided to track the cart. I initially wanted to follow it by rooftop, but it was clear that the option would likely cause too much noise. I instead did the more practical thing and climbed down to follow the wheel tracks the cart left. It was snowing, but there wasn't enough of it or a breeze to mar the tracks for another half hour.

The cart made a left and then another on the first chances it had, giving it a westward direction. It held this bearing all the way to the city limits. We passed a few guards patrolling the streets, with one even stopping the cart so that he could give it a quick inspection, but no one found the rider mistrustful enough to talk at length to. With the lack of buildings the farther we went, I had to keep a farther distance back to make sure the rider didn't get apprehensive and start taking a fake course.

A few miles later and a greater density of trees allowed me to better conceal my whereabouts. The cart was heading for the marshlands. A normally waterlogged area, the marshes were frozen over, with a fine mist hovering over the ground. The snow would have forced a slow crawl in an area where a wrong step could send one through the thin ice and into the freezing water, but the cart seemed to know where to go, and it did so for another hour into the night.

A twig snapped ten or fifteen yards behind me. It wasn't the first time I overheard nature moving, but the cracking stick was the final confirmation I needed to know that someone was following either me or the cart. In an effort to oust the second pursuer and to do it noiselessly, I made a turn at a bend, stopped by a tree, and cast my illusion spell. To anyone watching behind me, my illusion would make it seem as though I was still advancing. In reality, I stayed tight by the tree and listened intently for any approaching presence. The sound of crunching snow a couple minutes later was the fruitful result of my ruse. I timed it so that when I circled around the tree, I was standing behind the fooled tracker.

Unlike most I had seen at this time of year, the white haired girl was unhooded. She might have heard something behind her, but I had already sprung forward. At the same time I put a knife to her throat, I put a hand over her mouth. I noted how her skin lacked any kind of warmth. It was like I was touching a kind of pliable, icy steel.

"Scream and that will be the last thing you ever do. Understand?" She nodded. "Anyone else behind me?" She shook her head. "Who are you?" I removed my hand to permit an answer.

"Clarissa Lorraine," she said in a mousy whisper.

"You're one of the missing girls? What are you doing out here?"

"I saw you following Maxis back in town. I swear I was just trying to see if you could help me end all this."

"You seem free enough. Why not go to the guards or guild?"

"I can't. They'll see us no different from them."

"'Us'?"

"Trevon and I. Please, I'll tell you everything if you promise Trevon won't get hurt. He just needs to get away from *them*."

"And 'them' are?"

"Maxis and Belinda. They're the masterminds behind the missing people."

"Why are they taking people?"

"T-to get stronger. They either feed on them or, if we meet their measures, add us to their 'family.'"

"You're a vampire, then."

"Y-yes, but please, I'm not like them. I don't feed on people, only animals. They already don't trust me. Only Trevon is keeping me from being banished, or worse. I'll help you find their lair if you promise to leave Trevon and I alone."

"Where is your lair?"

"Do you promise?"

"No."

"But we only want to be alone together."

"That desire seems one-sided. I assume you've already tried and failed to convince your friend to leave the clan, correct?"

"H-he just needs to get away-"

"He sounds lost to me. You have to start thinking about yourself, and right now there's a knife being held to your throat. The only reason you're still alive is because your burden has not yet outweighed your potential usefulness, but the second it does will be the second when both you and Trevon have lost any chance at escape. So where is the lair?"

With a voice barely suppressing desperate tears, she answered, "It's a-another twenty miles to the northwest. I-it's a cave h-hidden underneath a bog."

"How many other vampires?"

"A d-dozen more, not including me."

"How many victims are still alive?"

"I don't know the exact number, but a few have died."

"What's the stone house for?"

"The house is over an old s-section of the sewer system. They use it to take the latest victim out of the city once the search for them dies down."

"Do you know where the sewer exits at?"

"Yes, just at the border of the marshlands."

"If they don't trust you, then why are you alone?"

"They don't outright say it, but they keep Trevon close to them because they know that I know they'll hurt him if I ever go against them. They think I'm out hunting right now."

I stayed silent a moment, trying to come up with a solution to the complications in my hands. "Listen, I don't care what happens to you or your friend. I just want to collect the reward for helping get the city guard on the right track, so if a couple of vampires are able to escape in the fray, so be it. I

112

don't think you're lying to me, but I can't let you get out of earshot, which means we have to end this tonight before your clan gets suspicious. Where is Trevon now?"

"He was helping Belinda hide the girl."

"Are there other vampires in the house besides those two?"

"It should just be them for now."

"Then my plan is to take the home first. After which, you'll lead me and the city guard to the lair."

"But if the guard finds out about me-"

"Do anything your way and it'll be my sword you have to worry about. Do as I say and no guard or guild member will know what you are. Deal?"

"Okay."

I freed her neck from immediate danger, allowing her to face me. Despite the makeup she wore to achieve the impression of color, her face was pale, as was common for her kind. My hand had smeared some of this makeup away to reveal the even lighter shade of skin beneath it. If she had some actual color to her, I would have thought her attractive. As it was, only her crisp blue eyes had any life in them.

"Let's get back to Mil'sith. We have little time."

I had her walk in front of me, not only to keep an eye on her, but knowing she had a better idea of where to step if we couldn't find our tracks. Our pace was a steady, wordless jog through the marsh. It was like this all the way to a real road, where we slowed to a hasty walk so we wouldn't draw the attention of patrols.

Probably tired of the silence I was comfortable with, Clarissa, now walking alongside me, asked, "You really don't care if two vampires go free?"

"We have a deal. Unless I catch you feeding on someone later, I'll continue to honor it. Anyway, it's obvious your only motive to becoming a bloodsucker was to join your friend, not infect the world. Your friend on the other hand…"

"He's not like the others. A few days away from them and he'll see that we can be happy together. *She* tricked him. *She* made him think he needs them. I've known him since we were little. He just needs reminding that a few simple things is all we need."

"I've heard stories on all the victims, why weren't you two connected in them?"

"Oh, well, he was just a street rat, so I had to keep my friendship with him secret or the stuffy orphanage I belonged to would have forced me to cut my connection with the 'bad' influence. He was a loner and a bit of a thief, but he had a hard life. After I started working for the orphanage instead of just living in it, I convinced Trevon to find real work so that we could someday start a new life somewhere. He didn't take to real work all that well at first, but I think he was starting to believe we could make something of ourselves."

"Then they offered another opportunity."

She hung her head lower. After a minute, she said, "He sounded so excited. He told me how he found a chance to become something greater than he was. A couple of weeks later and he returned as one of *them*. He made it sound so romantic. He said that if I joined his new family, that we would have a good life as children of the night. We wouldn't have to feed on people or work for them anymore. We would be our own masters. Gods, if only I knew what was really going on. That bitch manipulated him so well."

"What will you do if he doesn't choose to leave with you?"

"He will. He might be mad at first, but he'll see it was for the best."

"I'm not concerned with his resentment. If he attacks to defend his new way of life, what will you do? Will you follow his lead or continue to aid me? Even if the answer is to nail your feet to the floor, I would prefer to know what your reaction would be."

Her hands clenched. "If he doesn't choose me? Maybe the answer is 'nothing,' but I don't know. I certainly wouldn't attack you. I might attack *her*, but I know even in daylight she's quite powerful. All I know is a water spell that helps keep me dry getting to the lair."

"I would prefer if you retreated until the fight was over, but if you must do nothing, then that would be my second preference. I ask because it won't just be my ass at risk. There are two members of the Warriors Guild we need to meet before we get started."

With no more than three hours until dawn brightened the melancholy sky, I arrived at Francine's lookout spot. She had told me before that she watched the back of the home from an alley, and that's where I found her.

She looked relieved to see me, which was verified when she said, "Glad I didn't send the big lug to follow the cart with you. Who's this?"

Answering for her, I said, "Clarissa Lorraine."

"What? You found one of the victims?"

"She found me. She knows where the vampire lair is."

"Vampires? That's what we're dealing with?"

"And two are in the house. Listen, we have to end this tonight. How long will it take to gather the city guard?"

"I can get a dozen men to back us up in less than half an hour. That should be enough to take care of a couple vampires."

"Good, but to make sure they simply don't disappear in the sewers, Clarissa and I will infiltrate the house from an underground entrance they use to transport their victims. It'll take us about an hour to get in position. The moment you hear anything from within the house, send everyone in. If we're

115

lucky, there won't be any real fighting left by the time you enter. Once they're taken care of, Clarissa will take us and as many guards as we can gather to the lair."

Francine studied Clarissa carefully, but the hooded girl kept her face lowered. "Fine, I'll give you the head start, but in case something happens, I would like to know where the lair is now."

Clarissa said, "It's about twenty-five miles northwest of the city. You'll find a shallow lake free of any trees. At its center lies a cave system hidden beneath the water, which is kept back by a rune. You'll need guards to stay outside while others invade the actual cave, as some might try to escape through a tunnel system that leads back to the surface."

Not liking how critically Francine was studying her, I said, "Make sure Jacob keeps a good lookout while you gather the guard. One mistake and we could lose them all."

After a quick rundown of the plan and taking enough steps to get beyond earshot of the guild members, Clarissa said, "You didn't tell her about Trevon."

"We'll cross that bridge when we get there."

She took me back outside the city limits, where we then went another half mile before stopping at a cluster of prickly shrubs. We brushed past them to get to the center of the collection. Clarissa wiped away the snow and dirt to uncover a metal handle, which I grabbed to pull open a trapdoor. A short ladder led into a five foot wide tunnel that had a trench grooved into its center, however, even stepping down into this deeper tier would force someone to hunch over. I followed her down, where I already began smelling a modicum of human waste. It was dark, but Clarissa saying she saw well in the dark kept us from using a light source that could expose us.

"I can also smell pretty well, so what you're smelling is ten times worse for me."

116

"And your hearing?"

"I think that's pretty much the same as yours. If we're quiet enough, Belinda or Trevon will sniff us out before they hear anything."

"How noisy is it opening the secret trapdoor?"

"I've only been through it once, but I think it can open pretty quietly if we're careful."

"Then we'll be careful, but if Belinda hears us anyway, you'll have to pretend that you had to use the trapdoor to escape some trouble. You'll hopefully be able to distract her long enough so that I can get in a good position to kill her quickly. If you meet Trevon first, I'll let you talk some sense to him, but if he refuses to listen to you, I'll have to kill him. And here…" I pulled out two explosive stones. "Keep these."

"What are they?"

"A distraction in case they attack you. Drop them, close your eyes, and yell out 'Mercer.' I'll set them off in that instant."

"'Mercer'? Is that you name?"

"Yes. If your friend agrees to leave the clan, we'll hide him somewhere until we can destroy the rest of his associates."

"What are you?"

"What?"

"I mean, you talk like an old man, or like someone who has seen a lot."

"Something like that."

"So you're not with the guild or guard?"

"No."

"With anyone?"

"No."

"Why do you want the reward?"

"I need it to get somewhere."

"Where?"

"Away from chatty mouths."

She took the not so subtle hint and we focused and getting where we needed to go. There weren't many turns to take or hindrances to pass, though the increasingly fouler stench soon became like a gelatinous river we had to move through. Some hazy streams of light managed to seep through narrow slits from the streets above, and the old tunnel still connected to a few newer channels that spawned most of the stench. The older tunnel apparently acted as an overflow channel as we had to move up to the narrow walkway to keep from treading in shit.

When we moved back to near complete darkness, she slowed her pace when she thought us close to our destination. We then made a turn to a tunnel that led to a dead end a few yards away. She began patting the stone above her. Her fingers stopped.

In a whisper I was surprised my ears picked up, she said, "Here, help me lift it."

I put my hands near hers and, with great care, steadily began pushing upward. The stone that made up the bottom was actually very thin, making the trapdoor lighter than expected. The rest of the trapdoor seemed to be made of wood. There was resistance, but it wasn't a big problem. Lifting the flap allowed us to stand up, where our heads became level with a wooden floor. Stretching above the flap was a thick rug. Clarissa slowly pulled the rug away as I held up the flap. When the rug was cleared over us, I saw that we were in a basement, empty except for a couple of chairs, table, and a barren shelf.

I pushed the flap all the way and Clarissa cautiously pulled herself up. Before I did the same, I summoned some dragon stones and scattered them beneath the trapdoor and down the tunnel. To further bolster against the threat of enemy escape, I closed the trapdoor and had Clarissa help me carry

118

the shelf and place it over the access, forcing anyone in a rush to waste a few precious seconds removing the obstruction. I also placed a few extra deterrents on the flammable item.

Moving through the wooden floor and up the stairs produced some creaks and squeaks, but nothing responded to our tiptoeing. Once Clarissa opened the door to the first floor, we finally began to pick up some racket coming from the floor above. For someone who often found himself in the vicinity of two or more lovers in the spasmodic act during my Garf days, it was all too familiar to me. Clarissa was less sure, but the growing concern on her face told me she was grasping the only conclusion.

This conclusion was irrevocably reached when we were halfway up the stairway. On first clearly hearing the male's voice, Clarissa almost moaned a cry of heartbreak, but my hand on her shoulder reminded her of the mission. Ascending all the way to the top had us distinctly hearing the grunting and slapping of wet skin coming from an open room just off the stairway. I positioned myself next to the door and nodded. Clarissa nodded back and put herself in front of the entry.

She stopped time a moment so that she could take a long breath. On restarting the abstract being, she said, "Trevon?"

I heard something that sounded like "Shit" followed by some fumbling. This same person then said, "Clarissa? W-what are you doing here?"

Without surprise or worry, a collected woman who could only be Belinda, said, "Yes, what are you doing here?"

"Shut up, bitch! You ruined everything!" Her tears were possibly loud enough to attract the guards. "Me or her, Trevon? You have to choose now."

"There is no need to choose," said Belinda. "Now, I'll ask one more time, what are you doing here?"

119

"Trevon, we can leave right now. It's our last chance."

There was a crack in Belinda's voice when she said, "'Last chance'? Gods, you really did it, didn't you?"

"Did what?" asked Trevon.

"She's betrayed us."

"Just you," clarified Clarissa. "The guards have already surrounded this place, but you and I still have a chance."

"What?!" said Trevon, his footsteps getting closer to his friend. "You dumb bitch! What the fuck were you thinking?! They'll kill us all!"

"Step aside," said Belinda, walking toward them.

Knowing it was over, Clarissa dropped the stones and screamed, "Mercer!"

If her yell didn't cue the guards, the explosive stones did. To my great annoyance, Clarissa's body prevented a clean intrusion, so I had to grab her cloak and pull down. With the hindrance removed, I plunged Aranath into Trevon's leg. The instant I withdrew the blade, a powerful blast of air crashed into all three of us, sending us tumbling to the floor outside the room. In a blur, the naked Belinda dashed past us and headed downstairs. I recovered my footing and chased after her. When she reached the basement level, I set off the dragon stones. A howl of frustration shook my ears.

The front door burst open.

"Mercer!" shouted Francine.

"She's in the basement!"

A fast marching of steps came toward me, then the back door opened with a bang and more boots entered. There was a crashing of splintered wood in the basement as Belinda used a wind spell to knock away the blazing shelf. I arrived in a room full of writhing shadows. Belinda was ripping open the flap when I hurled a knife between her shoulders. She shrieked like a dying banshee as she turned to face me with furious eyes and bitter anguish on a

120

mouth that displayed her protracted fangs. Francine came down the stairs, a short sword drawn. Behind her were three city guards. Outnumbered, the vampire dropped down the shaft, which was the instant I triggered the rest of the dragon stones. I hadn't heard worse wailing in my nightmares. Francine and the others rushed for the underground access.

Remembering the other vampires, I headed back upstairs. I ran past some guards and Jacob on the way up. To make sure the guards didn't think I was the enemy, I told Jacob to get to the basement. He said something to me, but I didn't listen.

There were a multitude of thuds coming from the room I had been blown out of. In it I saw Trevon chocking Clarissa as she struggled beneath him. He saw me, which loosened his grip enough for her to push his arms away. He tried standing up, but the wound I had placed on him prevented any quick movements, making his neck an easy enough target to send my blade through.

Clarissa's eyes were shut and her head turned away from the scene as she wheezed and coughed. I wiped the sword on the bedsheet, sheathed it, and picked her up. She flinched from my touch, but offered no verbal protest. I pulled her hood over her face and moved out of the room.

As I carried her down the stairs, a guard coming up asked, "Is that the missing girl?"

"One of them, but there's another hidden somewhere here, so keep looking. There's a dead vampire in one of the rooms."

I exited the home and put down Clarissa on one of the stone benches in the front. She sat there languidly as I stayed watch over her, making certain no guard confused her with the enemy. Francine found me ten minutes later.

"Did you get the vampire?" I asked.

"Yeah. She couldn't get far with those cooked feet. We also found the latest victim in a hidden room in the first floor. She okay?"

"Physically."

"Well, we've gotta get moving soon. For all we know, there was a vampire watching over this place and is heading to warn the lair right now."

Minutes after she said this, Francine, Jacob, and some guards asked Clarissa and I to follow them to the western garrison. I had to induce her to her feet, but once on them, Clarissa walked well enough.

We met with a high-ranking guard outside the large garrison. He had already been informed of what was happening and had been organizing most of the available guards in the district. On a detailed map, Clarissa circled the area we were to head for. The captain then barked some orders that instructed different divisions to take different sides of the lair. As she stood meekly in the background, I agreed to have the captain and his top guards, along with the guild members, follow the undiscovered vampire and I to the lair's main entrance.

I requested a horse for Clarissa, but in her first words since yelling my name, she said, "I can walk."

So with just about everyone on foot, we began our trek.

Chapter Eighteen

Time always seemed to speed up unnervingly quickly when I was around large groups of people, no matter what they were doing. Tonight was no different. The vampire weakening sunlight wasn't far away, but as most of the fighting would likely take place within a cave system, this benefit would be of little use. Of course, if the assumption that a warning message about our approach was being delivered to the lair was correct, then perhaps meeting some fleeing vampires out in the open wasn't out of the question.

Dawn made her own approach when we were closing in on the vampire den. Luckily, the winter clouds remained thick enough to block the sun's beams from reaching Clarissa. Still, I saw her losing strength, or perhaps it was a waning will.

When the foggy lake was in sight, our group stopped and kept to the fringes of the tree line. We waited until a crow landed near the captain and cawed. Despite Francine's good word, the captain requested that I stay outside with a couple of his people to watch his back, though I knew he really didn't want an "amateur" fighting next to him. That was fine by me. I was sure I had already earned that reward.

So from the outskirts of the lake, I saw as two of the guards manipulated the lake's water with a spell, pushing it away as they walked toward the lake's center a hundred feet away. There was an outcropping of rock at the deepest part of the lake. At its center was a large cave opening that sloped beneath the ground, where runes kept the lake from filling the hollow space. The captain and rest of the guards moved in. What happened in the cave was of little concern to me. I just wanted everything done so that I could collect my coin and move on. Clarissa kept close to me, though I knew she wanted nothing more than to slink away to cry. She would have if there weren't surrounding guards on the lookout for her kind.

An hour into the operation, the captain—whose steel armor was charred in places and smeared with mud—finally exited the cave. Trailing him was a group intermixed with healthy guards, which included Francine and Jacob, and a second group of injured guards, a few of whom were being hand pulled inside the cart I had followed. Francine found me a little later and briefed me on what happened. They had killed all eight vampires they found in the lair, including Maxis, who had killed three of the five guards who didn't make it, and they found several of the victims still alive in the main feeding chamber.

"I'm done here, then?"

"Sounds like it. The guards will continue sweeping the area for any stragglers."

"And where should I collect my reward?"

"Ah, let me take care of that for you. You've been instrumental in this case, but the guards won't exactly admit that. Tell you what, I'll haggle for you and you can pick it up at the guild house in the center of town tomorrow morning."

"Fine with me. I'm taking Clarissa back into town."

"And Mercer, thank you for your help. You've done Mil'sith a great service, not to mention easing my own mind."

"I didn't do it for the city or your mind, so no thanks is necessary or even apt."

"Keep your aloofness if you wish." She stepped closer so that only I could hear her say, "But tomorrow morning we'll see if coin is all you'll take. Don't be late." She then walked past me to give an order to Jacob, reapplying a persona that made her seem as though she would never even think of suggesting something as titillating as she did to me.

124

The clouds were abating, so I knew I would have to carry the girl part of the way back. I had her stand up and we made our way back to town. When consistent streams of sunlight hit her halfway into the slog, she started to stumble, which was my cue to lug her myself. I did so until we came out of the marshlands.

"I'll rent a room for you. Tomorrow I'll give you some of the reward so you can do with it what you will."

She said nothing. I was sure this speechless response would have been the same if I had told her I was to kill her right then and there. She followed me to a relatively clean looking inn where I rented two available rooms for two nights. I saw her enter hers before I went into mine. There I slept on a stiff bed for a good chunk of the night.

I sought the guild house early the next morning. A request for directions soon had me finding the single story structure within the crowded space of Mil'sith's walled center. I knocked. Francine opened the door. She looked different in her casual linen clothing, her hair hanging loosely over her right eye, and a relaxed face that made her appear infinitely more appealing than the icy stone expression she had on the days before.

She stepped aside and said, "Come in, Mercer." When I did, she shut the door and locked it by sliding the metal bar in place. "I wasn't able to get every silver owed to you. Five silver standards were withheld since Clarissa was really the one to find the lair, but I think I can offer you some reward of my own, if you don't mind alternative payments." Along with something else, my left arm throbbed. She went over to a pitcher and poured some red wine. Also on the table was a little bag I assumed held my coins. "I know it's early, but my work day just ended. Would you like a cup?"

"No thanks. I'd prefer remaining lucid for my journey."

"You're planning on leaving town so soon? Where's a young warrior like you in such a rush to get to?"

"Ever heard of Riskel Rathmore?"

She paused in her drinking. She swallowed what she had and said, "I know the old guild vets talk about his death like it was the best thing our organization has done in a hundred years. I myself don't know all that much more than anyone else. What's your interest in him?"

"Depends on how much of his influence is still out there."

She raised an eyebrow. "I knew you were different the second I saw you. You'd make a good guild member."

"No I wouldn't."

"I was like you once. I didn't like the idea of taking orders and doing things a certain way, but the guild has good people, a good order to things."

"You're only giving me more reasons to avoid it."

"That so? Well, I'll stop trying to recruit you for life, but how 'bout for a few hours? There's a nice hot bath going in the basement we can start in." I must have looked hesitant, because she next said, "Is something the matter? Oh, I've taken some sariff earlier, so you don't have to worry about a little consequence coming out nine months from now."

"It's not that. I was just thinking about my left arm."

"Odd thing to think about." I rolled my left sleeve up to my elbow. I then unwrapped the cloth hiding the serrations. "What is that?"

"A fiend's tail."

I could see her shudder, though she kept a stoic face.

"You're corrupted?"

"Yes."

"You don't look it."

"Most corrupted become insane and wild after a few days or weeks. A special few can maybe hold out longer, depending on how they were corrupted. My enchanted sword thwarts my corruption from spreading

126

further, so I have more time than most, but I can understand if you're no longer in the mood."

"No, no, it's just I've never heard of a sane corrupted before, or a sword that can accomplish such a feat. Where did you find it?"

"Hiding behind a dead man."

"That you killed?"

"As with all things, I believe time killed him."

She set her cup of wine down and started walking closer to me, taking glances at my arm. The temptress didn't stop until her breath and chest were up against my own. She started rewrapping the arm and said, "Well, as far as I'm concerned, as long as one particular extremity isn't so sharp, I think we can still get along grand."

When she finished wrapping my arm, she leaned in the rest of the way and kissed me. I joined in on the act a half instant later. Everything else dissolved as primeval urges took their course. I kissed her thin lips a little longer before she coaxed me to the basement, where a roaring fireplace warmed the room to an almost uncomfortable level, giving the added incentive to remove what clothing we had. A third of the room was blocked off by a thin sheet, which was pulled away to reveal the large, steaming tub. Except for the wrap on my left arm, we undressed completely, putting our clothes and Aranath in a corner. The actions I did next were largely predicated in response to her own and what I had seen Garf's people do to one another. It was quickly obvious why they did such things as often as they could.

According to her, we had all morning before Jacob and the housekeeper returned, so we took things slow. A lot of that time was simply spent caressing and fondling each other. There was no part of her that didn't excite me—the toned muscles under her smooth skin, small but taut breasts, and an ass firm with muscle. She also couldn't stroke some part of me

127

without sending thrills up my spine. Then the real ecstasies of pleasure came when each of our most sensitive, slick areas tenderly met in rhythmic gasps and grunts. I was quick the first couple of times, but I recovered quickly and recognized from past gossip on how else to keep her engaged.

She seemed content by the time I could give no more, but I heard from other gossip that you couldn't always tell with women. In any event, I was tempted to take her offer to stay longer, but I had other forces pulling me away. We dried off, dressed, and I went upstairs to pick up my coin.

Before I left, I said, "The Warriors Guild has some kind of headquarters in most major cities, right?"

"In any nation that agrees to have us. Why?"

"Keep your ears open to any talk of corruption or any mention of Rathmore. Even if he's dead, his work might not be."

She nodded. I left.

It was noon when I reached the inn. I knocked on her door. I knocked again. She opened it. I gave her a small pouch.

"There's ten silver in there. Should be enough to take you anywhere you want."

She nodded dolefully. This felt like a time when regular people would say something, but I also knew saying anything wouldn't actually help. So with all the experience I had used up in nodding back, I left.

The rest of the day I went to the center of town to look for clothing that could replace the nomadic gear I was weary of. As I valued mobility and speed, I looked for and found a shop specializing in lightweight leather armor. They had a good selection, and due to few buying lightweight armors in the middle of winter, they were somewhat cheap. There were other samples I preferred the look of, but since I didn't want to spend the extra coin and wait to get fitted for anything, I bought a rudimentary cuirass that fitted me almost like a shirt. I also bought a thin undershirt, a right leather gauntlet, two greaves, and a pair of fingerless gloves. To cover my armor, I went to another shop and bought a sturdy linen shirt of dark blue and black trousers. Since my boots and cloak were sturdy enough, I did not replace those.

I then went back to the inn to eat and sleep the rented hours I had left. When I awoke in the early morning, I restarted my journey to Voreen.

Chapter Nineteen

On the second afternoon away from Mil'sith, Aranath said, "I hope you realize she's following us."

"Of course. Since the moment I left the city."

"So why haven't you chased her away? Pity?"

"It's no longer my business what she does."

"She'll make it your business sooner or later."

"Until then, I see no reason to chase her off. If she can keep up, so be it. Besides, she might think I'm too demented to stay around once she starts hearing me talk to myself."

"Have it your way."

Clarissa kept her distance from me for the next couple of freezing weeks. I would sometimes see her little campfire glow in the distant night, and less often I would catch her shrouded form fifty yards behind me, never coming much closer than that. The shade provided by the trees and winter clouds allowed her to follow me in the day, but I figured she would be slowed considerably once warmer weather arrived. I also assumed she would be forced to go her own way once I bought my ride across the Lucent Sea, but that was still hundreds of miles away. I tolerated her detached presence in the meanwhile.

In the third week since leaving Mil'sith, a fierce blizzard forced Clarissa to close the distance between us. It was midday, but the snowstorm had made the day as cold and opaque as any night previous. I was able to find a bit of cover against the ferocious gusts behind a large tree and, after digging out some snow, I used my usual method to create a robust campfire. About half an hour after making the only source of heat for miles around,

Clarissa trudged through the storm and collapsed on her knees next to the fire. As the passionate winds would have just carried any words into the ether anyway, neither of us spoke for a couple of hours.

When the carrier of air lessened its haste, the vampire said, "I'm sorry for intruding, but I couldn't get my fire to start."

"It's fine."

"How did you get your fire to start? I thought I had gotten good at living in the wilderness, but I guess I still have a lot to learn."

"I cheated." I pulled out a dragon stone, dropped it, and ignited it. She saw the stone burn for a few seconds before giving out. "Take it and hold it tight."

She gingerly picked it up, but when she felt how warm it was, she snatched it up and clasped it against her. "How do you get rock to burn?"

"I'm cheating there as well."

She rubbed the rock on her face for a few minutes before it lost its effectiveness. "T-thank you, and not just for the warmth, but for everything. It would have been so easy for you to kill me. Gods, how stupid I must seem to you. It was so obvious how he really felt and I never saw it, or didn't want to."

"You shouldn't be too hard on yourself. Most people I see seem to be too afraid or too weak to be alone. Some are even willing to take quite a bit of abuse for the sake of company."

"Then how do you do it?"

"Do what?"

"Be alone."

"I'm not."

"I mean before right now."

"So do I. I've had a voice in my head for the past few months. If I didn't happen to find him, I wouldn't be alive now."

131

She cocked her head. "I can't tell whether you're joking or not."

"And I don't care what conclusion you reach."

After a minute of studying me, she asked, "And where are you and the voice in your head going?"

"Voreen."

"What's there?"

"Information."

"On what?"

"Ever heard of a Riskel Rathmore?" She signaled in the negative. "Well, either he needs to die again, or if he really is dead, then whoever is continuing his work needs to die."

"What work?"

"I'm not entirely sure what's trying to be accomplished, but it didn't do me any good. Simple as that."

"Let me help you."

"No."

"Why not?"

"I don't like the idea of baggage."

"I'm no child. You don't have to keep an eye on me or hunt for my food. I have no obligations to anyone else in the world. I have nothing else in the world."

"That's no reason to join a cause that's not your own. It's the reason you're a vampire in the first place."

"Yes, I know I was foolish, but I also know what my choices are now. I can find another vampire den somewhere, live alone in the wilderness, or help the only person in the world who doesn't care that I'm a vampire."

"The first two options seem okay by me."

"Too bad, I'm choosing the third one."

132

I mulled over her strangely resolute eyes a moment. I sighed. "On one condition."

"Anything."

"The second you become a burden, you leave."

"Fine, but I'll show you how useful I can be. I'll stay guard during the night. I-I'll gather and catch food for you, and I won't even be within sight most of the time. I'll also-"

"Okay, I get it. Just get some sleep if you can. I'd rather you be alert in your first night watch."

In what was her probably her first in weeks, the edge of her lips cracked a smile and said, "Okay." She huddled by the fire and was fast asleep within a few moments.

"She'll now gladly die for you," said Aranath. "When the strong acknowledge the weak, the weak feel as though they've been given a grand purpose in life, no matter how selfish that purpose actually is."

True to her word, Clarissa continued to keep her distance, though a couple of more blizzards had us sharing a fire, and I actually did feel a bit more at ease knowing that someone was watching the area when I slept. She would also give me the animal she had sucked dry of blood, allowing me to eat more than I otherwise would have caught on my own. I thus awakened from deeper slumbers more refreshed and with greater energy to spare in my training regimens.

Speaking of which, when we were waiting out the second blizzard together in a cave, Clarissa asked me to show her how to be a better fighter. I didn't feel like teaching her anything, but I didn't mind directly showing her my abilities in some sparring sessions. Before I knew it, these sparring sessions became part of the routine. Her vampirism alone made her stronger than the average human, and since we didn't have many weapons or spells to practice with, hand-to-hand combat made up most of our sessions, though we also touched on her water spell and the best way to handle a dagger.

At one point I told her of my own corruption and the blade that prevented it from taking me over. I was even close to telling her about Aranath, but I ended up refraining from giving that away. I knew I wouldn't have to tell her that he was a dragon, but it seemed easier not to touch on it at all.

Both time and our roughly southwestern route loosened winter's hold, making travel less of a chore. According to a road sign, we eventually entered the country of Caracasa. After a couple of days crossing deeper into the nation, we saw a line of trees that began what my map labeled the Forest of Giants. The "giants" was a reference to the colossal trees that grew four hundred feet on average, with the tallest of them looking to be at least a hundred feet taller still.

The mighty woodland had once spread hundreds of miles farther south, but since the wood was prized for its resiliency and ability to hold prana well, people had cut down half the forest over the past two millennia. Clarissa and I crossed an area that was once the center of the forest, which had at one time been populated by an ancient people that used the trees as their homes. These people still existed, but they had been forced farther north hundreds of years ago by better equipped armies.

Getting out of the forest a week later correlated with temperatures becoming more bearable for travelers. The towns we passed were livelier, as though they were stirring from a hibernation many animals had taken as well. It was still mind-numbingly cold at night, but the sunlight was stronger in the day. One of my quick talks with Clarissa had me learning that she could continue following me as long as I didn't walk too fast in the middle of the day. I already thought I was moving slow enough, so instead of coming to a crawl, I decided to stop and train a little more in the afternoon while making up traveling time in the early mornings and evenings. I could tell Clarissa was very grateful when I altered my schedule to fit her form of corruption better. She often carried a look in her eyes that told me she wanted nothing more than to heap praise on me, but a stern look from me would stop her before she began the lauding.

The port city I headed for was a place called Abesh. It was Clarissa that told me the city was among the largest on this side of Orda. Its size and importance to Caracasa's trade economy ensured that ships were always coming and going from Niatrios. Moreover, I wanted to check with their Warriors Guild for anything regarding my goal.

Chapter Twenty

Spring arrived at the same time we reached Abesh one late morning. Unlike Mil'sith, almost no part of the sprawling city was walled in. Instead, I imagined the system of canals that encircled much of the outer and inner sections of the city was used as the main defense against land-based attackers. There were two major rings of ocean-connecting canals surrounding the city. Anything beyond the outermost ring was farmland or inns for travelers. The area between the inner and outermost ring appeared mostly residential, and anything deeper in was a business of some sort.

Before reaching the city itself, I had seen large forts sprinkled near major roadways, which were probably there to give the city time to raise the many bridges over the canals if an enemy army ever came, effectively dividing the city up into two islands. Even with the bridges currently lowered, I saw quite a few people taking advantage of the waterways by traversing them in small boats. Like Mil'sith, the tallest structures here were the six towers of the temple near the coast.

I put up Clarissa in an inn while I headed straight for the guild office located in the expectedly cramped business district. The guild building I found was only a single story, but it was wider than most others. Like most others, the structure was composed of both stone and timber. Entering it revealed a large entrance hall where two girls stood behind a counter taking job requests from several residents. Three of the petitions sounded reasonable enough, but one elderly woman had to be told a few times why she couldn't hire the guild to find the kids who wrecked her flower bed.

"What can the guild do for you, sir?" asked the taller of the girls when it was my turn to be helped.

"What do you know of Riskel Rathmore?"

Her forehead wrinkled as she rummaged through her experience. "Lot of ghost stories on that one. I don't know much. I was way too young to have been involved with that mess."

"Anyone not so young here?"

"Uh, hold on." Turning her head toward a hall that led somewhere to the back of the building, she said, "Hey Ping! Can you come a moment?!"

I heard the clunks of heavy boots treading on the wooden floor. The forty something year old man that appeared was actually only wearing some armored boots and metal gauntlets. A small axe dangled at his hip, but everything else looked less threatening.

"What is it?"

"The gentleman here wants to know about Rathmore."

Ping eyed me a second before asking, "Why the interest?"

"In the Onyx Mountains, near a little mining village called Bronzefrost, I found some corrupted. Not far from them I discovered a collapsed tunnel system. I asked around and someone close to the situation gave me that name."

"I bet they would. Someone hears 'corrupted' and his name invariably comes up. Wait, when did this occur?"

"This past fall."

"So you came all the way from the Onyx Mountains in the middle of winter?"

"Yes."

"Damn," said the still listening girl.

"Indeed," said Ping. "Listen, as far as I know, Rathmore is dead, but finding corrupted anywhere is a problem, but the Onyx Mountains are a bit out of this guild's reach."

"I don't need your reach. I just want to know everything I can about Rathmore. Who were associated with him? Are any of them still at large?"

"Well, if you're that curious, I suppose you should find Madam Rachel, the last guild master of this chapter. She was already an old woman at the time, but she only retired eight or nine years ago. I heard she was at death's door a few weeks back. It would be a big deal if she died, so I guess she's still living up at a little village about eight miles northeast from town. Most of the family works for the brewery her son owns, so just look for the biggest house and you'll find her."

"What's the village called?"

"Sunburst. They named the beer after it."

After thanking him, I left in a brisk walk in an attempt to reach the home before the old woman either slept for the day or died for life.

On reaching the village that fit Ping's description, I learned that the Sunburst brewery and the actual home was located another half mile to the north. There they grew most of the crops and brewed most of the beer. Following a little dirt trail someone pointed out to me led right to the house. From a hundred yards away I caught sight of a hefty three story house of brick and stone. An even larger structure of wood stood well in the distance, which likely held much of the brewing operation.

There came a point when two men sitting near the front of the house spotted me and both began walking up to the incoming stranger. They were garbed with some yellow shirts, but their bulk informed me of the obvious armor they wore underneath. Combined with their sheathed swords, figuring out their profession was a simple matter.

In a loud voice that was probably used to compensate for his smaller size, one of the men said, "Can I help you, son?"

"I need to speak with Madam Rachel."

"That so? On what business?"

138

"Old guild business."

"You a member?"

"No."

He looked up and down my frame. "Open your cloak a little." I did. "Why are you armed if you aren't part of the guild?"

"Dangerous world."

"I suppose it is. So, who do you represent?"

"Myself."

"Not an old enemy of hers?"

"From what I hear, any old enemy of hers would only have to wait a week to get their revenge. Just tell her Ping from the guild suggested I see her."

"You heard him," the smaller told the larger. "Go check if she'll see anyone."

Instead of going inside the house like I expected, the hired guard went around it. He came jogging back a minute later. He nodded at the other. They then both escorted me to the back of the house.

From this new angle I could see people working in the fields, and much closer than them were two youths sparring with wooden weapons on a large patch of bare dirt. One was a short girl with black hair that came down to her shoulders. She was equipped with a long pole representing a spear. The other was a boy wielding a sword-length pole. Sitting on a large cushioned chair up against the back of the house was someone bundled inside many layers of clothing, including a hooded cloak of bright blue that obscured the face from my position.

"This is him," said the larger guard.

In a stronger voice than I anticipated, the nestled old woman, without turning her head away from the sparring youths, said, "What's your name?"

"Mercer."

"And what does Mercer want with my past?"

"Rathmore. Tell me everything you know about him and his people."

She turned her head. Her left eye was milky white. The other was pea green. I noticed them more than her heavily creased skin and jutting chin. She soon went back to watching the sparring match. I kept them at the edge of my own vision for the minute she stayed silent.

The guards were ready to make sure she was alive, but she eventually turned back to me and asked, "What can you tell me about the young warriors?"

I gave them a glimpse before saying, "The girl knows her stances, but is too stiff in her movements, as though she wants to match illustrations more than real life. The boy has the opposite problem. He starts off with the right stances, but is not disciplined enough to hold them."

I couldn't tell if her nods were for me or because she was close to dozing off, but she did say, "I collaborated closely with my veteran colleagues to make certain my chapter was ready for Rathmore in case he made his way to Caracasa. Fortunately, he never made it this far north. Many good people died tracking him down. What is your concern with this horrible man?"

"His horrible work might still be continuing. If I can learn about his past, who his close associates were, then maybe I can find these people and end it."

She wheezed a chuckle. "Such conviction from a youth is rare! However, I only see it when the youth has been greatly wronged in some way. Am I mistaken?"

"No."

"How interesting. I've pretty much accepted that my only working eye has seen all it has to see, but perhaps not. Do you wish to sit?"

"I'm fine. Just give me every detail you have."

140

Looking at the youths—with the boy constantly being knocked down—she said, "No one knows exactly who Rathmore was. It can be pretty much assumed that he had been trained by Voreen's military, but they won't even admit that much. The secrecy has most suspecting that Rathmore belonged to one of their elite army units. That by itself is nothing unusual, but word was that these units were being prepared for a preemptive strike against Alslana."

"Did this word come from Voreen's Warriors Guild?"

"Maybe, but I doubt it. We are an organization that pledges to serve and defend all people. With that interest in mind, new guild members are often sent to cities they have no personal or official attachment to." She stopped to cough up some phlegm. She continued her trip to the past after drinking something steaming in a cup and clearing her throat. "What was I saying? Oh, yes, the guild. Our guild doesn't interfere with national conflicts, but the guild headquarters in Voreen has always been a bit too close to political matters for my liking. Perhaps they feel they have to be. Voreen has always been a place for conflict to erupt. Whether it's someone attacking them for their port or their own desire to take Alslana for their own, that country is never in a peaceful place for long. Still, my former colleagues have never found direct evidence to make them believe the guild there has become a Voreen puppet."

"I was planning of going to Voreen's guild to see what they had on Rathmore. That's beginning to sound-"

"Stupid? Yes, I agree. There might not be any direct evidence of collusion, but if someone starts asking around about the national disgrace that was Rathmore, they'll certainly hear about it. The best you can hope for is that they'll simply keep their mouths shut to you."

"When exactly was Rathmore considered a threat?"

141

"He was always a threat. People started disappearing around him for years before Voreen itself had to finally do something about his experiments. It basically happened overnight. There was suddenly word that a powerful caster dabbling in corrupted souls was on the loose, not to mention the dozen elite soldiers that joined his cause. He lingered in Niatrios for three years or so before he reached southern Iazali. He then hid for a decade before sprouting up again near Alslana. I really became interested once word had him moving farther north, but thirteen years after he was first pronounced an enemy of the people, an Alslana for-" More coughing. "An Alslana force was able to surround the mountain he fled to and a unit comprising mostly of *Voreen* guild members killed him and his supporters. That's the reason many people don't quite believe he's dead."

"What do you believe?"

"I believe he's dead, but I also believe there was some funny business going on. The official story says that the people there beheaded Rathmore and burned the rest, but someone ended up burning the head as well. It was never made clear exactly how that mistake happened. Without definite proof of Rathmore's demise, along with Voreen's involvement, the rumors of his escape began on that very night."

"And his supporters?"

"Most were pawns he converted to his cause in one way or another. The ones of note were his two mistresses and a younger man that is also thought to have been part of Voreen's secret training program. Proof of their beheaded corpses satisfied everyone at the time."

"But a decade is a long time to add more followers."

"Aye. I've always believed the guild moved on too quickly from the case. Voreen certainly wasn't going to release all they knew, and everyone else simply wanted to forget about the bad business. I might have pushed my

142

colleagues more if I wasn't already tired of the whole damn thing. I should have trusted my younger contemporaries to take over sooner…"

"If you could investigate now, who would you go to?"

"A fine question…" She stared at the youths. The boy wanted to continue, but the girl seemed to be explaining why continuing to kick his ass wouldn't do them anymore good. "What would you do if there was a dead end to your quest?"

"I know they're out there, and I know they need to die. I would continue looking for a way around the dead end. I'll still go to Voreen if I have to."

"Ah, I see. A child with nothing but death in his past and in his future… Those two are my grandchildren. They've heard most of my stories and they have it in their head that they can make good guild members, particularly the boy. My son hired expensive tutors to teach them, but they're too afraid to actually hit the kids of a rich man. I suspect you are not. Agree to help me whip them into shape and I will make sure your quest does not reach a dead end just yet." Sensing my objecting mouth opening, she lifted a hand. "Come back anytime tomorrow with your decision. You will receive payment, good food, and even a place to sleep if you so desire. They have another three weeks of training before they move to Qutrios' Festival of Lights. There they will compete in a tournament that the guild likes to use to evaluate young talent. And don't concern yourself if I happen to die. I will make arrangements for such an occurrence."

"I'm no teacher."

"Like I said, they've been taught. Now they need to be shown what someone their age can accomplish."

"How do you know I can accomplish anything?"

"I would have allowed myself to die by now if I didn't enjoy employing my wisdom every now and again. All the same, even if I am wrong about you, I'll know after tomorrow. What do you care, anyway? I can see you're willing to die to find who wronged you. A little sparring shouldn't deter you."

"I find dying less annoying than people."

She snorted. "You just haven't met anyone worth living for."

Knowing I could not dissuade this old warrior woman, I sighed and said, "Three weeks?"

"Aye."

"Very well, I'll take your extortionist offer."

"Ah, you've amused a timeworn woman. The gods will smile on thee. My grandchildren appear too tired to continue training for the day. We'll start again at noon tomorrow. Do you wish to stay over?"

"I have to notify someone of the change in plans."

"You may bring them along if you want. It's a big house, and my son will welcome anyone I wish him to."

"It'll just be me. I'll return by noon."

I bowed and left the old woman to wallow in her victory.

Clarissa couldn't help chuckling when I told her what happened.

"Sorry, I just know you must hate this."

"Hate that an old hag is using me for her amusement before she croaks? What gave you that idea?"

Putting down the history book I had already read, she said, "I know you don't like it, but I think you'd make a good tutor. You don't even talk all that much and I feel like I've learned a lot."

"What are you going to do for food?"

"Oh... I guess I'll just have to adopt a couple of stray cats or something. I'll be fine here while you're gone."

144

Chapter Twenty-One

I was at the Sunburst home by noon. The same two house guards from before met me and took me to the old woman. It was like she hadn't moved since I left her the day before. She waved away the guards.

The larger guard said, "Master Bolin wanted me to watch over the stranger."

"Nonsense, Britton. *I'm* here to watch the stranger."

"But Mada-"

She waved her hand. "If my son was truly concerned about me or his children, then he'd be here himself. Now shoo. I'll scream if the stranger starts stabbing everyone."

The guards shrugged at one another and left.

"Where are his children?" I asked her.

"They warm up with a run. They'll be here shortly. As you saw yesterday, each have been tutored with the fundamentals. I simply prefer to see how they respond to actual hits."

"And you believe they're three weeks away from impressing the guild?"

"They'd be much more ready if I had things my way. Ethan has been eager to train and join the guild since he was a lad, but his parents didn't think him serious and ignored a crucial development period. He and his sister are thus latecomers. However, ever since my son realized they were indeed serious about becoming warriors, I have seen them blossom with the little guidance they've had. I love my grandchildren. If I didn't believe them capable in this endeavor, I wouldn't encourage them."

Her grandchildren showed up a few minutes later.

After catching his breath, Ethan asked his grandmother, "Is our new tutor here yet?"

"This is him. Meet Mercer. Mercer, this is Ethan and his sister Catherine."

"What are you talking about, Grandma? This guy is the same age we are!"

"Age is a number. Experience on the other hand…"

"Who are you?" the bright-eyed girl asked me.

"All you need to know is that your grandmother thinks I can help train you. In exchange, she'll tell me something I need to know."

"Come on, Grandma!" continued Ethan. "This is an insult! Get one of your guild friends to come over."

"Their time is too precious for such a meager goal. No, you will see the wisdom of my choice when this young man shows you exactly what I have seen. What have you seen from them, Mercer?"

"The boy is reckless and watching the girl is like watching a painting fight."

"*Boy*? I'm already seventeen! And there's no way you're that much older."

"This can be solved simply enough," I said. "We spar. I win, you shut up. If you even put up a good fight, I leave."

"Good enough for me." He headed for some training poles of various lengths leaning against the back of the house. He chose one that represented a longsword. "Come on! Let's get this over with!"

"Gods," said Aranath, "I've never wanted you to strike somebody more."

Agreeing with the dragon, I went to choose a pole that represented a short sword and met Ethan on the grassless area a few yards away. Already knowing what I wanted to do, I held the training pole with my left hand.

146

Ethan looked at his grandmother and reluctantly gave me a small bow. I did the same.

As I had seen yesterday, he held a stance well enough, but I knew he wouldn't be disciplined enough to hold it when something went against the obvious. To induce him out of his defensive stance, I charged at him. Showing that he believed the match was even, he immediately moved in as well. I pulled out a dragon stone and lobbed it at him. There was no point in igniting it. A rock in the air was all I needed to distract my opponent. By the time his eyes were back on me, he panicked and swung with little purpose. My pole easily blocked his and I lunged forward to land a hard punch right above his stomach. Seeing he wasn't going to fall, I grabbed the arm that held his practice weapon and head-butted him. This sent him falling backward.

"First lesson, if you're not sure what the fuck is happening, keep back." Looking at the girl, I said, "Catherine, right? You're up."

The raven haired girl looked at her elder, who directed her to me with a wave of her hand. Catherine grabbed a spear-long pole and eyed her brother trying to stand back up as she walked over.

"A spear is a good choice," I told her. "If they were easier to keep hidden, I'd carry one to gain a longer reach. Let's see how well you can keep me back."

I didn't go all out on her as I did on her brother, but I didn't want her comfortable either. Using the same information I had gained the day before, I was very quickly able to attain the upper hand. She was just too predictable. Within a few moves, I had grabbed the shaft of the spear and pulled her in so that I could land a kick to her gut.

As she laid on the ground, I said, "I don't know who your teacher was, but they ingrained too much of the basics in you. The stances are a guide, not a universal truth. Get this through your head and you'll easily become a menace in the battlefield. You're already better than your brother."

"What do you mean *better*?" asked Ethan behind me.

I turned to say, "I mean her problem is easier to fix. She just has to open her mind a little more. You, on the other hand, have to actually grow up. That might not happen in three weeks."

"I'm growing up just fine. Grandma says I only have to focus a little more."

"For your sake, I hope that's true. Now, what can you each cast?"

"I can do a little of everything."

"Which really means you can do nothing well. What's your most competent spell? And if you say 'fire' I'm going to bash your head in with a rock."

"Uh, it's actually an earth spell for me."

"I've concentrated on wind," replied his sister.

"Good," I told the sister. "Extending your reach further is a good strategy. As for earth, you'll have to show me how you employ that."

Ethan, probably wanting to surprise me, shot out his arms and I felt the ground beneath my feet shifting. I jumped back just before the ground cratered and became a sand-like consistency. It was Aranath that told me this was a sand-trap spell. Tricky to get out of for those caught in it.

"A bit faster and you might have something there," I told Ethan, "but it will matter little if your enemy can still ward off your attacks without moving their legs. All right, I'm tired of talking, so we'll just spend the rest of our time today focusing on physical attacks. Both of you come at me at the same time. We'll see if you two can work together to take me down."

It was plain they had never worked as a pair before, making it easy to repel their attacks. When I did talk, it was almost always to correct Ethan, which I reinforced by whacking the limb that needed correcting with my

148

practice sword. By afternoon's end they each had bruises and bloody scrapes on every visible part of their skin. As they weren't completely incompetent, they each were able to land the occasional strike on me, but I always returned the favor immediately afterward. Neither of them seemed troubled by their signs of inadequacy. If anything, they looked pleased that they had something to strive for. Their grandmother held a similar expression in her single working eye.

With the first training session over, her grandchildren helped lift Madam Rachel off her chair, but once she was up, she walked under her own power. I took Madam Rachel's offer to take a little guest room they had during my three week stay, which also meant I would take some of their food as well. Most of the many family members who saw me gave me a wary look, particularly the mother of my students, but I did my best to avoid them, taking my dinner up to my room. The bed in my chamber had clothes for me to wear. Not needing leather armor during my time here, I removed them and accept their attire, though I kept on my cloak when I exited the bedroom.

Exempting the people I had already seen, I learned that Ethan and Catherine had an older brother, who was the next in line to own the brewery, and a younger brother. The parents of their mother also lived in the home, and while these were the permanent residents, there were always other people over, which included friends or more relatives. In any event, many of these people would barely get glimpses of me, and what they said behind my back was of little concern to me or the old matriarch of the home. Most of my off time was spent in my room reading from a large collection of books they had.

Apart from the times I had to speak, I enjoyed the training sessions. It was an opportunity to sharpen my abilities against some active opposition, and it never not felt good to hit Ethan. He had warmed up to me on realizing my superior skills, and started seeing me as something of a rival, which he

149

indicated as much near the end of a training session when he said, "It's nice having someone else besides my sister as my main rival."

In response to this declaration, I said, "A rivalry implies two participants at around the same level. We are not."

"Not yet we're not, but there's plenty of time for me to catch up."

"Unfortunately for you, I have certain advantages that have given me too far a head start."

"Yeah? Like what?"

"Nothing you need to concern yourself with."

"I guess I'll just force you to think differently. Hey, if you're so good, then why don't you want to join the guild? Or do you want to join something else?"

"I have my own goal."

"Let me guess, you won't tell me what it is. You know, girls might like guys who are all mysterious and shit, but you don't have to put on that act all the time."

"It's not an act. I don't like people and most won't like what I am, so there's little point saying or doing anything more than what's necessary."

"Why won't people like what you are?"

I sighed. "You talk way too damn much."

"And you don't talk enough. Come on, you can't be so bad if my grandmother hired you to train us."

"Why do want to join the guild?"

"Uh, well, because I want to get stronger and help people while I'm doing it."

"I too want to become stronger, but only so that I may someday kill the people who took away my past and what I could have been. Nothing else matters."

150

He was quiet for a long moment, but his mouth invariably opened to ask, "What did these people do?"

"All you need to know is that they've given me the power to beat your ass."

Not long after the conversation ended, his sister came up to me and said, "Sorry about Ethan. He's always been a little unfiltered with his thoughts and emotions. I personally think he might be too sensitive for the warrior lifestyle, but he really wants to join."

"And why do you?"

"Well, at first I just wanted to get out of this village, but the more I dwell on it, the more I think I just want to keep my stupid brother out of trouble. Ugh, please don't tell him I said that."

"Just keep in mind, the less he's around me, the less chance I have to tell him."

A week after I started training them, Ethan came out to the session shirtless. A few minutes after we began sparring, some of Catherine's friends came over to watch, giving me the reason why my student was showing off his musculature. Of course, I went at him with fiercer conviction. Catherine's girlfriends seemed to both encourage and mock Ethan as we fought, and sometimes in the same sentence. I wasn't quite sure what to make of that, but I had a feeling this was how most people treated the annoyingly outgoing boy.

Near the end of this training session, Ethan asked me, "Hey, can I borrow your sword?"

"No."

"But I just want to show off with some real steel. You see that cute blonde over there? She's this close to giving me a nice goodbye present before I have to leave."

"Very well. Who am I to stop young love?"

I unsheathed Aranath and handed him the hilt. He had to drop it the instant he grasped it.

"What the fuck was that?"

Picking up the snickering blade, I said, "Remember when I told you I have certain advantages over you? This is one of them."

"What kind of enchantment is that?"

"An old one. It only accepts those who have their head in the right place during battle. Catherine!"

Separating from her friends to come to us, she said, "What?"

"Hold my blade as long as you can." Knowing what I wanted him to do, Aranath allowed her to hold him, though I could tell from her scrunching face that he wasn't making it easy. "See? She's more ready than you are."

"Bullshit, I'm ready! Give it to me, Cat!" She handed him the sword when I nodded my assent to her. His grip and face were tight, but he was no match against Aranath's power. He had to drop it. "Fuck."

"We have two weeks more to get your head straight. If you truly want to act like a warrior, then you'll learn to hold your fucking stances. Your unpredictability, while a benefit in some situations, won't take you far on its own."

This "proof" of his shortcomings appeared to finally settle him down. I wished I had thought of it sooner. I soon found him studying books on stances, and his performance on the field was less chatty and more focused. The minor adjustment actually did make him a better opponent, especially when he worked together with his sister. Over the next few days the siblings seemed to come up with a system that played off what their stances were, giving them a better understanding as to how to keep me off balanced, since I could not effectively counter two different styles at once. It was finally making things interesting. By the end of the second week, I could only prevent myself from losing by using my explosive distractions.

152

With his physical attacks more honed in, I allowed him to train as much as his sister did in his casting. Catherine's capacity to cast a wind spell as she jabbed or swung with her spear made her a difficult target to get close to. The job was made even harder when her younger brother timed his own attacks well. As he stated when we first met, Ethan could cast a bit of everything, but his flame spell was barely hot enough to cook an egg, a water spell was only useful enough to create a patch of mud, and his own wind spell was a nice breeze on a hot day. I thus instructed him to focus on his earth spells. If he correctly predicted where I was going to step, this earth spell was able to grab at my feet, forcing me to slow down to smash its hold. Sometimes Catherine took advantage and pushed me down with a strong blast of air before they each closed in.

Three days before they were set to leave, I was forced to show them my last ace up my sleeve. I had scattered several explosive stones and ignited them when the time came. The blast created a cloud of dust that hid the fact I was casting my illusion spell. So as Ethan swung at a fake copy of myself, I forced his sister to the ground. Once she was down, Ethan was much less of a threat.

As he brushed off the dirt coating him, Ethan said, "So you can combine an earth and fire spell, *and* cast an illusion spell? You don't play fair, do you?"

"'Fair' is not a word that should exist in a warrior's vocabulary. You've heard of Edith the Great?"

"Yeah."

"Then you know how she died?"

"Yeah. A kid killed her."

"Specifically, Etoc, through a supposedly neutral party, sent a bunch of war orphans across the border, knowing that the warrior queen had a soft spot for them. When she went to visit the group of children, one of them took

153

out a dagger from beneath his rags and stabbed her in the heart. A great warrior, caster, and tactician was undone by a mere child."

"Caracasa still won the war."

"Five years later and at great cost, yes. Her absence then led to a civil war that lasted a decade. If you believe my using an illusion spell to be unfair, be prepared to die from much more ordinary schemes."

The day before our last training session took place, I told Aranath to allow Ethan to hold onto him for a few seconds. We both didn't care much for the idea, but I suspected if Ethan wasn't shown "evidence" of his improvement, then he would revert back to his unfocused self. It was also on this day that Madam Rachel called me down to her room soon after dinner. Her bedroom was large and brightly lit. She laid on a small bed with her shriveled head poking out of some thick blankets. Her servant stepped out of the room at her request.

"You're not finally dying, are you?" I asked, my tone unchanging.

"Ha! You wish. I know how death feels like, and it isn't close yet. The Reaper stands at my door, but the lock is still hardy. Even so, it's time I give you what you came here for. First, you will tell me about your sword. Why did Ethan change when he couldn't grasp it?"

"Hand me over to her," said Aranath.

I untied the scabbard and stepped up to her bed. "See for yourself."

She sat up and her skinny fingers clasped the item. She laid it across her body. Her eyes widened, pushing out the wrinkles around them. They kept their wider shape until she turned to look at me a minute later. She said, "To think that this power will appear in someone like you after five hundred years. I suppose options are limited." She handed me back the blade. "No matter, I don't believe you're a lost cause just yet. I only regret I will not be able to see what happens for myself."

"Rathmore."

154

"Yes, yes. The man I worked most closely with during the Rathmore case was Braden Silver. He works for the main Alslana guild chapter. Last I heard, he evaluates young talent for the guild, so he'll certainly be at the tournament."

Seeing where this was going, I said, "You're going to want me to travel with your grandchildren, aren't you?"

"Nonsense. I was simply going to offer you a free trip that happens to include my grandchildren. They'll be going on a ship, giving them plenty of time to enjoy the start of the festival before the tournament begins, but you may wish to run all the way if you prefer."

After a heavy exhale, I said, "Pay for another companion of mine, give me an extra five gold standards, and I'll accept the joint trip."

"Done. Now then, Braden will be easy to find. He's a large black man, who was already quite bald the couple of times we met, so I imagine he's without all his hair by now."

"Is he as old as you?"

"No, but his retirement isn't far off. Anyway, I suspect that of all the guild members I connected with in those times, he's the most likely to have kept an ear out for Rathmore's dealings even after his death. He also has the seniority to ask what questions he wants to Voreen's chapter without getting stonewalled as much as most others. Tell him I sent you and that alone should warm him up to you, but I would of course mention what you saw up in the Onyx Mountains."

"Anything else?"

A hoarse sigh escaped her. "I would say so much more if I wasn't so damn tired. For now, I'll simply say you need to relax more. I understand what you're seeking, and I have no right to dissuade you from it, but do everyone a favor and don't spill your angst on us. There's enough of that going around."

"I'll keep that mind."

"It's all I ask."

I emitted something that was between a scoff and a chuckle. "When was the last time you didn't get things your way?"

"Just before I developed breasts. It's been smooth sailing ever since."

Chapter Twenty-Two

The evening after my last training session, I brought Clarissa to the wharf so that I could settle her in our transport, which turned out to be a single-masted sailing ship called *Dawn's Hammer*. It was the day before Ethan and Clarissa would board, but I didn't want to have to introduce Clarissa to them when their family and friends would be there eyeing her. Like most transports, the ship's main purpose was to move cargo, but the well-kept little cabins in the central deck showed that "cargo" could include about a dozen well-to-do passengers.

Early the next morning, Catherine, Ethan, and a handful of other travelers showed up with their family and friends to see them off. It took about half an hour for everyone to board and say their farewells, and it required another half hour for the sailors to send *Dawn's Hammer* into her eight day voyage to the city of Qutrios.

The fat, jolly captain wasted no time sharing personal stories with his new passengers. It was obvious he exaggerated his tales about the pirates he evaded and the sea monsters he'd seen, but as his aim seemed to be to frighten everyone, it was the way to go. I wasn't afraid of the sea, but as I had yet to practice swimming in it, I wasn't too thrilled with his stories either.

Giving the excuse that she wasn't feeling well, I didn't introduce Clarissa until the sunset cast its long shadows on the top deck. Ethan was unremitting in his questions, but Clarissa handled him well. In truth, the vampire likely welcomed the chance to exercise her mouth after weeks of using very little of it, and all without hinting at exactly how we met and what bloodthirsty community she belonged to. Though they wouldn't use them in their matches, the siblings brought their respective weapons and did a few half-speed practice sessions with them on the top deck.

"They're nice people," Clarissa concluded after she entered my room later that night.

"I wouldn't mind if you take a taste of Ethan."

She giggled. "He does smell kinda good."

"Does your kind find anyone revolting?"

"Believe or not, yes. Most people are more or less the same, but some do smell either really good or pretty bad. I'm not sure why, but they do."

"I can guess that I don't smell all that appetizing."

"How did you figure that out?"

"Based on what I've heard and read, the main impulse of your kind isn't really to feed, but to spread your corruption. I'm already corrupted with something, so there's no point in trying to turn me."

"That makes sense... How do you think they'll react if they find out what I am?"

"Ethan is too dense to figure it out on his own. Catherine might begin piecing things together if she sees you only in the twilight hours and never eating real food, but she'll come to me with any concerns."

"That's not really what I meant."

"I know, but it won't get to that point."

"Hey, since we're going, will you enter the tournament?"

"Why would I do that?"

"I heard the winner gets fifty gold standards."

"I have enough to get by for a little while."

"Or you could have a little more to get by even longer."

"You should know by now that drawing attention to myself isn't exactly my thing."

158

"But I think it'll be fun."

"I know what else you think might be fun, but I'm not indulging that craving either."

"And why not? I just want to thank you."

"Because right now it'll mean more than just a 'thank you' to you. You still rely on others too much. If I ever believe that you're finally standing on your own two feet, then I'll fuck you."

"Maybe I'll use Ethan."

"Provoking me is not helping your chances."

She stuck her tongue out at me and left.

I mostly read the time away. I would have spent more time training, but the rocking of the boat and the limited space it offered prevented any lengthy sessions. The weather was perfect for sailing. Aranath even commented on how an old pastime of his included flying over calm seas. The ship rarely moved beyond the sight of the coast, though morning fog, night, and a few showers often hid it.

Despite the smooth sailing, I discovered that I held no love for the sea, so I experienced more relief than I liked to admit when an afternoon sun revealed the ship nearing the port city of Qutrios. As the name implied, Qutrios once belonged to a nation in Niatrios, specifically, an older version of Voreen, but that was hundreds of years ago. Since then, Alslana has had firm control of one of the largest and most important cities in all of Iazali. Only a handful of other cities, which included Alslana's capital several hundred miles farther south, were brighter gems.

The two week festival was a week and a half away, and the town already teemed with more people than it could handle. Simply glad solid ground was supporting me, I agreed to Clarissa's request for us all to stay at the same inn. We found one spacious and well-maintained enough at the fringes of the city a couple of hours after arriving. I then went to find the guild headquarters to find out if anyone knew where Braden Silver was. The answer to the inquiry—given to me by a well-ordered, prim clerk whose voice was wasted behind a counter—was that he wasn't expected in the city until the start of the tournament, meaning I would have to spend two and a half weeks waiting for him.

More travelers arrived in the city over the next week, and though the official revelries had not yet begun, many newcomers already started celebrating in the evening hours. As this mostly consisted of drinking games, I wasn't interested in joining in. It wasn't until the actual festival started did I begrudgingly unify myself with the siblings and Clarissa in their search for festive events. As the more interesting parts of the festival happened during the evening and nights, it was easy to keep Clarissa indoors during the heat of the day and come out at her preferred hours.

As to be expected under the bluish moonlight, the entire city was alive with stranger folk. The rich intermingled freely with the poor, rambling drunkards were treated like great entertainers, and I once saw a fully-armored knight looking aimlessly for someone. Many people wore a mask so that they were free to enter one of the many masquerade parties happening all at once. Music came from lutes, drums, violins, flutes, throats, harps, and a dozen others I could and could not name. Nearly all played within the city squares, and they were often accompanied by jesters and entertainers from foreign lands with foreign animals. I was surprised to find myself charmed by the little performing monkeys dressed in tiny clothes. When no one was looking, I dropped a bronze standard in the hat.

There were also plays with the best and worst actors in the very same act, casters showing off the beauty of spells large and small, and dishes spicy and meaty. A handful of these I enjoyed more than I assumed I would, but what caught my attention the most were the often gimmicky fighting pits. Full-scale fights were being saved for the real tournament, but that didn't stop others from creating brawling competitions with sometimes odd rules, such as fighting blindfolded or on their knees. The one that intrigued me took place on the third night of the festival. It was a fighting ring on a raised platform that involved contestants fighting with their hands tied behind their back. As I believed this a real world possibility, it took little convincing from Clarissa for me to volunteer for the next match.

The competitors I faced were brutish things that had as much grace as a rotting stump, but after I had kicked and head-butted them with little trouble, I witnessed a new contestant enter the dirt covered platform. She was a tall young red head, with long slender legs that allowed her to stand almost a head taller than most, including me. She easily beat her first opponent in a quick blur of precise kicks. What worried me wasn't her reach and limberness, but her unmistakable training history. The other competitors appeared to be nothing more than inebriated louts trying to win a few coins and impress their friends, but from her single match I knew that she was skilled enough to be in the main tournament. Was she using this competition as a warmup, then? Whatever her reason, we met after we each disposed of the next challengers.

I couldn't go easy on her, so when the arbiter yelled over the rowdy crowd for us to begin, I ran right at her. When I closed the distance between us by half, I sent prana to my feet. When I was just out of her range, I focused on Aranath's training and collected the prana in my airborne foot. On coming back down, I received an even bigger burst of speed. She had backed away some, but I mimicked the speed enhancing ability in my next step and quickly got within kicking range. She dodged the initial swipes of my legs, but she was limited to an uncomfortable position as she retreated to the edge of the platform, unable to extend her own legs fully.

Still, she didn't panic. She even got me on the defensive a few times, since I couldn't simply take one of her kicks and expect to shrug it off. In any

161

event, my speed training was paying dividends. It wasn't second nature or effortless, but I held my blur of speed just long enough to give me an opening. If I had an arm free, I would have given her an uppercut to the jaw. Instead, I used a head-butt to her gut to get her stumbling. One last dash and I landed a sweeping kick on her lower left leg. Without arms to rebalance her in time, she crashed to the ground. Match over. My last opponent was the official championship round, but he wasn't half as worrisome as the red head. His defeat meant two whole silvers.

As Clarissa handed me back Aranath—with Ethan infinitely perturbed that Clarissa held the blade so readily—the lofty red head came up to us. Behind her was a masked young woman carrying a masked little girl on her shoulders. A waterfall of wavy blonde hair enveloped the older girl's masked face. The blue half-mask had a faded floral design and did not prevent one from thinking she must have been a gorgeous sight, and even if I was wrong about the upper half of her face, her plush pink lips alone looked worth climbing a mountain for. The smaller girl also had fine hair, but its color was a shade closer to brown than not, though I still guessed she was a sister or cousin to the other.

"Expensive looking blade," said the red head. "I suppose that means you aren't a commoner."

"Neither are you. I suppose it was a bit unfair for everyone else that we practiced on them."

"Hey, I joined up to try and stop you. From the first match I could tell that no one else had a chance to give you a real fight. I didn't want you to win some coin so easily."

"Coin wasn't my goal."

"Are you here practicing for the tournament, then?"

"Talk to these two if you want to talk about the tournament."

"Are you gonna enter?" asked Ethan to the crimson haired woman.

162

"No. It wouldn't be fair."

"Someone once told me not to expect fairness in battle."

"What are you, then?" asked Catherine. "You're too good not to be fighting for something."

"She's a bodyguard," I replied, putting on my cloak. "Isn't that right?"

"Whoa," stated the child. "How did you know that?"

Answering for me, the blonde said, "Because Bell can't help but be in a half stance between us and our new friends here."

"Not only that," I began. "I can also assume that your masks are someone's idea of remaining incognito as you walk among the common rabble. Only nobles who can afford bodyguards are worried about such things."

The little girl clapped. To the girl beneath her, she said, "I want him for my beau! He can fight and he's smart."

"She's so cute!" said Clarissa.

"What's your name?" continued the little girl.

"Tell you what," I said, "I'll give you two brand new silvers if you make Ethan here your beau."

"Done!"

In the moment I stepped up to hand over the promised standards to her outstretched hands, I stole a more scrutinizing glance at her human beast of burden. Her half-mask didn't hide her two brilliant emeralds, which were studying me with the same latent potency I was examining her with. Her full lips looked as slick as butter and gave me the impression that she pouted them to get her way in anything. Gods help me if she licked them at that second.

A little further south, her dark mantle presented a nice bulging bump that had the space to balance Aranath on. If I didn't have to make sure that I

163

didn't drop the coins, I would have probably been caught gawking too long by everyone around me. As it was, I knew she noticed, but I didn't really care. It was something she must have lived with since the day they sprouted.

Displaying her nobility more than anything, her tresses had a fine sheen to it, and the night breeze that swayed them carried a hint of its fruity scent to my nose. She had me going now. I made a mental note to keep an eye out for any vulnerable looking, voluptuous women primed to spend a wild night with a stranger.

With the transaction complete, I said, "Congratulations, Ethan, you're now at least second in line to this family's fortune."

"Third in line," corrected the little girl.

The blonde jostled her passenger. "We're supposed to remain completely mysterious."

"But I can't keep secrets from my new darling. Oh! I want to dance with him to make it official!"

"I wouldn't mind treating my future bride to a dance," said Ethan.

The others began yapping all at once with their opinions on the matter. Meanwhile, I started linking a couple of unrelated ideas together.

In a moment the blonde wasn't speaking, I asked her, "Does the name Braden Silver mean anything to a noblewoman who knows her stances?"

After half a second of thinking, she said, "Yes, in fact. He's a well-respected member of the Warriors Guild, though I have not met him personally."

"I know he won't arrive until the tournament begins, but would it be possible for you to introduce me to him?"

"If I believe your reason to see him justified."

164

"I already know the words that will get him to give me what I need, but it occurs to me that a well-respected veteran warrior might be difficult to meet in this mass of people."

"And what is it you need from this man?"

As I began walking away, I said, "Talk that will ruin the mood before a dance."

Our newly formed group ultimately found a plaza where music was being played and crowds danced to it. After generously giving Clarissa my best notion of a dance, which felt closer to fighting than actual dancing, I slipped away and sit on a bench under a shadow of a closed shop. In the middle of wondering whether I should just head back to the inn on my own, the disguised blonde found my silhouette and sat herself next to me.

"I've seen few people able to match the speed I saw you reach."

"I couldn't have kept it up much longer. Your friend would have had me dead to rights if I didn't get her when I did."

"You know, comparing your movements in the fight to your dance with Clarissa reminded me that sparring and dancing aren't so different."

"Their goals are."

"You don't enjoy people much, do you?"

"I enjoy people just fine when they have what I need."

"Geez, even the way you talk is so tense. It's like you're always expecting a fight. Or are you just worried I might start prying into your life?"

"Something like that."

"Well, based on the fact you stopped talking about Silver by heading for a place you're clearly uncomfortable in, I can guess that your reason is highly personal. Of course I'm curious about it, but you shouldn't think I'll pry into something that will offend somebody I only just met."

"Others should take a page from your book."

"We nobles are taught some manners. They come in handy sometimes."

"Is that what the mask is for? Joining the common folk for a couple of weeks before you have to get back to manners and snobbery?"

"A little of that is in there, but I mostly just want to have fun with my sister."

"Where did she get the idea that dancing with someone makes a relationship official?"

She chuckled. "That's the first time I've ever heard her say that. She's an odd one, but most children are to adults."

"You should get back to her."

"Don't trust your friends around her?"

"It's the other way around, actually."

"Well, I'll let you wallow in the darkness, then."

"Couldn't have said it better myself."

As Clarissa and I headed back for the inn, she told me that the blonde called herself Garnet, the smaller version of her was Pearl, and that Bell's full name was Isabella. Expect perhaps the bodyguard, I figured that the rest of the names were false. Clarissa also informed me that they would meet up with us again at our inn in a couple of evenings and treat us to more exclusive celebratory fare. A fleeting tinge of disappointment came when I learned it would take that long to see this "Garnet" again.

Chapter Twenty-Three

The evening before we were to meet up with the trio of high-class girls, I felt my blood yearning for the peace of nature. When I told Clarissa that I was going to take a break from the crowds and take a walk outside the city, she said she wanted to tag along.

Though it only lasted a few hours, it was a nice respite from cramped streets and boisterous mobs. It also made me realize that I had enjoyed Clarissa's company during our travels more than I thought.

As we headed back toward the glowing city, I said, almost in a whisper, "I know I'm not the most amicable person in the world. I'm sorry I'm not better around people. I guess I'm really trying to say I'm sorry I'm not better around you."

"What? Oh, don't be silly, Mercer. I don't care that you're not the most social person in this realm or any other. I mean, when I think about it, saying little makes every word you say that much more important."

"Still, I see how you are around regular people. The social environment suits you better."

"But it's not an environment I can ever truly be a part of. Regular people can help me forget that I'm a vampire for a little while, but it's what I am. Really, the only reason I can get away with intermingling with people at all is because you act as an intermediary for me. No, Mercer, you never have to apologize for something as silly as your social ability. If anything, that kind of talk is worrying me. What brought this on?"

"I'm finding that my goal will only have me encountering more and more people. You say I'm an intermediary for you, then I'll have to ask that you act as my intermediary with those I meet. I'll try tolerating people more, but I fear that'll be a slow going process."

"You can count on me."

My first deliberate attempt to endure the company of ebullient people happened the evening the girls returned. Garnet and her sister still wore their masks, and they brought some for us. I wouldn't have worn the black mask she offered, but Garnet threatened not to tell me the favor she had done for me unless I donned the pointless disguise.

"Okay," I said, "It's on. What's the courtesy?"

"I've learned that Braden Silver will arrive around noon tomorrow. I already threw around my real name and informed the proper people to expect someone named Mercer to ask for him. He'll be at the Coliseum of Genesis in the northern district of town. Now then, with business out of the way, we can get to the real matter at hand."

"Magic show!" exclaimed Pearl.

That was indeed our first stop of the night. Garnet had bought seats to an open air stage that had several casters display a spectacle of sharp light and precise sound.

When most people think of spells in action, they can't help envisioning balls of fire raining down on an enemy, summoning an otherworldly creature to tear someone's flesh apart, or raise an army of corpses, but according to Aranath, that's what selfish, narrow-minded humans used it for. Even the casters twirling, weaving, and jumping on the stage as they fired patterns of light into the air and produced cracking sounds with whipping vines were only skimming the surface as to what a true universal understanding of magic could someday achieve. With that sentiment too far in the future for me to worry about, I simply tried concentrating on anything that might help me become a better warrior.

The rest of the night's entertainment was agreeable enough. My favorite part was when Garnet paid for us to try an assortment of lavish dishes at a city square full of food carts and stalls. I had never stuffed my stomach so much before, especially with sweets. There was also some fun seeing Ethan trying to make Isabella fall for him. She humored him, but she was only having fun of her own. Pearl eventually threw a half serious fit at her new sweetheart's lecherous ways, forgiving him when Ethan groveled at her feet. I wanted to throw up from the sight, mostly because I wanted to laugh, but I kept my self-possession.

It was late morning by the time I awoke the next day. Leaving everyone but Aranath behind, I went to meet with Silver. The Coliseum of Genesis was a rounded stadium that fit sixty thousand people. It was the main amphitheater in the city and it was set to hold the biggest fights during the later stages of the tournament. For now, it was largely barren of people.

I walked up a few flights of stairs within the wall of the building to get up to an exposed viewing platform I saw a clutch of people grouped in. A few guards stopped me from going down a hall, but when I mentioned my name, they acknowledged that I was expected. One of the guards escorted me down the hall until we reached the open air room filed with ten people. We walked up to a large ebony-skinned man reading a scroll. He wasn't just tall, but broad. As Madam Rachel predicted, he was also bald, though he did have a short beard. Strapped to his back was a double headed battle-axe. The rest of him was donning less hostile garb.

"This is Mercer," said the guard when we walked up to the seasoned warrior.

"Thank you, Fredrick," said Braden without taking his eyes off the scroll. "You may leave us." As the guard walked away, he said, "Be quick now. Some people are busy."

169

"Of course. I'm only bothering you now because Madam Rachel told me you were the man to go to if I wanted more information on Riskel Rathmore."

His eyes stopped perusing the parchment. He then rolled up the scroll and looked into my own eyes with a brief amount of intensity before they faded to a lighter shade of composure.

"Madam Rachel, eh? I thought the next time I heard that name would be in an invitation to her funeral. She still alive, then?"

"As far as I know."

"That's good." He started walking to the edge of the narrow balcony overlooking the arena floor. I followed him as he leaned on a railing. "What do you already know of Rathmore?" After I told him what was rooted in my head, he said, "That's pretty much spot on."

"Anything more you can add?"

"Nothing too solid, but it makes sense that the freshest news of his possible work comes from such a remote place."

"How would one know what his worked looked like?"

"Scale and brutality. What you found in the Onyx Mountains hints at both."

"What exactly was he trying to accomplish?"

"In truth, I'm not certain even he knew what he was trying to accomplish. The hideouts we found were usually destroyed to a point, but skilled eyes could still distinguish the many forbidden experiments he attempted on man and beast. Most know him for his research on corruption, but his tests encompassed many horrific things. Nevertheless, I do think Rathmore believed the power of corruption to be the key component in whatever his main goal was."

"Do you trust he's dead?"

"Can't say whether his physical body is dead, but I do believe his influence is alive and well somewhere, which is a harder thing to kill."

"He was on the run a long time."

"Yes. He could have spread his research to dozens by the time he died. There was even rumors he created followers with his mistresses."

"Children?"

"Aye. Soon after he made the jump to Iazali, there were witnesses that reported seeing a man fitting Rathmore's description carrying a child. Other reports told upwards of four children. This was actually something I wanted to investigate more in depth after his death, but the guild just wanted to move on. It doesn't help that most of the southern Iazali nations keep only a minimal guild presence."

"What's your best lead?"

"Now it's the Onyx Mountains…" With a shake of his head to clear some cobwebs, he said, "Wait, you're not a guild member, are you?"

"No."

"Where are you from?"

"I don't know."

He rubbed his hairy chin. "Ah… I see. So what else do I need to know?"

"Before that tunnel collapsed, there were at least two people using it—a brown haired boy not much older than me, and a red haired woman."

"Red hair, eh? One of Rathmore's mistresses was a red head. Shiri Mason."

"I never caught any names. I know she mentioned a master."

"Could she have been around thirty?"

"That sounds right. Are you thinking she's Rathmore's daughter?"

171

"I'm thinking coincidences are a myth. Still, age and hair color don't lead us anywhere." He started mumbling random words under his breath before I heard him say, "Gremly."

"Who's Gremly?"

"It's a place. A forest in the heart of southern Iazali. About four years after Rathmore's demise, I became head of my chapter. I used the position to quietly send a couple of feelers to learn what they could of Rathmore in the southern nations. Along with some other tidbits of information, they were able to come back with a map of missing people they believed Rathmore might have been responsible for. Nearly all of them bordered the fringes of Gremly Forest. I suspect he had a base camp hidden somewhere within that wild place. Most people don't enter that forest and come back, but Riskel was no average caster."

"If Rathmore had a comfy hiding spot there, then why did he come out of it?"

"He obviously needed something, something important enough that he risked exposing himself. Whatever that was, the point now is wondering if someone else is taking advantage of Gremly at the moment. Or, even if they're not, if it's possible that Rathmore didn't destroy the base and now sits with a trove of forgotten information."

"What happened after you learned of the Gremly connection?"

"Oclor was already embroiled in their civil war when my feelers returned. For five years the southern guild chapters were overwhelmed with their obligation to the citizenry and to do all they could to make sure it didn't spill over to Brey Stor. Once that matter settled down, I had a thousand more immediate responsibilities to attend to. For a few years I honestly just forgot about the whole fucking thing. Now here you are, biting me in the ass."

"As nice a painting as that is, do you know what part of Gremly would be a good place to start looking?"

172

"It wouldn't discourage you if I told you Rathmore was on the moon, would it?"

"If he got there somehow, then it means I could get there too."

"I suppose it would. Listen, I may no longer be head of a chapter, but I still carry some authority around the guild. If you're willing to be patient, I can request that copies of my old documents be sent to me here within the week so that I can figure out a good place to start. Might even help me remember something I've forgotten. If you're truly serious about seeing this through, then you should also wait until I can get a couple of my subordinates to aid in the search. You'll need the support if this forest becomes your next visit."

"By when will you have more answers for me?"

"Go to the main guild house in town the day after the festival ends. We can ponder over this in more detail then."

An hour later and I was back at the inn. Clarissa must have heard me entering my room, as she asked to be let in.

"Find out anything?"

Her voice betrayed the apprehension she felt, but I eased her worry when I answered, "He'll give me more answers at the end of the festival."

"So we don't have to go anywhere until then?"

"Correct."

"Good. I want to see how well Ethan and Cat fare in the tournament. Oh! And Garnet said she knew of a wonderful little hot spring in town that we can bathe in tomorrow evening. It's kept hot with a rune and used only by the rich. It'll be the fanciest place I've ever been in!"

"An elite bath house, eh? Suppose that means they separate the sexes."

"Drooling over Garnet as you gawk at her won't help us get good seats for the matches."

"Let me think, would I rather see Garnet naked or get a good close up view of Ethan as he fights? Such a difficult question to answer."

"Gods, it's a good thing she doesn't know what you're thinking."

"I'm sure she knows based purely on the fact that I'm a male of our not so subtle species."

"We're lucky to have met her and her companions. Why do you think they've been so nice to us? It's not like pity or something, is it?"

I shrugged. "Maybe, but I doubt it. If you remember correctly, it was in the moment Pearl declared she wanted to dance with her new boyfriend that Garnet had to make a choice—either allow the dance to happen with a complete stranger or politely move on from a group she met near a dirty fighting pit. No amount of pity would overtake a feeling of wanting to protect her sister from possible lunatics, so she's either a great judge of character or a terrible one. For whatever reason, Garnet took a chance on us. Then, probably because all the girls got along splendidly and found Ethan as harmless as an excitable dog, kept the group together."

"I noticed you left yourself out. You don't think she likes you?"

"At best, she's only curious about me… You know, I bet every year she finds strangers to hang out with."

"Maybe she's giving some peasant boys a chance to win her heart."

"No way she's not already attached."

"Then why haven't I seen her suitor around?"

"First, we aren't with her every hour of every day, so she might be with him at this very moment. Secondly, even if he's not here, it's probably because he's a busy noble or warrior doing his shit somewhere else. Lastly, Pearl seems to want a beau simply to copy what she sees at home, though I suppose the older sibling might be the example there. Oh, and even more lastly, nobles are always in a hurry to marry off their daughters."

Clarissa giggled. "Geez, you haven't dwelled on her at all."

174

"You can get out of my room now."

Chapter Twenty-Four

The early rounds of the tournament began two days later. I was honestly intrigued by the upcoming spectacle. There were hundreds of young warriors from Iazali and Niatrios, and I wanted to see if there was anything to take away from the variety of spells and fighting styles I was sure to witness. The rules were as straightforward as they come. Each contestant was permitted to pick a single weapon from a rack that fit their style best and wear either light or medium style armor. So as to not debilitate young warriors for life, every weapon choice was made from a hardy kind of wood, though I heard they had been enchanted to feel much like their real life counterparts.

For the first two days the dozens of matches took place in smaller arenas all over the city. Clarissa wanted to join the thousands of bettors, and while I was certain I could safely bet on Catherine to make it to the third or fourth rounds, I didn't humor the vampire's wishes. As the smaller venues didn't really have bad seats, Garnet had informed us on the last night we spoke that it wouldn't be necessary for her to buy seats for us until the fourth round. When that round arrived, we were to meet Isabella at the Coliseum of Genesis' main entrance and follow her up to our saved seats.

Meanwhile, I had to see what would become of the siblings. The first one up was Ethan. He went up against a lithe girl in thick leather armor, which had some small metal plates attached. Seeing her brandish a large wooden maul as though it were no heavier than a table knife made it clear that she trained to use her prana in devastating physical attacks. At the same time, she had a small round shield strapped to her left arm. Ethan was simply armed with a two-handed wooden longsword, a light leather cuirass, and the training I had put him through.

He started off badly. As soon as the arbiter began the match, the girl became the aggressor. It was all he could do to retreat away from her maul's wide sweeps. He was taking too much time evaluating her obvious strengths and weaknesses, but he eventually did act on a plan.

He realized that, despite the speed of her attacks, they still required a long windup and that a swing became impossible to stop once she chose a direction. So in the same moment she commenced her next swing, Ethan, and everyone else with eyes, knew where it was going to end up. The instant the head of the maul passed his nose, he dashed not toward his opponent, but to the maul's end. Unable to readjust her weapon's course, Ethan used his own to pin the head of the maul to the ground. He next used his free hand to grasp the maul's most blunt end and cast his earth spell. The soil under the head erupted and enclosed around it. She could probably pull it out if given a half moment, but Ethan was already bringing his sword down onto her. She had no choice but to react defensively.

For the next few seconds Ethan vigorously swung his sword into her shield, with the apparent goal of wanting to shatter it, but this made him predictable. His opponent timed it just right. She grabbed a hold of his weapon and pulled him toward her. The stumbling Ethan couldn't prevent the cracked shield from bashing into his shoulder. She was about to land a second blow, but he had the sense to roll out of the way. He next tried trapping her feet in his earth spell, but with nothing obligating her to standstill, she easily avoided it.

Within a handful of swift moves, she had once again taken hold of his fake blade and snapped the weakly enchanted weapon in half with the rim of her shield. He threw what was left of his blade at her and ran to release the maul from the ground. He wasn't too familiar with the type of weapon, but it was better than a fractured shield. There came a point when she almost took back her own weapon from him, but even Ethan wasn't dumb enough to allow such a thing. She couldn't recover after being hit squarely in the stomach by her former weapon.

Catherine fared better in her first round, facing an opponent who couldn't even get close to her. A weak fireball spell would be extinguished in midair by a surge of wind, and her long pole was employed with grace, strength, and lightning speed.

As to be expected from young warriors, most incantations they displayed were simple elemental and physical spells. Of course, as Aranath explained in his own volition during a random match, there was still something to be gained by paying careful attention.

"Do you see how this fire spell is different from the one Catherine faced? How their form is weaker but the power is stronger? Sometimes even the fiercest training can't elevate one beyond another who is naturally gifted in a particular style. As no mind is the same, no spell is the same. It's the reason why one being can boil an ocean while the other can barely light a candle with the very same spell, or why a thousand years from now this world will see new incantations learned. Keep this in mind as you fight and you will never be surprised. Surprise is death in a battlefield."

The second round began in the evening hours of that first day. Both siblings recovered their energy quickly, and though Catherine experienced some trouble from her portly adversary, they each moved on to the next day's matches.

Clarissa and I were waiting for the third round to start in the same venue as the day before. Not long after the breakfast hour, with the sky clear of any clouds, a suspicion creeped into my vision when a thin line of black smoke started to rise above the brim of the arena. Suspicion turned into unease when two more smoke plumes made themselves known. I stood up

178

from my seat and began making my way up the steps until I ascended the highest step in the squat structure. More smoke columns popped up throughout the city. By the time Clarissa joined me, far-off screaming reached the proper sense. Other spectators had begun to notice the disquieting signs that something was wrong.

"What's going on?" Clarissa whispered. "Is the city being attacked?"

"Let's see if we can reach Catherine and Ethan."

As the murmuring crowd became increasingly nervous with rumor of unplanned violence nearby, Clarissa and I jumped down into the fighting pit with the goal of entering the hall that led to the waiting room for the participants. The arbiter, a man in his mid-twenties, was sitting just inside the hall's entrance chewing on a toothpick. He stood up on seeing us.

"Whoa there. You two aren't allowed down here."

"I think the matches are about to be canceled for the day. Listen closely... Hear the people getting restless? They're seeing smoke and screaming rising outside these walls. While you go get the people in charge here, we're going to see our companions."

The arbiter stepped into the light to see the agitated people for himself. "Just stay here," he said before leaving.

Disregarding his request, we went deeper into the hall as soon as he left our sight. We found the sunken waiting room to our left a few strides later. There was a horizontal gap in the wall that the waiting warriors used to watch the matches taking place and give light to the room. Most of the youths stood by this gap, talking amongst themselves. Not a second after Catherine spotted us, the city's loudest bells began clanging.

Putting together our sudden appearance and the ringing bells, Catherine said, "Are those warning bells? Is the city under attack?"

"Where do you keep your real weapons?" I asked.

"What's going on?" asked one of the contenders. "Who's attacking?"

179

"We don't know," said Clarissa, "but there's smoke and screaming not too far from here."

"I doubt our attackers are using wooden weapons," I said, "so where do you keep the real ones?"

Ethan opened a shabby door to expose a small storage room that held both wooden weapons and the real articles. He grabbed his sword and gave Catherine her spear. The others were hesitant at first, but seeing the conviction of the siblings helped spur them. When the arbiter returned with two other men, all were armed.

"Is the city under attack?" someone asked the older adults.

"It looks like you're all ready to find out," answered who I could only assume was a guild member. "That's what I like to see! But remember what the goal of a guildsman is—to protect those who cannot defend themselves. If you see soldiers fighting soldiers, do not interfere. Our business is not to meddle in wars. Now come! Do as we say and you might not need any more tournament wins to impress the guild."

Clarissa and I followed the rear of the group as they made their way out of the building. The arbiter was told to help the city guards handle the crowd in and around the arena. Whatever fighting was happening, it wasn't yet that close to us, so the guard wanted to keep everyone contained, despite some wanting to get back to the streets. The guild member I had not heard speak jumped onto a roof and took point. The bells continued tolling and the air started to smell like burning wood. The group, which the guild captain had split into two lines, headed for the nearest shouting.

If I had been alone, I would have stayed in the background of all this and waited to see how this was going to shape out, but the presence of Clarissa and, to a lesser extent, the siblings forced me to act sooner than I would have otherwise. The benefit of putting myself in harm's way was getting information quicker. With a few silent signals from the guildsman on the roof, the captain directed the aspiring guild members and had them surround a small group of men raiding a small temple. By the time Clarissa and I reached the place of worship, two of the three men were dead and one laid on the ground with the captain's longsword at his throat.

"What is this?" the captain asked a man donning scale armor under his blue cloak. "Speak all you know and the guild will spare you."

"We'll be here all day if I spoke *all* I know," sarcastically answered the raider. The sword punctured skin. "Fuck! All right, all right! I'm with the Blue Swords."

"And who hired you?"

"Don't know. I just know we're about to have a lot of backup soon."

"From Voreen?"

The mercenary shrugged. "Probably."

After knocking him out with the hilt of his blade, the captain ordered his lieutenant to restrain him inside the temple. A couple of city guards came over and were told to spread the information we received about a possible incoming army. The guards said they had already heard the news, giving me pause. Our assembly began heading for the next area of need.

I found that something wasn't sitting right with me as we jogged onward. There were too many questions. Why would Voreen attack at a time when the city held thousands of foreigners that would be caught in the fray? Why would they even hire an undisciplined mercenary group to cause a little chaos beforehand? I suppose any amount of disorder before a battle would benefit the invading army, but the city guard alone could handle a mercenary organization while the main army concentrated on assembling for a real battle. Indeed, the Alslana army defending Qutrios now had a warning to prepare to.

Why would a low level member of the Blue Swords even be aware that a surprise attack was to take place? Surely the plan would have been

181

kept secret from them. There was also the question of how an entire Voreen army could move out without anyone knowing it. As soon as a fleet of ships left Voreen's ports, Alslana's spies would send word of the development. Only one conclusion made sense—someone was being played.

My contemplations were interrupted for a few minutes when someone summoned giant millipede things to attack us. It was the first time seeing Clarissa truly afraid of something. She shrieked from a bug crawling over a rooftop and rushed into a shop. In any event, the giant insects and their summoner were dispatched easily enough. To be sure, with a group of two dozen mostly competent warriors, I never felt in danger of meeting true resistance. The mercenaries were too scattered and not well organized. I actually felt sort of useless. This only added to my supposition that something was wrong with all this.

About half an hour after the attack started, I stopped running with the squad.

"What's wrong?" asked Clarissa on noticing my standstill.

"By now, thanks to some low life sell swords with flapping tongues, the Alslana army believes a Voreen fleet may be heading our way, so what do you think they'll do?"

"Um, set their army by the shore?"

"Right, meaning less eyes to the east."

"Wait, what are you getting at? You don't think a fleet is coming at all? Gods, you don't think they're already on shore somewhere?"

"I don't think there is an army coming."

"Then what is the point of all this? No way are these guys attacking a major city for no reason."

"Of course there's a reason, but maybe not the one they think… The guild guys have things covered here. I want to head east."

"But shouldn't we tell-"

182

"They'll be fine. We'll meet up with them later."

Restarting my run, I steered myself eastward. I wasn't sure what I expected to find, but if I was right, then something important was going to happen where the least amount of eyes were concentrated. Concern for the city itself stayed far back in my mind. I simply wanted to know if my theory turned out to be correct.

I ran as though I was expecting to run for miles more, so I didn't dash at my fastest speed, but it was still fast enough to outrun anyone not using prana. The bells had sent most people hiding in their homes or any accessible building, so I stopped seeing citizens altogether as I neared the city's eastern border. Really, even the enemy appeared most concentrated in the north and west. No coincidence, I thought. At one point, when a row of low buildings made it possible, I scrambled up to a home's roof and ran across the rooftops. Clarissa followed me from below.

Then, not three hundred yards away, a massive surge of fire shook the air and trembled the ground. I stopped to see the immeasurable embers exploding out from an arena not much bigger than the one I had left. Something powerful was there, and it pulled me toward it. I had to jump down to street level to head south. Now closer to her, I saw an exhausted Clarissa.

"Stay here," I told her. "You'll be killed if you're too weak to dodge whatever created that flame."

"But-"

"I know you want to help, but rest until you catch your second wind. I'll wait for you at the arena."

She nodded reluctantly as I pushed myself to full speed.

A smaller but perhaps fiercer upsurge of flame flared out from the arena's brim. I actually felt the heat it wrought when I was still thirty yards outside the structure. When the shockwave passed me, the metallic, guttural sounds of battle reached me. I spotted the combatants when I went through the arch of the main entrance.

To my left were some acquainted faces. The first, with his right forearm lying a few feet away and the other holding a cracked battle-axe, stood a beleaguered Braden Silver. The stump just beyond his elbow was as clean a cut as I had ever seen on a living thing, though a spell stopped it from bleeding too profusely. Behind him was a spear-wielding Isabella standing next to an unmasked Garnet, who held a golden, curved, short sword as her weapon. At her feet rested an insensible young man. No red stains did I see on the blonde youth lying face up, so I guessed he wasn't dead. Enclosing them was a transparent, crystal-like bubble. I only saw it due to the sunlight it reflected.

A dozen bodies lay scattered around them, many having been charred to the point where they were nothing more than blistering black masses. A couple of them looked to be Braden's subordinates, but the majority belonged to the Blue Swords, guardsmen, and a few of the civilian populace.

The sound of clashing steel came from my right. One of the participants was a vaguely familiar knight I had once seen in the night streets looking for someone. His heavy steel armor was blackened and he had a gash in his nose gushing out blood. He swung a huge claymore that sliced with terrifying speed, but it was hitting nothing but air. His swift foe was a cloaked, but currently unhooded, effeminate looking man. He was tall, lean, and had long white hair. His fleetness alone made the claymore ineffective, but in the few times the heavyweight came close to landing some kind of blow, the cloaked man's long halberd parried it without difficulty.

On seeing me running toward the fighters, Braden shouted, "Attack his left side! I was almost able to sever his arm there!"

The enemy jumped back from his fight. "Hey! No sharing of information! I'm already outnumbered…"

The tip of his halberd became wreathed in pulsating flame. A swing released this concentrated blast of heat in a feverish wave that looked as solid as an ocean swell. The knight put his hands to the ground and cast an earth spell to raise a wall of rock. I took advantage of the wall as well, though I was still too far back to get the full value of its shield. The wave of scalding heat first hit the arm I used to protect my eyes. Starting from the sleeve, my cloak caught fire, compelling me to remove it. Getting behind the wall of rock gave me the opportunity to cast my illusion spell away from the enemy's line of sight. Seeing that our enemy as no small fry, I cast two illusions. I then sent each of my false selves around the wall's right side. At that same moment, the knight placed a hand on his wall and most of the wall became shards of projectiles that fired outward.

The defensive slab turned offensive rush hit nothing but the arena wall, and my own distractions were diverting no one. The enemy was already fifteen feet in the air and charging up another inferno. However, before he released it, a twisting jet of water caught his attention. A glance back showed that it was the one armed Braden who had cast the spell. The enemy had no choice but to send his wave of fire to counter the airborne river. An explosion of steam was the consequence. Not wanting to give our enemy a chance to use the mist to his advantage, I threw a couple of explosive stones and triggered it in the center of the cloud.

The airburst cleared away the boiling fog to reveal that the enemy had landed in the first row of stands and was observing us nonchalantly, his weapon resting on his shoulder. He shook his head and said, "You all should be embarrassed of yourselves! Five scary warriors against one man with only one working arm. Ugh, I'll never hear the end of it, but it's better than hearing nothing at all!" At the same time the end of his halberd's shaft hit the ground, a thick cloud of black smoke burst forth.

Everyone retreated from the rapidly expanding cloud, and I used another explosion to clear my area. Once the hungry smoke cleared away enough to see shapes more than a few feet away, no one could find our white haired adversary anywhere.

I began running toward the last spot I saw him, but sensing my intent, Aranath said, "He's too strong for you alone. Even unleashing your corruption might not guarantee a victory."

I took his counsel seriously and slowed down back to a halt. As the knight hastened back to Garnet and the insensible man she was tending to, Braden ambled up to me.

"Glad you came when you did. I was foolish for underestimating him. Just five years ago I could get away with that type of mistake. Not anymore it seems."

"He appeared to be more than just a mercenary."

"I agree, but I can't say yet what he is, except he's one tough fucker."

As I stared at Garnet, I asked, "Can you say what he was after?"

"I'll let the girl decide what she tells you."

With that goal in mind, we walked up to the others.

"How's the kid?" Braden asked the knight.

"He's been hit with a powerful sleeping spell. A good healer should be able to dispel it without too much trouble." Looking at me with bushy eyebrows and a chiseled, stubbled chin, the knight asked, "And who's this?"

"His name is Mercer," said Garnet. "Mercer, this is Sir Abelus Stone."

Sir Stone ignored the introduction and picked up the youth as gently as someone in heavy armor could. "Come, milady. We need to find a healer."

To Braden, Garnet said, "Your aid and the sacrifice of your men will not be forgotten, guild master."

"Unfortunately, more sacrifice may be required before the day is out. Let's find your sister and move to a more secure location."

She nodded and headed for a hallway leading to the rooms below the seats. We all followed her as she called out for her sister with the name "Elisa," enlightening me what her own real name was. She found her little sister huddled up in a weapon's storage room. Odet gave her blade to Isabella and picked up her sister. The little princess was shaken up, but she put on a brave face, which lit up a little when she saw me.

"Mercer! Did you save us? Where's everyone else?"

"They're fine. Clarissa should appear soon, in fact."

As we moved back outside, Odet told her sister to bury her face in her shoulder so she wouldn't get an eyeful of the desiccated dead, though nothing could prevent her from smelling the cooked flesh. Stepping out of the arena had us meeting an incoming Clarissa. I told her in my succinct way what happened, including letting her in on who Garnet really was. She obviously wanted to comment on it, but the time for such things wasn't that moment. Not long after, some city guards that had seen the fiery turmoil came over to assist us. Braden requested for one to send out a message to all the city guard, asking to make certain that the other valkrean were safe.

"I see," said Aranath. "So the golden haired boy is a valkrean." For my benefit, he continued with, "Most simply think them as powerful summoners, but it's a bit more complicated than that. The most relevant element to know is that some summoned entities align themselves with certain bloodlines, not just individuals. There isn't much difference between these and regular pacts, except when they involve eidolons. Most eidolons keep to themselves in their respective realm, acting as aloof sovereigns in the territories they inhabit, but several have allied themselves with human clans, just as the elder dragons once did. Valkrean families have helped shaped your history ever since the pacts first formed, and there isn't an era when nations and cults aren't looking to harness their power in some manner. I suspect the man with the halberd belongs to one of these mad sects."

I absorbed this information as the remaining guards helped escort us to some barracks where a few healers were treating both injured guards and civilians. As I thought over what Aranath told me, I realized that these valkrean would be observed closely by their families and benefactors at all times. It was also likely that they weren't all that many in one place at any one time, except perhaps when some youths gathered for a certain festival.

I suddenly had a worry that the tournament group I left had a valkrean in it. What if someone as strong as the halberd wielder attacked the group the siblings were in? I didn't think so. If a valkrean was within the group, they would have been watched over by more than just a handful of guild members. Still, there was a chance they simply ran into one. I tried not thinking about it, not when I couldn't do anything about it at the moment.

Braden was tended to in his own room while the rest of us followed the knight, who carried the valkrean into another room with multiple beds.

"Is Owen going to be okay?" Elisa asked her sister.

"Yes," she answered, sitting on a nearby bed. "It's only a sleeping spell." Turning to me, she said, "Thank you for your help, Mercer."

"All I did was show up."

"And it was enough to force him to retreat… I suppose you've figured out who I am."

"I already suspected a noblewoman, though that you're second in line to a powerful kingdom was beyond my guesses."

"I don't know how powerful we are if a lowly mercenary group can infiltrate so easily and create this much disorder."

"There is more at work here than a mercenary group. They are mere pawns in this, I suspect."

"He's right," said Isabella. "That man was no simple sell sword."

"He could be from a Voreen special unit," speculated Stone.

"That would imply an incoming army," I said, "One that most likely does not exist, even if your army is now forced to prepare for one. How many valkrean are in the city?"

"Four I'm certain of," replied Odet. "Owen here belongs to an Alslana noble family, who are close friends with my own. Two others are from Niatrios and the other is from Oclor. All were here to test themselves in the tournament. There are undoubtedly others, but as their interest is merely to watch over their kin, they have not made their presence known. Owen's mother would have been here if she weren't ill."

"Then it all makes sense. Someone knew the valkrean would be here, they hire the mercenary group to cause some chaos, and they snatch up what valkrean they can and leave east before anyone knows what hit them."

"And stir further animosity between Voreen and us," said Isabella. "Don't the Blue Swords have their headquarters there?"

"Aye," said Stone, "but even if this theory is correct, you cannot stay here, Your Highness. We need to get you home as soon as we organize an escape."

"We can't leave without Owen," said Elisa.

The woman healer that had been examining the valkrean said, "The spell is deep, Your Highness. We can revive him, but it will take at least the rest of the day to dispel it safely."

"Stone," began Odet. "Find out when leaving here will become possible." The knight seemed reluctant to leave, so she said, "I'll be fine. I'm sure Mercer here will gladly lay down his life for us maidens."

"Well, maybe not gladly, but you can be assured, knight, that I'll unhesitantly risk another burnt cloak for your princesses."

He did not look amused by my light banter, but he bowed and left the room. Odet, taking Elisa with her, fell backwards to lie on the bed.

"You don't think Daddy will be mad at us?" Elisa asked her older sibling.

"No, not mad, but expect him to get even more wary about where we go and who we meet."

"Um, dumb question, uh, Your Highness," said Clarissa. "Do we still call you 'Garnet' and 'Pearl'?"

"The façade is over, Clarissa, so 'Odet' and 'Elisa' are fine now. Oh, and friends never call us 'your highness' or anything like that, even if Sir Stone thinks they should. Please, I hope you don't treat us any different than you were because of our status."

"N-no, not at all. I just know there's a bunch of etiquette and stuff when it comes to nobles."

"But not with friends."

"This guy isn't one of your suitors, is he?" I asked.

"No, but he is an old friend, though I suppose we might also be distant cousins if I remember my family tree correctly. However, I am currently being courted by someone back home, in case you were thinking of trying to make yourself royalty."

"No, I'm waiting for Elisa to get a few years older for that."

"We'd already be together if you had danced with me," Elisa pointed out.

"Until then," said Odet, "What are you going to do?"

"Have you spoken with the guild master about me?"

"I told you I wasn't going to pry."

"But he told you something."

190

"Only that you might be going somewhere after the festival was over, but now that it has ended prematurely..."

"I actually need to talk to Braden before I make my next move. There's information he can still give me."

Braden himself entered the room a few minutes later, his stump bandaged and in a sling.

"How do you feel?" Odet asked him.

"It will take getting used to, but I know of a few comrades who have had much worse chopped off. I'm actually glad this didn't happen when I was younger. Where is Sir Stone?"

"Preparing our leave back to the capital."

"When do you leave?"

"As soon as Owen is revived, which the healer says will take at least a day. It might have to be faster if a Voreen army attacks, but the city is well defended enough to give us time to move out."

"I'll have to stay if an enemy fleet arrives, but if no sign of that army appears by the time you move out, I would like to gather what men I have and become part of your escort, if you'll allow it."

"Of course."

"If you wish, Mercer, you may join me so we can get to your business when we arrive at the capital."

I nodded and was about to open my mouth, but I was interrupted by a loud, distant chirping coming from somewhere outside.

"What was that?" Clarissa asked.

My response, along with Braden's, was to head out of the room. Clarissa followed, and Odet sternly order Isabella to keep an eye on Elisa as she stepped out with us. The deep chirping was heard again on reaching the open air. Its origin was eastward and skyward. It was maybe a mile away, putting it over the edge of the forest line, but everyone in the street could

191

plainly see a brilliantly blue bird soaring a thousand feet in the sky. Every flap of its huge wings glistened sunlight and its four long tails left a trail of bluish sparks in their wake. The size relative to distance meant it had to have been twice the size of the jengsing hawk I saw with the nomads.

"A marcuno," said Aranath. "She's an eidolon."

Wanting a better vantage point, I chose the easiest looking building to climb and did just that. With a jump on top of the stones protruding out a window, I pulled myself up onto the one story roof.

Just as I gained my bearings, the magnificent bird suddenly pulled in her wings and dove to the ground. She opened her orange beak and fired off what initially looked like blue fire, but when it impacted the ground, great blocks of ice pushed away fifty foot trees. Shattering part of the newly created ice was a discharge of inverse lightning that almost hit the bird as she swooped over the leafy canopies. The marcuno made a seeping turn back at the spot she had attacked, but she must have found nothing more to assault with her ice spell. She chirped and began climbing the sky until she was smaller than an ordinary bluebird.

When my trance was over, I noted that Odet and Clarissa were standing alongside me.

"What a beautiful creature," said Clarissa. "And what power."

"If it takes summoning an eidolon to beat this opponent," I began, "you should hope there aren't too many of them involved."

I saw Odet tilt her head from the corner of my right eye. My right ear then heard her say, "How did you know that was an eidolon?"

"An old comrade described her to me once."

"Your old comrade is very knowledgeable, then. Valkrean families don't like to attract attention to themselves when possible. There aren't even many illustrations or books on the matter."

"There aren't illustrations or books on many things, but the information is out there somewhere. Sometimes even in the heart of a mountain."

Chapter Twenty-Five

Clarissa and I stayed in the barracks with Odet for a few hours longer. When word came in the early evening hours that all the violence had been quelled, the vampire and I decided to head back to our inn and wait for the siblings or news of them. Darkness fell before they finally showed themselves. As usual, I didn't have to add much to Clarissa's explanation of our doings. The siblings reacted as one would expect when told of Garnet's true identity. They also accepted Clarissa's offer to join us in attending the royalty's escort, who we planned to meet up with before dawn.

As for the siblings' side of things, they had stuck with the same group of prospective guild members after we left them, helping to clear the streets of mercenaries and anyone else taking advantage of the disorder. The guild captain had taken down their names for consideration, but their optimism increased when they learned that we would be traveling with a former guild master who would likely recommend them further.

After getting a couple of hours rest, we headed for the barracks. With two princesses to protect, quite a few soldiers guarded the area, but knowing we were due, Isabella was out waiting for us and we slipped through the assembly of shiny armor, bulky shields, and pointy things without trouble.

After Ethan asked for the latest news, Isabella replied, "It doesn't appear as though a Voreen invasion is imminent. The mercenaries seem to have been hired to mask the true goal of their employers."

"The valkrean," said Catherine. "Are they all safe?"

"No. Two who had entered the tournament are missing and one of their protectors was found dead not too long ago. We have hundreds of soldiers and guards scouring the city and woods, but no luck finding the missing so far."

"Your enemy is likely receiving help from within your government," I said. "They didn't infiltrate without help and they definitely won't be able to escape without it."

"This has been troubling Odet's mind as well... Elisa was still asleep when I left, so try being quiet when you enter."

Opening the door showed Elisa slumbering next to an awake Owen, who was sitting up on his bed and talking quietly to Odet. Catherine tried acting as though nothing had changed between her and the royalty, but Ethan couldn't help being somewhat reverential.

In a naturally soft voice, the first thing Owen said after introductions was, "Thank you all for your help in this. I only wish I could have joined in the fight."

"That would have simply made you an easier target," I said.

"You sound like Odet."

"He sounds like a rational fighter," said the princess, who was garbed in a marvelously pristine white cloak of silk.

"And you sound like my mother."

"With the risk of sounding like someone else," said Catherine, "is there any word as to who our enemy is?"

"That will take time," answered Isabella, "but there's little chance some people strong enough to take on an eidolon can group up without anyone noticing."

"Do you know what your parents will do in response to this?" Clarissa asked Odet.

"They'll get our best people to look for the missing valkrean and watch the borders. I'm sure security on all valkrean will be strengthened as well. Not to mention all the di-"

Stone came in and, in a boisterous tone that woke Elisa, said, "We're ready to move out, princess. Ahh! Forgive me for not being more delicate, little madam."

We went outside to see a large horse-drawn coach waiting for the nobles. Surrounding it was a small army of soldiers on horseback. Several horses were brought up by Braden for us to ride, and since I did not yet know how to ride competently, I became a passenger on Clarissa's mount. Half an hour before sunlight cracked above the horizon, the escort began a ten day ride to Ecrin, Alslana's capital city and so called brightest jewel in all of Iazali.

The trip was a largely nonstop affair for the carriage, only stopping to trade for new horses or simply when Odet wanted it to stop. The rest of us couldn't switch for fresh horses as often, so our stops came a little more frequently, though we never fell that far behind Odet. It was during one of these brief rest periods that Braden learned that Catherine and Ethan were the grandchildren of Madam Rachel, telling them that this alone was worth a recommendation to the guild.

"We like to use the tournament for more precise evaluation," he continued, "but there are of course other methods the guild uses to choose new members. I can easily get you two into one of these plans and lower the requirements for you to pass."

"That would be greatly appreciated," said Catherine.

"Yes," added Ethan with barely suppressed enthusiasm. "We'll be willing to do any menial work for as long as it takes."

"That's good, but I'll try not to make it too menial for too long. We'll need every guild member we can get if we meet any more like that arm-taking bastard."

According to the map, the Alslana Isthmus began to rapidly narrow its land area. It had been about 350 miles wide in Qutrios' latitude, but that

196

shrank each day we moved farther south. By the time we reached the extreme fringes of the capital, we were on a strip of land no more than thirty-five miles wide. It was a moonless midnight, but thanks to the lit braziers on top of the six massive towers of day and night, both man and ship could make out exactly where the city lay from many miles away.

As our paths diverged from this point forward, Odet ordered her carriage to stop so that she and everyone else could say their goodbyes. She and her sister took their time saying their personal farewells to everyone.

When Odet stopped in front of me, she said, "I've told guild master Silver this already, but if you need aid in any honorable cause of yours, you and Clarissa can write to Silver's guild house and ask me for whatever you need. Well, any *reasonable* thing you need."

"I'll keep that in mind. I wish you luck in your own honorable endeavors, princess."

"You must not think us friends if you insist on being so formal."

"I don't."

"Oh? So what would it take for formality to fall between us?"

"I wouldn't wish for such a thing to occur."

"You wish to bar friendship with me?" she asked, looking honestly confused for the first time I've known her.

"Yes."

"Why the sentiment?"

"I'm of the belief that no man could befriend you and not eventually wish for something more."

"Oh, I see, but when it comes to what men want from women, don't they all wish for something more?"

"I would describe that as wanting something *else*. Understand, if I believed myself capable of withstanding your effortless wiles, I would gladly

197

accept a connection deeper than decorum. As it stands, however, I find the idea of our friendship more cruel than satisfying."

"Well then, in an effort not be cruel, I'll make sure to keep any future exchanges between us as businesslike as possible."

"I would appreciate it. Of course, if you're ever just feel lonely one night, you can leave a note with Braden. I'll be right over."

"So it's either a lifetime or a single night, huh?"

"I don't see the point of doing anything in-between."

"It's good to know where we stand, then."

Not half a minute later, we had remounted our conveyances and entered the city by following our own road.

In reality, Ecrin was comprised of three cities. The one I headed for was known as Central Ecrin. It held the main guild house, most of the lower class citizenry, and the oversized temple at its center, where one could climb to the top of any of its six monolithic towers and stare out into the Lucent Sea and Parsillion Ocean at the same time on a clear day. Western Ecrin held the Diamond Palace and most other noble houses, and thanks to its location by the sea, was a prime trading port that made many merchants wealthy. When someone mentioned "the capital" they normally meant Western Ecrin. Eastern Ecrin also enjoyed its advantage as a major port, though it had more merchants and farmers than nobility.

When one included the trading that occurred between Alslana's northern and southern neighbors, it was easy to imagine a nation waging a war to take this strip of land. Indeed, this area hadn't seen a peace last longer than two or three decades, or the length of time it required a new generation to replace the dead from the previous war. Still, the current family regime had not lost any significant territory in over half a century. Someone realized at one point that defending a smaller kingdom was easier than holding on to an empire, which Alslana once touted itself as over a century before. The

198

only other Iazali nation that challenged Alslana's wealth, with their fields of sariff and their own strategically significant ports, was Oclor.

Even at night the city was more bustling than most towns would have been at any time of day, and a consistent eastern breeze from the Parsillion Ocean blew away the humidity that would have otherwise collected in a similar environment, making the night cooler than one would think. Just about every street I saw was paved with flat stone or brick, and no structure looked debilitated. Due to the lack of quarries in the region, the vast majority of homes and shops were made of a light colored wood. As for style, many homes seemed to keep their outer segments open to the outside world, with roofed porches encircling much of the building. Also pointing to the people's fondness for outside living were the many gazebos strewn about.

The guild house itself was a four story building of a reddish stone with three major entrances in the front. Some people greeted Braden as we placed our horses in an adjacent stable and from then on I never saw him alone. He took us to the top floor and allowed us to use a couple of unused rooms as our own for the night.

The royalty, thanks to messenger birds, or perhaps through magical means, had days before learned of what happened in Qutrios, meaning they had already paid for the services of the guild to seek out the missing valkrean and learn what they could of their unknown enemy. So with a short crew on hand, Braden, despite not having official responsibilities beyond appraising the youth, was busy helping to handle requests for the next couple of days, but I didn't mind waiting.

One of the things I did during the delay was to buy a replacement cloak. Liking the idea of making myself hide better in shadow and night, I chose one dyed in black. The shop owner also said it wasn't as flammable as other clothing, but since she said this soon after I mentioned my last cloak had caught fire, I knew it to be bullshit.

199

My wait ended when Catherine knocked on my door and told me Braden was ready to see me. With Clarissa having just went to sleep, Ethan on an errand, and Catherine going to have some breakfast, I went alone to Braden's office in the second floor. Covering his desk was a map a little larger than its surface. On top of the map were a pile of papers and scrolls neatly stacked in the corners.

"This is all I have on Rathmore," said Braden. "I went through just about everything again late last night. Bad idea. I dreamed I was facing down a faceless Rathmore with only one arm attached."

"Was the bad night worth it?"

"It will be if you find something in Gremly." He motioned for me to get closer to his map of southern Iazali. Near the center of the inverted v-shaped subcontinent was an almost perfectly round forest located within the confines of western Oclor. Surrounding this forest were some x's, dates, and notes written with ink. "As you can see, there's a rough path to follow once Rathmore makes his jump from Niatrios to Iazali. He heads east until he reaches southern Gremly. Then things get quiet for a few years before towns around the forest begin reporting an abnormal amount of missing people again. I'm sure a few of these are cases unrelated to Rathmore, but no doubt most are."

"That town northeast of Gremly…"

"Yes, Holmfirth. I remembered my prior interest in it when I saw the dates. They imply he returned there often, and was also the last place he seized victims before moving north."

"So Holmfirth will be my first stop."

"It's a fairly large town, but we have no permanent guild presence there. Unfortunately, with this valkrean mess going on, I won't be able to send any official guildsman with you, but if you wish to ask your friends to join y-"

200

"Their goal is here, and you need what help you can get."

"Very well, I won't give them the choice. However, I doubt you'll refuse a free trip to Oclor."

"The guild will allow you to fund a trip for a couple of strangers?"

"Not normally, but a quick note to the royal family and I'm certain your newest acquaintance will compensate us. I've already sent a request and I should have everything organized in another few days."

"This would be much simpler if you could summon me," said Aranath with a grunt.

"I appreciate the effort," I told the human entity. "If you don't mind, I would then like to use the rest of my time here learning how to ride."

"Of course. You can even use my Jasmine in the endeavor. She's a sweet old thing that even allows hollering kids to ride her."

"There isn't a place I could also learn how to swim, is there?"

"There are some good public baths that are warm and deep, though it does require a few bronze standards to enter the better ones. Now, I don't know what the latest rumors of Gremly are, but keep in mind that it holds its reputation for a reason. People have been entering that place only to never return long before Rathmore ever arrived. Not to patronize you, but approach that place with great caution. For all we know, Rathmore himself is there."

"If alive, then I pray he is."

Much of the next three days was spent with Clarissa teaching me the fundamentals of how to ride on the easygoing Jasmine. I wasn't planning on actually bringing or riding a horse to this leg of the journey, I simply wanted to make sure I wouldn't need to rely on somebody else when the next opportunity arose. It was a little more painful between the legs than I thought it would be, but after already having a pretty good idea of what to do, I thought I had built a solid enough foundation to learn the finer points later.

The other half of my free time was spent in a public bath nestled inside a large stone building, its interior decorated with marble and beautiful murals depicting different landscapes. I bought a little instruction pamphlet that contained illustrations showing children how to swim. Again, a foundation formed, but it still wasn't strong enough to stop me from fearing a sinking ship and the drowning that occurred afterward. Or did good swimmers fear that too?

Braden soon got word that our ship was ready one drizzly morning. Catherine and Ethan came to see us off. Braden didn't show up, but he had given his farewells the day before when he gave me a rough copy of the Gremly map, which was inscribed with what he believed to be the most important notes. He couldn't get us the fastest ship, but the two-masted *Cheska* looked sleek and her large sails easily gathered any errant breeze. The vessel was strictly a cargo ship, but the captain had often hired the guild to help defend against pirates and so we were able to use the quarters they would have otherwise occupied.

Even before Clarissa cleared her blurred vision, which she shared with Catherine, the anchor was aweigh.

Chapter Twenty-Six

Our destination was a ten or eleven day voyage, assuming favorable winds most of the way. As it turned out, a foul storm struck our part of the ocean three days after we set sail. One sail tore, but it didn't take long to repair. Getting out of Alslana waters brought us into the waters of Brey Stor, a close ally of Alslana. The southern neighbor became free of Alslana's direct rule when the empire broke apart a century before, but they still shared many cultural similarities. It likewise acted as an important buffer to the more belligerent Oclor nation.

As for the country I was heading for, the reading I did before and during the sailing told me that Oclor was ruled by two major factions. The most influential were the owners of the vast sariff fields deep within the country. While the pregnancy preventing flower could be grown in well-maintained gardens, it did not thrive as readily as it did in Oclor's naturally rich soil and rainy environment, giving the nation a valuable monopoly on the plant. About a hundred families controlled the majority of sariff farmland and potion production, with each having a small army at their disposal. More often than not, these armies were employed to defend their territory from their fellow farmers, not invaders.

A tier below the sariff growers were the merchants who did the actual work of selling the sariff and the various byproducts it created to foreign ports. Both these groups were intermixed with the old nobility, who now acted as a glorified mouthpiece for the country. Keeping a loose hold over the lower and upper classes were the priests and priestesses serving the gods of day and night. The rulers seemed well aware that a weak sense of unity among the people would create dissatisfaction and disorder. Still, one of these factions would occasionally challenge these state of affairs, but nothing had really changed internally since the War of Dragon Fire. For now, the land was quiet. On the other hand, with its rarely unified navy, its waters were always subject to pirate attacks, hence our captain's penchant for hiring the guild.

Speaking of the captain, he was an old sea dog who had a son and daughter among his crew. His daughter in particular was a good caster and helped direct the winds into the sails whenever they went too much against us. On the sixth evening, as the grizzled captain sat smoking a pipe on the top deck, I asked him what he knew of Gremly.

"My path will take me near there," I answered his subsequent inquiry. "I've heard it's always had an unwelcoming reputation."

"Aye, but I suspect Oclorans takes pride in that repute. It's like they think no other people could survive with such a terrible forest in their midst."

"You've boasted about surviving great storms, have you not?"

"Plenty… Ah, I see what you're getting at. I suppose the sentiment would be comparable. Ha! Perhaps my land loving friends think me tiresome with all those tales of tempests and pirates."

"And what of your tales about Gremly?"

"I've never gone in deep enough to experience any firsthand accounts, but plenty of second and third hand accounts have reached the coasts. From what I gather, that place used to be much grander. It was a forest three or four times as large as it is now."

"What shrank it?"

"More recently it's been farmers seeking more land, or locals burning its fringes to either extend towns or simply to be rid of the ghostly place. But most of the reduction came well before the dragon war, when Oclor hardly had control of its own shores. What caused the forest to recede, if it really did at all, is what tickles the imagination of everyone."

204

"The history book I read didn't even mention that Gremly used to be larger."

"Historians just put what they know, don't they? Like I said, no one can say for sure the forest was even that much bigger all those years ago. I bet your history book didn't mention why people even call it 'Gremly.'" I shook my head. "They say 'Gremly' is actually the name of a town or stronghold deep inside the forest, built by the first people who arrived long before northerners ever came to southern Iazali."

"First people? Where would have they come from?"

He shrugged. "Some say they sprouted in Gremly itself, or even came from Degosal before it became the Corrupted Island. My favorite theory is that they came from another realm altogether."

Repeating Aranath's words, I said, "Or they might not be human at all."

"Ah, maybe, maybe. Whoever they were, or are, the theory goes that they feared the newcomers so much that they retreated into the deepest reaches of their forest. Without anyone to tend to those twisting trees, the forest died. Others say they warred among themselves and ended up burning everything in less than a century. Whatever you want to believe, everyone knows that some kind of ancient magic permeates that place. How else can so many people go missing? Entire armies have to avoid it, so you know even mighty generals take respectful heed of whatever's in there."

"And what of recent news?"

"I haven't heard anything in particular, but I trust that you'll satisfy your curiosity as soon as you walk a dozen steps into Oclor."

When the ship finally docked five days later, I decided to keep my curiosity to myself until I was closer to Gremly itself. Holmfirth was five hundred miles away, which a steady pace would have me reach in about twenty days. I was tempted to buy a horse, but I didn't want to take care of

205

an animal unless I had to. Besides, as I walked away from bustling crowds for the first time since leaving Abesh, I began to feel more in my element. Nothing beat strolling wordlessly under a waning moon and a thick layer of starlight.

We did at one point hire a carriage service that conveyed us to a town twenty miles away, but we found the ride too uncomfortable to hire similar services again. The weather was too humid and hot to travel in the middle of the day, so Clarissa and I slept most of it away. By staying clear of other people as often as possible, the vampire and I made good time and didn't become diverted by problems that were not our own.

Chapter Twenty-Seven

Holmfirth became visible one sweaty midafternoon. It looked like any other typical town, but there was a mire in the air that seemed to have gotten stronger the closer I came to my aim. The outer reaches of Gremly's trees could be seen a few miles off. As a kind of reward for reaching this place, I bought a large lunch and stuffed the entirety of the chicken, bread, fruit, and spell-cooled water down my throat in practically one gulp.

Once I ate the large sweet roll I ordered, I asked the corpulent woman behind the tavern counter, "What news of Gremly?"

"Most don't need to come to my tavern to hear the most recent stories. Where do you hail from, stranger?"

"A question I would like the answer to myself, madam. If you wish to know the first place I remember, then northern Etoc is my only truthful response."

She raised a nearly nonexistent eyebrow. "Stranger indeed. I've always wanted to travel beyond this land. Tell me, what is the far north like?"

"The biggest difference so far would be the lack of overbearing humidity."

"That would do me good right about now. Unless you enjoy being constantly drenched, I can't imagine you've come all the way down here because of the weather."

"I followed a man's name down here, but the name 'Gremly' is my current interest."

"I don't see why. Nothing good comes out of there. Don't go in or you'll bound to become part of the undead that guard it."

"Undead guards?"

"That's right. Everyone knows the dead watch over that misty place."

"For what purpose?"

"Who knows, but they've been doing it all this time."

"And people have seen these corpses or ghosts?"

"Seeing them means you're soon to be dead yourself, so no one alive has seen them, but what proof do you need besides the people that always go missing? Beasts and men leave trails to follow. I personally believe it's an ancient cult of vampires, though that wouldn't quite explain what they do with the corpses they take."

"Corpses have been taken?"

"Aye, and not just from our town, but half a dozen others to the south and a few in the north. Every few weeks or months a grave will be missing its occupant. Sometimes they've been dead ten days, sometimes ten years. As though our living aren't enough for them, they have to defile our dead."

She spoke a little longer, but about other topics that had less and less to do with Gremly.

I rented a room for a few days, giving Clarissa and I time to accrue more stories and rest up a bit before we began exploring the peripheries of the forest. What we heard more than anything else was how foggy the interior of the forest always was, no matter the time of day. Despite all the ghost stories, no one ever seemed to actually experience anything amiss. And since locals knew better, most people that ended up vanishing were either new arrivals looking to forage under the winding canopy or adventure seekers wanting to make a name for themselves. Still, these were perhaps not as common as they once were. The stolen corpses really did seem like the most up-to-date piece of news.

208

When a clear sky and a half moon was rising one late evening, we headed for our first venture inside the forest itself. To keep from getting separated, I tied a thin rope to one of the strings that connected Aranath's scabbard to my belt and tied the other end to Clarissa's right wrist. We could separate as much as ten feet before the rope became too taut for comfort, but we usually stayed half as close as that. Knowing I couldn't be too careful here, I had Aranath unsheathed the moment we were out of sight from other people.

Not including the sluggish air I had sensed thirty miles out, the first hundred yards of Gremly wasn't anything special, though the wild shapes of the thin and distorted trees played with the imagination. The mist we heard about was forming around us, and anytime a big enough puff contacted our skin, it felt like a licked finger of an old woman stroking that exposed area. I used the blade to mark the trees as we went along, hoping not only to use them as a guide to head back, but also when we returned later.

Clarissa was the first to notice the almost complete absence of sound. I was trying so hard to see something, I hadn't realized there was nothing to hear. No owl hooted on a creaking branch, no snake hissed as it slithered in the fallen leaves, and no trapped fly buzzed in a spider's web. Clarissa couldn't stand it after a while and started humming a song about a clumsy prince we had heard in the festival. I think she expected me to say something against it, since I was expecting much the same, but I never did.

"Interesting," said Aranath about an hour into the excursion. "I wasn't convinced at first, but now I know it's no mere delusion. Something is disturbing your prana. It's subtle, but it's there. I cannot be certain what type of spell it is, but it's safe to say that it's affecting either the whole mind or a specific sense, likely in an attempt to disorient someone without their knowing it. As I do not see what else could be causing it, I'm going to assume the fog or something it's concealing is to blame. But to think an

209

entire forest is enchanted. Deep magic indeed… Stay still a moment and let me sense what it does in response

I did as he asked, telling Clarissa to stay still so that I could plan out our next move. For the next several minutes I sensed Aranath sending a trace of his power into me, a power that felt a great deal like the kind he used to remove my mind rune.

The sword finally said, "It's not the fog, or at least it's not *only* the fog. I suspected as much. A spell meant to ward off invaders wouldn't be very effective if it could simply be blown away. Wherever it comes from matters little. Walk slowly and I will be able to learn how to nullify the spell's effectiveness."

This was one of the few times I heard Aranath excited about something. Not only was he diverting himself with work, but with a new challenge. I don't think Gremly had intrigued him until now.

His amusement helped ease my own nerves, but I was still glad when we left the damned place a few hours later. It was strange. Not once did I see or hear danger approach, not even the sense that I was being watched, but I had never before felt as though I was in greater risk of losing myself. I speculated that Clarissa's vampire nature helped her cope better than if she were a human, which she said as much herself after we reentered our room. Informing her of what the dragon told me, I said that another night in the forest and we likely wouldn't have to worry about suffering from the disorientation that others had experienced.

"So you're corruption can sense the spell over Gremly?"

"Not my corruption, but the sword holding it back."

"The sword? How is it letting you know these things?"

I sighed, knowing I shouldn't have said my last sentence. "It's not just enchanted. It's connected to a summoned beast."

She cocked her head. "So that's the voice in your head?"

210

"Yes."

"Why didn't you tell me before?"

"Because at first it wasn't your business, and now it's because I don't want to lie to you."

"Lie about what?"

"About exactly what summoned beast I have in my possession."

"Why do you have to lie about that?"

"Because you might start thinking I'm something I'm not, or, gods forbid, other people more knowledgeable about history find out who it is I carry."

"You don't trust I could keep it secret?"

"I think I trust you with my life, but this is really something I don't want to touch on, not until it can do me any good, anyway."

"You trust me with your life?"

"Yes."

"Does that mean we can have sex now?"

"No."

"Aw, why not?"

"Because you're still not quite at the point I need you to be."

"What point?"

"Don't worry, you're close."

"You're just being annoying."

"I don't care."

Chapter Twenty-Eight

The next night was spent inside the vaporous borders of Gremly, with Aranath requesting another night to definitively make certain he had familiarized himself to the spell's eccentricities. When he finally believed he had, I felt prepared to begin exploring the verdant depths. Since the vampire couldn't profit from the dragon's power, we still kept the rope secured to one another.

It was quite a difference walking through the forest with Aranath at the helm. Sound seemed to return to the forest, and while it wasn't as though birds sang with glee or herds of deer stamped nearby, I at least picked up the sporadic sounds of a beating bat's wings and a mouse skipping into a shrub. Of course, all this did was make a nearly impossible goal into a foreboding one. The forest covered a huge area, and my guard still needed to be up for any corporeal enemy. Without having to worry as much about the enigmatic sway of the imperceptible spell, I was determined to spend the next few days in the forest and dare something to show itself.

The daylight did not alter the mood at all. The mist stayed dense and the tree tops held back most of the sunlight. I began to think that even if vampires weren't the ones behind everything, some had to have been benefitting from the sun's lack of power here. For two days we walked deeper into the woodland, not seeing or sensing any threat around us. Our main trek remained a westward one, but with a zigzagging design to it, hoping that gave me my best chance at stumbling to anything suspicious. When we could, we also climbed a tree to better observe our surroundings. It was this very technique that produced something of note.

I was perched on a high branch that provided a view above the canopy. Clarissa watched with me on another, slightly lower, branch. For several minutes we waited to see if anything stirred under the ineffectual morning light peeking over the horizon. Then, in the middle of deciding whether I should head back down, I distinguished something a little different from everything else. It looked like a tendril of mist at first, but its color was a shade darker, and it rose higher and faster than the hovering fog around it. I ogled it a little longer to make sure I was seeing it correctly, and once I confirmed that it must have been steam or smoke, we climbed down and headed in the northern direction it laid some thousand yards away.

Seven hundred yards closer and a small flock of sparrows fluttered away in front of us. They flew over our heads as fast as their diminutive wings could take them. We froze and stared intently to see if whatever spooked the birds would appear. Standing fifty feet away, a pair of twenty foot tall trees quivered. I expected the ground to rumble or a gust of wind to reach me as a result, but neither happened. Instead, the trees shook more and their bark creaked and groaned like an old man waking up on an even older bed. One of the trees curved its cylindrical body, revealing a kind of warped pair of stiff, hollow eyes ten feet up its gray trunk.

"A woodland sprite," said Aranath. "Mostly mindless flora that help guard precious areas of forest in their natural realm. They can manipulate anything their long roots connect with, so watch every flank."

Verifying the dragon's warning, the ground under the tree facing us began to spasm. Then, like striking snakes, some vines dangling on the tree near me propelled toward my sword wielding arm. One of the vines curled around my elbow, but it alone wasn't strong enough to prevent itself from snapping from a jerk of my arm. The ground under the other tree began stirring as well. Its attack came from beneath us. Tree roots sprang up from the dirt and wrapped itself around the rope, pulling it down that same instant.

Before the rope dragged us down with it, I cut the link and told Clarissa to stay beside me. I backed away, pulling out two dragon stones at the same time. I threw them at one of the trees, but before they got halfway across, some vines knocked them out of the way.

"I guess trees can see pretty well," I muttered. "Let's try to get around them."

An hour after some careful prodding, I discovered many more awakened sprites encircling the area. Almost all of them were grouped in pairs, if not trios. The entire forest seemed to be rasping and moaning as they tried grasping at us, but we found their range to be limited to about sixty or seventy feet. None also appeared to have been all that fooled by several tries of my illusion spell. Aranath speculated that they used their roots to sense vibrations, or lack of them, so they didn't react to something that couldn't affect its environment.

"Now what?" Clarissa asked.

"This place won't be defeated subtly. My fire will work, but we need a way to make sure they just don't slap the stones out of the way."

After a minute thinking it over, Clarissa said, "Oh! What if we protect the fire stones in my water spell so that- Oh, I guess wet stones won't ignite, will they?"

"Actually, I think you're on to something. My fire stones should remain potent enough to burn even after being doused in water. Let's test that now."

As I took out a stone, I felt somewhat ashamed that the strategies I tried concocting didn't bring in Clarissa's abilities. I had to keep that in mind for future reference. Once I set the stone on the ground, she cast her water spell, creating a bubble of water around the rock. With the water still enclosing it, I set off the stone. The water burst in a hiss of steam, and while

214

it didn't last as long as a dry stone, the dragon fire still lasted long enough to melt the outside of the rock.

"That's quite a flame," she said.

"It can burn down half this forest if we're not careful. Let's find the best clearing we can so we don't have to worry about running from a forest fire."

We ultimately found a pair of sprites surrounded by only a relative handful of regular trees. I summoned ten dragon stones, which Clarissa then wrapped around with a ball of water. She breathed in and out a few times before firing her sphere of water at the first sprite. As before, vines and roots whipped at the threat, some with sufficient force to knock away several stones out of the watery barrier, but not all. The instant the projectile crashed into the sprite, I triggered my spell. The exploding steam made it difficult to see what happened, but a red flame glowing behind the fading haze soon made it clear that the plan was a success.

As the dragon fire spread, a disturbing moaning came from the dying sprite. Its bark popped and the ground beneath it shivered until the crackling of the fire became the only discernible sound. With some regret, Clarissa fired off the second water sphere. A few minutes after that and we freely slinked past the charred trunks of the dead sprites. There was of course the chance more sprites lied deeper in, so we continued to move with the heightened attentiveness we had been carrying the last few days. However, except for the sprites we already knew of, no others made themselves known.

What did appear a hundred and fifty yards later was what initially looked like a pile of black boulders, but what turned out to be the collapsed corner tower of a small fort. This buckled left half appeared to be sunken into the ground itself, as though it were in a mire, though the ground here was as firm as anywhere else in the forest. The right half appeared less debilitated, though the top of its squared tower was overgrown with vines and curtains of moss dangling from every crack. The tower stuck up for fifty feet, but every tree nearby dwarfed it. Just behind the visible part of the fort stood a particularly tall tree, which likely sprouted from a courtyard the rubble now hid. At the lowermost portion of the intact tower was a large wooden door. I wanted nothing more than to burst in, but reason reined me in.

We circled the fort, finding that the other corner towers and the walls they connected to were nothing more than an unmovable ruin. I couldn't tell where the steam or smoke originated from, but it couldn't have been far off. For a while Clarissa and I watched for any signs of movement or traps, but there eventually came a point when there was nothing left to do but open that door.

We inched our way to the seemingly dead structure. I tapped Aranath on the soil ahead of me, making sure no rune was hidden there. I finally tapped him into the thick door itself. Only the magic of sound echoed back. I slowly pushed open the heavy door. The metal fasteners squeaked and a mustiness escaped from the inside. Nothing else reacted to the opening access. The tower's empty innards were swathed in darkness and looked no bigger than a large room of a small house. The obvious way to go was a staircase that hugged the wall. A somewhat less obvious way was a trapdoor at the far corner of the room.

After finding that the stairway led to nothing but dusty rooms, I hovered over the trapdoor and grabbed its metal latch.

Before I started lifting it, I said, in the quietest whisper possible, "I'll go down first. Don't follow me until you hear some commotion."

The crack created when I lifted the flap half an inch revealed a sharp light streaking out the opening. Luckily, the hinges were discreet as I wanted them to be. I opened the flap completely, allowing me to see the sturdy ladder leading down to a stony floor. I waited by the admittance for several moments, taking in the odd mixture of smells that stemmed from the

216

underground level. Every whiff I sucked in either gave me the impression that I was in a garden of blossoming lilacs or standing over a rotting corpse. I then heard humming, though whoever was producing it couldn't carry a tune very well. It sounded far away enough for me to begin climbing down the ladder, which I did with equally parts speed and stealth.

The basement I entered was larger than I anticipated, and would have been larger still were it not for the wall of black stone that came from the sunken side of the fort. The ladder was near the middle of the room, and all of the light came from four runes etched on the ceiling. Shelves filled with scrolls and books lined up against every wall. There were also a dozen tables of different sizes strewn about. As well as being topped with texts of some kind, they had dozens of vials and flasks chaotically scattered about on them.

Two doors were closed, but an open one led down to a dark hallway, which did not have the benefit of light runes lining the ceiling. Alongside one of the walls were a pair of beds. One had a petite young girl with short brown hair sleeping on her side. The other I assumed belonged to the man sitting with his back to me. He was topped with shaggy red hair and wore a long green tunic.

With the nimblest steps I had ever taken, I made my way to the seated figure. Aranath was at the ready in one hand and I clutched an explosive stone in the other. The bad humming continued unabated as the skinny figure jotted down something in a hefty tome with a small quill pen. The oblivious writer never paused to breathe or look about himself. A light rune shining directly above him bent my shadow away from him. I let the stone to fall so that I could grab his frayed hair. At the same instant, I slipped my blade against his throat. The cold steel pressing against his damp skin made him yelp, stirring the girl awake.

When her groggy eyes saw what was happening, she jumped out of bed and shrieked out, "No! Don't hurt him!"

217

Unware that running toward me was not a good idea, I had to say, "Stay back, girl. The way this works is that no one does anything foolish and just maybe no one gets hurt."

Her feet stopped, but her words still rushed at me, exclaiming, "Please! Rathmore hasn't hurt anyone!"

I pulled his hair in a way that made part of his face visible to me. If I didn't feel the body heat his head leaked out, I would have been sure that the pale, gaunt face tentatively staring up at me belonged to a vampire. As it was, he merely needed a great deal of sunlight.

"You're Rathmore?" I asked.

He cleared his dry throat and said, "Um, I'm *a* Rathmore, not *the* Rathmore, if that's what you're thinking. I'm Ghevont Rathmore. Who might you be?"

Clarissa had by now made herself known, to which the young girl said, "Rathmore! There's another one! What do I do?"

"Wonderful question."

"Uh, Mercer?"

"Stay there," I replied to Clarissa. To Rathmore, I asked, "You're Riskel's son? Is your father dead?"

"As far as I know, or, at least, most of him is, but perhaps even less than that."

"You have a sister, right?"

"Oh, you're acquainted? When did you meet? I haven't seen her since… Let's see, how old were you when Vey was last here?"

"Eleven," answered the girl.

"And how old are you now?"

"Fourteen."

"Ah, that's right. Three years, then."

"What are you doing here?"

218

"Oh, this and that. Mostly this, but sometimes other things too."

I tightened my grip on his hair. "A little more specific."

"That'll take a while. I do lots of specific things."

"Including taking people and corpses?"

"Oh, I only do the taking corpses thing. Real people unnerve me. I couldn't take a living person if I wanted to. I'd freeze up."

"Then who takes people? Is anyone else out here with you?"

"Unless Vey takes the time to visit, then only Gremly takes the living people, just as it's been doing since before the memory of this nation."

"See!" said the girl. "He's hurting nobody! Let him go!"

"She's right," acknowledged Ghevont. "I'm out here because everyone leaves me alone. Frankly, I find it fascinating that you two have made it so far. You're not lost, are you? Though it sounds like you were looking for my father, or signs of him, meaning you're here on purpose. That's quite a feat. The tricks this forest plays on people normally ends up killing them. It's the man reason my father came here all those years ago."

"Do you know where your sister is?"

"She doesn't keep me notified of her doings. Vey only comes when she wants something from me or this place, which is usually bodies or information, or information on bodies. She's always been a little obsessed with father's work."

"Why? What does she want?"

"She wants what father wanted."

"Which is?"

"From what I can gather, it was to break the barrier between the mortal and immortal, though I realize that's a broad statement. Don't many healers attempt to reach the very same goal? Albeit with more morals involved. Ironic, really. Dad's pursuit to immortality was his undoing. Very sad. I often wonder what it would be like if he and I used our insatiable curiosity to propel our search for knowledge together, without the fear of looming death that so worried him."

"So he believed corruption held the answer to his problem?"

"How could one not think so? Corrupted are short-lived due to their madness taking them to life shortening situations, but keep them isolated and their advanced healing trait can stave off death from hunger and injury far longer than a regular mortal could sustain. Hey, you want to kill Vey, don't you?"

"Yes."

"Good," said the girl.

"Now Marcela, that kind of temperament doesn't suit you."

"I don't care. I hate her. She would have hurt me."

"Oh yes, very much so. Uh, Mercer, was it? I'm beginning to find that talking with my throat up against your sword is rather uncomfortable. I'll be glad to continue our charming conversation under less threatening circumstances. While I do know all kinds of spells that a more competent fighter could use to separate sword from neck, I can assure you that I do not have the mentality or physique of a warrior. Look around you—I'm a scholar, a seeker of truth and admirer of the arcane. I'm not like the rest of my family."

"And you don't care that I want your sister dead?"

"Well, I wouldn't go that far. I care as far as she's been my only real connection I ever had outside of Marcela here, but if I had to choose between her and me, I have no problem choosing my own welfare."

"You never answer anything simply, do you?"

"Few answers are ever simple, no? It's why you didn't slice my throat when you heard the name 'Rathmore.' How many others would condemn me for that alone?"

I let go of his hair and removed the potential for an easy kill. Marcela ran up to her companion and leapt up to hug him. Going by Ghevont's awkward patting of her head and back, I figured that physical contact between them was scarce. Over his shoulder, Marcela gave me the dirtiest look anyone had ever given me. I was close to placing Aranath in a different place, but Clarissa walking up to me broke up that desire.

"Yes, yes," said Ghevont, "I'm okay now." As she unwillingly slid off him, he stood up and smoothed his ragged cloak. "She's been quite attached to me since I found her wandering the forest a few years back."

"I heard your sister mention a master she served. Does that mean anything to you?"

"Hmm, I don't know about a 'master,' but the last time she was here she spoke of wanting me to meet with an old friend of hers, but as it required a relocation of my presence, I refused. She really despises the fact that I won't actively aid her in her goals, you know. I've never thought of her as someone who takes orders from someone else, but if they were powerful enough, I suppose anything's possible. Now that I think about it, some of her actions do imply servitude. Perhaps she believed her friend could convince me to leave my hermit lifestyle."

"If she believed that, then why not bring them to you?"

"Oh, she might serve someone with real influence and power, but I'm quite positive that she would never trust anyone with this place. This is sacred ground to her."

"Is it possible to bring her here?"

"Oh, err, yes."

"How?"

"There are certain runes in this fort and in the two other ruins nearby that will alert a rune seared into her forearm if ever tampered with. I suspect she will come running if that ever transpired, but she will come ready to battle, and she will make for a powerful opponent. I'm also pretty sure she'll kill me if you fail."

"Then you better make sure I don't."

"No!" said Marcela. "You don't have to help him! You hate fighting, and bringing her here will ruin everything! I like my life here. No one bothers us."

Ghevont studied my unyielding eyes a moment before saying to his little friend, "Well, look at it this way, if we can remove Vey from the painting completely, we won't have to worry about her any longer." This did not appease the girl. She stomped her barefoot on the ground and went to sit on her bed. Ghevont sighed. "I feel much the same, but I kn-" He stopped when he saw Clarissa. "Oh my, you're a vampire, aren't you?"

"Uh, yes."

Marcela shrieked and pulled the blanket over herself. Ghevont walked up until he was inches away from Clarissa, walking in a circle around her a couple of times.

"Fascinating. How many people have you fed on?"

"None, though I have drank some human blood before."

"Even more fascinating. You only drink animal blood, then? How different is it from our own?"

"Well-"

"Ghevont," I interrupted. "Will you destroy these runes for me?"

"I don't really have a choice, do I? Refusing will only force you to start arbitrarily destroying my place of work, and I would prefer to avoid that at most costs."

"Can you do it now?"

"Oh, I suppose nothing is preventing me from doing so. Very well, I'll go ahead and ring the bell for you. You'll be staying here until she arrives, I take it?" I nodded. He exhaled. "Then let's get this over with."

Ghevont went down the hall, which he lighted by activating a small light rune on the low ceiling, and entered a storage room that held a sundry of items stashed in shelves and open crates. He had to push a shelf a few feet to fully expose the etching of a large rune. He splayed his hand in the middle of the imprint and began pouring his prana into it, making it glow with a red hue. This bloody radiance then altered to a white incandescence. A few seconds later and the glow faded entirely.

When he finished, he asked, "So why does my sister need to die? I mean, I know why she needs to, but why you?"

I knew both girls were watching us from the hall. Seeing as I was probably going to spend some time with these people, I decided to make Marcela less irritating in my presence by fostering some pity. "She corrupted me."

"Really? And you're not deranged?"

"Not completely, at least."

"How were you corrupted?"

I undid some of the cloth wrapped around my forearm. He put his face an inch away from the serrated tail.

"How far does this go?"

"All the way up my arm."

"When?"

"It's been about five years."

"Direct exposer to corrupted prana and to be sane for five years afterward? Does this explain how you were able to make it this far into the forest?"

"I used a different method for that."

"Which one?"

"My enchanted sword, and no, you can't examine it."

"Where did you obtain it?"

"The depths of a mountain."

"And how close are you to madness? Do you sense it creeping up on you? Wait, before you answer, would you mind answering a survey I'll prepare for you? Ahh! So many questions! I never thought I could personally ask a vampire and a corrupted the questions I've had in my head!"

"Help me prepare for your sister and we'll answer all we can."

Chapter Twenty-Nine

Not long after learning that Ghevont and Vey were actually twins, with her being the older by ten minutes, I asked, "Can you cast any spells that can paralyze her? I would prefer not to kill her before I can get a chance to find out who else was involved with my corruption."

"Certainly. One in particular comes to mind, but she is far stronger than I am. No spell I know will hold her all that long unless she's weakened first. At best it would give you a nice opening. Give her a few good strikes in that time and hopefully she won't be able to fight at all, but she'll be a handful if she does escape with full mobility. I've seen her practice, and even before she slept with men she killed them."

"How does she fight?"

"That's her strength, really. I've seen her seamlessly switch between any number of weapons and tactics. I can say that one of her favorite techniques is when she wreathes her whip with lightning. Quite a show watching her train with that sparking and crackling about."

Clarissa came out of the kitchen area carrying a tray, setting it on the table Ghevont and I were sitting beside. The tray had three little bowls of vegetable soup. "I hope this is okay," said Clarissa. "I haven't cooked since I was in my orphanage."

After taking a couple of bites, Marcela said, "Hey, this is good! I wish I can cook, but I never really learned. Some stuff comes out really, really bad."

"Nonsense," said Ghevont. "I enjoy all your meals."

"Dummy, you're too starved to care what you eat. He's so into his work he would forget to drink water if I didn't dump it on him."

"Where do you get your water?" Clarissa asked.

"A small lake north of here," answered Ghevont. "We also grow most of our food around there."

"I'm surprised you can make any kind of life here. How have you been able to live out here without the forest affecting you?"

"I have to cast a singular spell my father created to guard against the special magic here, but even he would not dare get much deeper than we are now. The odd magic becomes too strong near the center of Gremly."

"And why is this fort here?"

"It was built in a time when Oclor made a concerted effort to conquer this land. It did not go well, of course. The other two ruins are sunken deeper than this one, and one of those has an unusable basement level. I someday hope to use all my knowledge and uncover the heart of Gremly. That aim is still a decade or two out, however."

"Hey," said Marcela. "What will happen if Vey wins? She'll kill us, won't she?"

"You won't be here," I clarified. "Clarissa will be watching you at an inn until my business is done."

"Wait, why can't I stay?" said the vampire. "I can help."

"You can help by making sure Marcela stays out of harm's way. I can't spend any thought worried about either of you being killed if things go bad."

"But I don't want to leave Rathmore!" said Marcela.

"Ghevont," I said sternly.

"Hmm? Ah, yes. I agree with Mercer. It would be best if you're not here when she is. It would also ease my mind knowing you'll be safe if we fail to subdue Vey."

"But I don't want to be in an inn. Can't I at least stay in one of the other forts?"

226

"There's a chance she'll visit them before coming here," I said. "It's probably a small chance, but it's still more than the alternative. We'll head to town tomorrow or the day after and rent the room for you two. You'll have the coin to stay a year if you have to." Clarissa said my name in a pleading tone, but before she continued, I said, "If Marcela wasn't here, then I would have you help here, but she is, and neither Ghevont nor I will need that distraction as we prepare and wait for Vey."

Clarissa mimicked Marcela's crossed arms and expression of vexation, but seeing I was not going to budge on this matter, neither of them protested beyond their body language.

We decided to escort the girls to Holmfirth the following morning, not wanting to take the chance that Vey would arrive much sooner than expected. On exiting the fort, Ghevont cast his special spell on himself and the girls.

"How does this spell work, exactly?" Clarissa asked Ghevont as he cast the spell on her.

"My father discovered that the forest has the ability to imperceptibly change the way someone's prana pulses in the body. This in turn affects our senses. Some sensitive souls even hear voices in their head. They otherwise become too disoriented to think straight and get hopelessly lost until they finally die from exposure."

"Right, but how does the spell work?"

"Oh, right. Well, once my father discovered this, he figured out a way to match his prana's pulsations with that of the forest, canceling out most of the negative effects. He then taught Vey and I the spell when we were young. It was basically the first spell I learned. Still, even after all this time learning to master it, it is not sensitive enough to take one deeper in the forest."

"Can Marcela cast it?" I asked.

227

"Yes," she answered, "but don't worry, I'm not going to use it to sneak back."

"Also," began Ghevont, "she can't cast it for longer than a few hours."

"And how do you get past the sprites?" Clarissa asked.

"How did you?"

"We had to kill two," I replied.

"Aw," said Marcela. "You didn't have to do that."

"Actually, they would. Strangers are habitually attacked, remember? You see, sprites are a bit like dogs. Take care of one as a seedling and they become loyal protectors for life. Most of these sprites I've known since my father summoned them as saplings. As long as they sense my presence, they won't attack us."

Our way to the town was largely spent with Ghevont asking Clarissa all the questions he could on her life as a vampire. This was intermingled with Clarissa using her social charms to ease Marcela with the idea of spending the following weeks as a pair together. For her part, I knew Marcela didn't like me, and I could tell she wanted to say so, but since she did seem to take some pity from my corrupted state, she simply chose to ignore me— the best possible consequence for me.

One of the talks between the girls had me overhearing a little of Marcela's past. She was a runaway, leaving her overbearing parents when she was eight or nine. I got the sense that her parental guardians were not abusive, simply strict, so I imagined Ghevont would have been better off sending the child back to her rightful parents after finding her.

This line of thinking forced me to wonder how my own parents were doing, if they were even alive at all. It was odd, despite the questions about my past, there was no great urge to reunite with them. I wanted to discover what happened to them, but it was more out of curiosity than anything.

Would they be little more than strangers if I saw them again? Would the event trigger my old memories, or was there no getting them back? What would they think of their corrupted son?

Without having to move so cautiously, the trip to Holmfirth was only a day and a half long. Ghevont stayed at the outskirts as I made sure the girls were all set at the inn. I made my way back with the reclusive scholar as soon as that was done.

"All this is feeling more real," said Ghevont as night veiled the sky. "Either Vey or I will really die, won't we? I always expected she would be killed at some point if she insisted on following father's familiar path, but I never imagined I would be directly involved with it. I figured I might not even hear of her death until long after it happened, or perhaps I would simply never see her again."

"Are you having regrets?"

"Not regret so much as I'm ruminating about our relationship. We really did enjoy each other's company once, but ever since receiving word of our parents' death... Well, she was never the same. She became angry that I wasn't seemingly as upset as she was about the whole thing. That rift only increased the following years."

"Wait, who was taking care of you after your parents left?"

"Riskel moved us out of Gremly and into a little village before he moved north. One of his more casual mistresses watched over us for a few years before Vey went off on her own and I moved back into Gremly."

"Another mistress? Who was she? Where is she now?"

"You know, I haven't thought about her in a long while. Gwen Prothoro was her name, or is, if she's still out there."

"Does she know anything about your father's work?"

"Gods no. She was a lovely woman, but a simpleton not worth trying to breed children with."

229

"What else can you tell me about your father's work? I mean, you really don't know why he moved north when he did?"

"My early work involved searching for that very answer in his research. I do recall my father was confident he would return to us or I'm certain he would have told us more about his undertakings, whether personally or in clearer notes. Vey took a more pragmatic approach, but if she discovered why Dad left, she hasn't told me."

Getting back to his home had us begin setting up the groundwork needed to trap his sister, much of which involved the actual ground. I burrowed groupings of explosive stones around the fort, while Ghevont went ahead and dug some pieces of parchment inscribed with paralyzing runes. Most of these were near the tower's entrance, but with weeks of waiting ahead, we placed more and more around the fort each passing day.

Ghevont also set up an early warning system to alert us of his inbound sister. He buried hundreds of paper sheets about a hundred yards from the fort, each etched with a sensitive rune that, when stepped on, would trigger a particular light rune in the basement. The problem with this system was that it was easy to trip. The red warning light would glow and we would rush to our planned spots just inside the entrance, only to have no one arrive after hours of heedful waiting. Ghevont would go out and conclude that an animal or falling seed had been the cause. This happened two dozen times.

The scholar likewise began practicing using spells for offensive and defensive purposes. As he mentioned before, he could cast a wide variety of incantations. He knew how to levitate objects and hurl them at a target, how to manipulate every element, and create a short-lasting shield of magic strong enough to deflect the swing of a sword, but his weakness was the speed in which he cast these spells. He would have been a formidable opponent against the average bandit, but if his sister was as half as skilled as he said she was, he was better staying in the background of a fight.

230

I also trained, though never too arduously, not wanting to be too fatigued in case Vey showed up that day. I was especially vigilant after the first week of waiting went by, though I was aware it could be months before she showed up, if she came at all, but the more days that passed, the more I felt that wouldn't be the case. It was as though my old mind rune was sensing her dreadful presence ever nearing. Of course, it was barely more than a hunch, a hunch that gnawed the back of every thought I had.

Though difficult to tell under his natural fidgetiness, I saw that Ghevont was growing more nervous at the impending meeting. He would dive into his books when his twitchiness reached acute levels, becoming a statue for hours at a time, stopping only to go about doing the most critical of bodily needs. Something else that calmed him down was when he asked me new questions he would come up with. Some of these came just a few days after we left the girls in town. He came up to me as I watched the outside world from an arrow slit in the tower.

He couldn't hold back a look of incredulous wonder in his eyes when he asked, "Did you know woodland sprites have bark like iron? They are incredibly resistant to fire, yet I saw two sprites burned nearly to ash. I can only come up with three possibilities for a flame that potent. The first is that you are already a master pyromancer at such a young age. The second is that you have access to phoenix feathers, but in lieu of feathers, I found stones melted to their core, bringing me to my third theory-"

"Let's go with the master pyromancer thing."

"I'm aiding you in your retribution against my last remaining family, you would think that would give me some trust from you."

I sighed. "Fine, what was your third theory?"

"You told me you picked up your sword in the depths of a mountain, and you also told me you saw my sister in the Onyx Mountains. Most may

231

have forgotten what happened there, but I've read all I could on the War of Dragon Fire. If you're not Veknu Milaris, then you're something close."

"Let's go with 'something close.'"

"Does anyone know?"

"No."

"Is this why your corruption is being held back?"

"Mostly."

"Do you know what will happen when word spreads?"

"I'm not planning on letting you or anyone else spread that word."

"Oh, it won't be me, I can assure you. It'll be when someone else figures out you use dragon fire, or when someone sees you summon or riding a dragon, and if you wish your power to mature, you'll be doing such things. The Warriors Guild have done their best to supersede the dragon knights of old, but their influence is nowhere near that zenith. You'll have to be wary of how your actions are perceived. People will either believe you are a threat to be rid of or a guide to follow—likely both, actually."

"I'll move to Gremly if that happens."

"Can I study your dragon fire?"

"If it'll make you shut up about the whole damn thing."

Chapter Thirty

One and a half months twitched by when the warning light started to burn for the twenty-sixth time. We climbed up to the first floor, where the always open door allowed us to see the diluted evening light shimmering off the warm mist. I put my back against the wall by the entrance as Ghevont stood next to the trapdoor facing the outside world. We waited patiently as before, and after half an hour of doing so, I began thinking it was just another false alarm, but Ghevont squinting his eyes and leaning his head forward told me he spotted something of interest.

"Gods, it's her," he whispered a moment later.

I nodded and tightened my grip on Aranath's hilt. Though he was already inside the shadows, Ghevont couldn't help taking a step back to press his back into his wall. I didn't hear anything for a few minutes, imagining that Vey was being cautious in her approach to a place she believed had been attacked, especially if she passed the dead sprites. I knew she was close when Ghevont took a deep breath. A few seconds later and tender footsteps crunched some leaves we had purposely placed in the way.

After another deep inhale, Ghevont said, "Thank the gods you're here, Vey."

"Ghevont? What the fuck is going on?"

"Just hurry up and I-I'll show you." She took a couple more steps toward us. Then, for my cue, he thrust his arms forward and said, "Stop!"

With all the prana I could muster in my feet and arms, I whirled out from my hiding place. A bright yellow light was glowing from underneath her as the rune of paralysis was activated. She was temporarily helpless as I took the second I had to aim the longsword's point to where I wanted it—her right shoulder. The chainmail she wore under her brown mantle was not enough to prevent the blade from puncturing her skin and muscle. By the time I sensed the tip of the sword grating the chainmail over her back shoulder, the rune's light was gone, but I no longer needed it. Aranath began pouring his power into her, dropping her to her knees.

When time once again flowed at its normal pace, she used a laboring voice to say, "What the fuck is this, Ghevont?"

"Show her," I said.

Ghevont cast a little ball of white light over his palm, lighting up the room.

She looked up to see a face she quickly recognized, going by her widening hazel eyes. She laughed. "I'll be fucking damned."

"That's the idea. Who's your master?"

She chuckled. "That's the question you ask?"

"What would you recommend?" I asked, twisting the blade a bit.

Through clenched teeth, she replied, "It doesn't matter. I won't say shit to the likes of you. As for my dearest broth-"

I pushed forward with Aranath, sending her to the ground. "Ghevont, restrain her."

He shuffled forward with some rope he had enchanted to be stronger than normal. As he was finishing up binding her legs together, the corner of my eye saw something come out of the forest and rush with terrible speed at me. It was instinctual more than anything that I rose my sword in time to shatter an incoming javelin of ice. I was more mindful when a second spear came hissing out of the shadows. I ducked to allow the projectile to break behind me and made sure Vey didn't try anything by placing Aranath's point against her throat.

"Who's with you?"

She snickered. "The answer to your first question."

234

A large humanoid shade stepped out from the darkest part of the forest. He was a tall man with bronzed skin and arms like tree trunks. His graying hair told of an older man, but he exhibited few wrinkles and his black, vibrant eyes had a sheen of vitality not seen in most people my age. Beneath a waistcoat of dark purple was a thick sample of leather armor. Sticking out from behind him were two hilts.

"I'm disappointed in you, Vey," said the newcomer with a voice that vibrated through that meaty neck of his. "Your attachment to this place lowered your guard far too much."

To Ghevont, who had hid himself behind the wall, I said, "Keep your sister secure."

"Err, right."

A yellow glow enclosed Vey as I stepped toward my new opponent. The big guy stopped his unhurried walk when I asked, "What's your name?"

He bowed and said, "Corbin Tolosa, at your service. You, on the other hand, I already know. I'm impressed that you've been able to be rid of my mind rune. Perhaps it was a mistake selling you so cheaply. I suppose allowing me to examine your living body will be out of the question." He unsheathed both swords at his back. Both were katanas, the right one being a few inches longer than the other. "No matter, a dissection of your corpse will do just as well."

I triggered the explosive stones nearest him and dashed toward the dirt cloud's left flank. I expected to hear scuffling feet or the casting of a spell, but he seemingly didn't move at all. When the dirt haze dissipated somewhat, I cast my illusion spell and followed the false me into the cloud. I saw his dark figure react to my illusion, swinging down a blade to destroy it. The impact the katana made with the ground was powerful enough to blow away some of the cloud. I had my opening. I swung at his wrist. The edge of my sword cut through a leather gauntlet, but it then hit something as hard as iron. Aranath glanced off this second armor. Corbin now had an opening of his own.

The brute lunged at me with his left blade thrusting out. I felt his steel nick my neck as I twisted my body out of the way. His right blade was next able to swing upward and scratch my left knee as I leapt backward to reassess the situation.

When my feet were back down, Aranath said, "There's a dense concentration of prana around his body. It's likely that he's enchanted his flesh to be as hard as stone. He won't be easy to cut. Only your strongest thrusting attacks will have an effect."

By his last words, Corbin was already swinging away at me with blurs of steel. I was forced to move backward and could not break from my defensive stances. A peek at the others showed me Ghevont trying very hard to make sure his resisting sibling did not escape. It was over for us both if she did. When Corbin stepped near another hidden cache, I set them off. I spun and blindly shoved Aranath at the darkest spot in my field of vision. The leather armor gave way, but unlike before, there was also some give in the second layer of armor.

Shortly after Aranath sent his power into the body, I heard one of his weapons drop, but before I could send more of my own strength to pierce deeper into him, one of Corbin's shady hands grabbed a hold of my blade. I was pulled in closer, bringing me in range of a downward swing. A fountain of hot blood poured out of the deep wound that started from the top of my collarbone and went down five inches more.

"Aranath!"

The dragon knew what I needed. My left arm flared up and pulsated waves of ice cold energy. I freed my weapon from his grip, watching as droplets of blood leaked from his palm. He was now in the defensive, barely able to deflect most my flurry of strikes with his single sword. I couldn't find

236

a good opening to puncture a vital organ, but the loose corruption now allowed my swings to cut through his armored skin with ease, so whenever we exited or cleared away the clouds of chaos I created, he would have new wounds somewhere on his body. I especially enjoyed giving him the laceration above his bushy left eyebrow. Corbin's eyes quivered every time our blades clashed, though he wore no expression of concern.

"Shit," said Aranath. My prana took a sharp dive in that instant. The opening was enough for Corbin to send a spinning kick at my side, sending me rolling for a dozen feet. "I cannot stabilize your corruption much longer, boy. End this."

I rolled away from a javelin of ice. I jumped back to my feet expecting to evade or deflect a blow, but I instead caught Corbin about to propel a ball of fire at my ally.

"Ghevont, watch out!"

He looked up in time to realize a fireball was hurling toward him. He dove out of the way just in time to see the roaring shooting star impact the inside of the tower. His sister used the opening to begin freeing her legs.

I felt my prana take another dip. With my options dwindling just as quickly, I set off every explosive stone in my circle of influence. The fort itself was overtaken by the dust that erupted. I knew she would target Ghevont before me, so I rushed in Vey's direction. It was impossible to see her, but I steered toward her grunting and couching. I tossed and ignited an explosive stone in the spot I thought her to be. The little clearing the explosion made permitted me to see her standing form. She had a whip in her right hand and a mace in the other, but it was too late for her to react. A swing of my sword created a large gash that went from the side of her hip up to her navel. I was actually aiming for her thigh, but my own begrimed eyes, lack of time, and wildly fluctuating prana prevented a decent aim.

She groaned and dropped to the ground as she clutched the severe injury. "Fucking bastard," she moaned more than said.

I had no time to contemplate her feelings about me. A fireball exploded at my feet, chucking me to the ground. I rolled to use the momentum to get on my knees. I did so just in time to raise my sword to block a downward swing, except Corbin's sword went straight through Aranath. When the Corbin in front of me dissolved away, I knew I was left too open to live.

The real Corbin came out of the dust cloud and was about to hurl a harpoon of ice at point-blank range. Then, just before he brought his arm forward, a whip wrapped around it and pulled him backward. I wasted no time in taking advantage of the miracle. I charged with all the power I had remaining. Aranath punctured both his armors to get to his ribcage. I only stopped charging when the crossguard met his waistcoat. His heavy form trembled before slumping. Withdrawing the sword had his body crumple lifelessly to the ground.

Behind the dead Corbin was a half dead Vey on her knees. Her hateful eyes wanted to attack me with all her ferocious spirit as well, but she had wasted all her energy lashing her whip in the last attempt. She fell on her side. I went up to the heavily breathing Vey.

Kneeling beside her, I asked, "Why?"

Before she could answer, her brother crawled to her. "Vey?"

"Ah, my stupid little brother. Why couldn't you just help me? We could have avenged Dad and Mom much sooner."

"Avenged?"

She coughed up blood. "Hurry up and use a spell to ease my fucking pain."

He searched my face for permission. When I gave it, he placed his hands over her gash and cast a spell that made his hands radiate a golden hue.

"Stay with me, sis. What do you mean by avenged?"

"Corbin Tolosa, the fucker who betrayed father and let him die. He was the one who gave him up to the guild, all because he believed he got what he needed from him."

"I don't understand."

"Of course you don't. All you're good for is reading his dusty scrolls. *I* actually went out and did shit. *I* learned of father's last living associates. *I* learned of who was the only person close enough to him to expose him at his most vulnerable. *I* spent years gaining his trust so that *I* would end him when the right moment came." Her fading eyes shifted to me. "Then *you* showed up. Don't fucking point out the damn irony in this, I see it."

"What exactly did Corbin want out of your father? Who is he?"

"He was many things. He was once a young ambassador of Voreen. To most today he would be known as an influential business man, but to me, he belongs to a cult who wishes nothing more than to raise a dead god."

Aranath grumbled a low growl. "I see. Them again. She speaks of the Advent, a cult who I'm now certain is involved with the targeted valkrean."

"He belongs to the Advent, then?"

With effort, she raised an intrigued eyebrow. "Yes."

"Why did you bring him here?" Ghevont asked.

"I could always give him some excuse to hold off bringing him here, but he was losing trust in me. He would have forced my hand sooner or later anyway, so I brought him along when the rune indicated something was wrong. I also thought it would be a prime chance to kill him if things were indeed bad here. At least that part turned out to be true."

"So the Advent were after what your father was after?" I conjectured. "What was it?"

239

"The map to a dead god's grave."

"Did they find it?"

"The short answer is 'yes,' but Daddy made it difficult."

"So they found the grave as well?"

"A few years ago."

"Where?"

"Neither Corbin nor I were high enough ranking members to know such a thing. Corbin's main job was to find ways to strengthen the cult either financially or with little projects like you."

"Projects like me?"

"That's all you are. The Advent want to see if they can create loyal foot soldiers from corrupted souls, but it's merely a minor goal of theirs." Her mouth opened to say something more, but only a great deal of blood spurted out.

Ghevont gave me an expression that said, 'She won't last much longer.' For the first time since knowing him, he wore an emotion on his sleeve—sorrow.

After a moment of raspy breathing, she said, "Corbin might have been the one to betray us, but it was that cult who wanted it done."

"Why?"

"Dad knew where the map was and he wouldn't share."

"What was he going to do with it?"

"Anything he fucking wanted. What do you call yourself?"

"Mercer."

"Well, Mercer, promise me you'll try and kill every Advent you hear of and I'll tell you where you can begin to find out who you are."

"I'll promise you if you tell me everything now."

"I don't know the stupid details. Corbin kept the records and hired the bandits to take the people and resources we needed. Besides, you think I

240

would tell you everything even if I knew? It's your blade that killed me. Hurry up and promise, or I'll die with the information I do have."

"Fine."

"Say it, fucker."

"I promise."

She sighed and rested her head on the ground. "I saved your fucking life, so gods fuck you if you break it… Go to Dranall. Do you remember my assistant?"

"Yes."

"He's there… Magnus Nissen. He'll be in the shipyard offices Corbin partly owns. After we learned of your body's natural resistance to corruption, Corbin targeted the rest of your family. I do not know the results of that venture. I was sent to support a more important mission."

"The valkrean."

"Yes."

"Why do the Advent need them?"

"You need power to resurrect a dead god. Now leave me with my brother. We have a family matter to discuss."

A doleful nod from Ghevont had me step away from the pair. The corruption still left began to recede, permitting me to feel the unbroken throbbing of my deepest wound. The corruption had helped stop the worst of the bleeding, but it would take weeks for it to properly heal. I sat against a tree and watched as the siblings spoke to one another, with the dying woman doing most of the conversing. Killing Corbin a second after I was certain death had come to me had been exhilarating, but seeing the increasingly lifeless Vey did not bring me any such feelings of conquest. Was because I didn't see all that much difference between me and her?

"What do you know of this 'dead god'?" I asked Aranath.

"So you're planning to keep your oath, then?"

241

"I have a feeling that finding out who I am and eliminating some Advent might end up being one and the same. Besides, we can't have your blade getting too dull on weaker opponents, and these Advent promise to keep things challenging."

"If you wish. I personally believe this 'dead god' is nothing more than some ancient eidolon with thoughts of grandeur, but old myths say it was once a seventh god of day and night. I'm sure the scholar can give you different tales as to how this god lost its divinity. Whatever its origin, the Advent have long believed that awakening this 'god' will have the grateful being reward them with eternal life and power. If they've truly found its grave... Well, if a lost god is to be raised, it'll help having a dragon by your side."

Vey died when evening completed its metamorphosis to full blown night. Ghevont came and sat by me, casting his healing spell over my shoulder, making it feel slightly less worse than before.

"Sorry I'm not better at this healing thing," said Ghevont. "I've only really practiced with rats. Turns out that wasn't good enough."

"I'm sorry about your sister."

"I am too. Makes you think, doesn't it?"

"Sure."

"I mean, she was right about one thing. I'm insanely curious about the world, but all I do is read about it."

"I know where this is going."

"You do?"

"Yes, and my only answer to you now is that I'm in enough pain as it is. Let's wait a bit longer before we start contemplating things that annoy me."

"Oh, all right... but it would make sense, no?"

"I really don't want to have to bury another Rathmore tonight."

"Can I request something regarding that?"

"You better make it quick. I'm pretty sure I'm about to pass out."

"Oh my. Well, I realize this is a sacred thing to ask of you, but I was wondering whether I could use some of your dragon flame in her burial."

"Sure."

His increasingly nebulous voice spoke about how this was a grand opportunity for him to study the effects of dragon fire on a human body, but that was all I caught. My head went limp and I blacked out.

45792238R00137

Made in the USA
Middletown, DE
20 May 2019